Death
on the
Menu

BOOKS BY EMMA DAVIES

EMMA DAVIES

Death
on the
Menu

THE ADAM AND EVE MYSTERY SERIES 3

Bookouture

Published by Bookouture in 2022

An imprint of Storyfire Ltd.
Carmelite House
50 Victoria Embankment
London EC4Y 0DZ

www.bookouture.com

ISBN: 978-1-80314-436-8
eBook ISBN: 978-1-80314-435-1

For Holly, Dylan, Ethan and Angharad

1

_____

Fran stared at the woman in front of her.

Even after all these years it was like looking in the mirror. Olivia Turner hadn't aged a bit. Well, obviously a little bit – when Fran had last seen her they were nine and that was thirty-odd years ago, but she'd know that face anywhere. The same dark unruly hair as Fran, the same grouping of freckles across her nose, the same deep-brown eyes which were only just beginning to crinkle at the corners. And the same lack of height. Clearly, Olivia's longed-for growth spurt hadn't arrived either.

'Like two peas in a pod,' their teachers had said, and always with a sigh. It wasn't big stuff they got up to, it was only primary school after all, but rather antics of the mischievous kind. Whenever there were shenanigans afoot, Fran and Olivia were at the root of it, and to this day 'shenanigans' remained one of Francesca Eve's favourite words.

Back then, of course, she'd been Francesca Williams. Jack hadn't come into her life until much later, giving her all the things she had ever wanted, as well as a new surname. But she had never been a *Francesca*. A name like that was too much of a straitjacket. Too uppity, too severe for a child who didn't like to sit still and wear pretty dresses, and Fran had been aware of that almost as soon as she had been old enough to pronounce it. So, when Olivia came along, calling her Fran without any hesitation whatsoever, she felt as if she'd been born again. Of course, her mum had hated the use of the shortened version of her name and would insist on everyone calling her daughter *Francesca*, correcting Olivia countless times. But all that did was make Olivia even more determined, and make Fran love Olivia all the more.

And now, looking at her, it was as if the years had simply rolled away.

'Olivia! My God, it's so good to see you!' Fran stepped forward ready for the hug which, despite the passage of years, she knew was coming, but then she stopped and looked up, suddenly acknowledging where she was. The imposing edifice of Justice House towered above her. Fran might run her own catering company but Olivia had clearly spent her time since school wisely.

Olivia followed Fran's gaze and laughed, and it sounded just as Fran remembered: wicked and very infectious.

'I know! Didn't I do well? Little Olivia who was always getting into scrapes.' She adopted a matronly pose. 'So sad... Olivia has such a good brain if only she would learn how to use it.' It was a perfect impression of their class teacher. Olivia laughed even harder. 'Actually, I didn't do that well. This place belongs to my employer.' She rolled her eyes, and reached forward for the hug that was becoming long overdue.

'I can't believe it's you,' said Fran, grinning from ear to ear. 'There's so much to say, I don't know where to start.'

Olivia took a step backwards. 'Well, come in first of all. It's flipping freezing out here.'

Fran smiled as she hurried across the threshold. 'And I'm really sorry, Liv, for your loss, I mean.'

For a moment, Fran wondered if Olivia was about to cry,

but then she smiled, warm and wistful. 'Clarence was a wonderful man, the best boss I've ever had. I keep reminding myself he was eighty-two, with a wonderful life behind him, it's the only thing which makes me feel better. He wasn't ready to go, though, not by a long stretch. It would have been his eighty-third birthday in a couple of months and he had a lovely party planned... It's just so sad.'

Fran held her look. 'Aw... I *am* sorry.'

Olivia nodded. 'Come in quick or you'll start me off again.'

And for the second time that morning Fran was caught off guard.

'This place is incredible...'

'Isn't it?' Olivia smiled. 'Fascinating history, too. But I can tell you about that over a cup of tea.' She paused, eyes twinkling again. 'I think we're going to need several gallons.'

Fran's first impression of the house was of majesty. She couldn't think of another word to describe the entrance hall into which she'd just walked. From the towering oak staircase which rose in a graceful, vaulted arch above their heads to the warm stone walls which lined the space, it was grandeur at its finest. Deep ruby-red carpet stretched ahead of her and— She stopped, peering at a series of arched recesses cut into the stone. Except they weren't recesses at all.

'Trompe l'oeils,' said Olivia. 'Aren't they incredible?'

Fran stared at what she knew were flat, painted scenes. Masterfully rendered, they did indeed trick the eye into believing you were looking at a scene in three dimensions. Although each painting was slightly different, the 'view' in each was of rolling fields dotted with sheep. It was as if you'd just opened a door and stepped outside to admire the scenery.

Olivia gave Fran a moment more to drink in what she was seeing before raising a hand to indicate a doorway at the end of the hall. 'The kitchen's this way.'

Fran followed, conscious that there was little point in trying to close her mouth as more jaw-dropping sights caught her eye. She certainly hadn't imagined her visit this morning would turn out to be quite so surprising.

By contrast, the kitchen was very modern, sleek, and filled with light from a line of windows which *did* look out over the gardens. No pretend imagery here. And the reality was every bit as pretty as the scenes back out in the hallway, even though the view was decidedly wintry, the trees and lawns glittering from the hoar frost which had come in the night.

Fran laid her bag on a huge, glossy white table. 'I can't believe I didn't realise it was you when your email enquiry came in,' she said, taking the seat Olivia indicated. 'But then again, who'd have thought it after all these years?'

Olivia smiled. 'Especially as the last you heard of me I was in Australia. Besides, I would imagine there are plenty of Olivia Turners in the world, it's not an uncommon name.' She pulled a face. 'I did have another name for a while, but... that episode in my life is probably best glossed over. Not my finest hour.' She frowned a little as if wondering what else to say but then thought better of it.

'So how long have you been back here?' asked Fran. 'You didn't keep the accent.'

'No... Things didn't work out quite the way my parents intended. We had five wonderful years out there, Fran, and then I lost them both, in a sailing accident.'

'Oh, Liv...'

'No, it's okay. It was a long time ago. But it meant I had to return to the UK when I was fifteen. I lived with my aunt down in Cornwall, right on the edge before you fall into the Atlantic. And Megan wasn't what you'd call conventional...' Olivia paused, a fond smile on her face.

'The one with all the dogs?' asked Fran. She nodded. 'Yes, I remember. You used to spend holidays with Mad Megan, didn't you?'

'My mum's batty sister... Not surprisingly, we got along like a house on fire. My life would have been very different if it wasn't for her. She saved me, I think.' Olivia stared across the kitchen as if she could still see that part of her childhood even now. 'Anyway, what about you? You're married, obviously, and an exclusive caterer, obviously, but what about the rest?'

'That's pretty much it. I'm married to Jack, have been for fifteen years, and we have a daughter, Martha, who's twelve. Left school, went to uni, did loads of jobs, most of which I hated, and then about eight years ago I decided to retrain and become a chef. I've been running my own business for the last four.' She undid the buttons on her coat, grateful for the warmth in the room, and lowered her bag to the floor. 'Which is how I ended up on the receiving end of your email.' She gave her a warm smile. 'It's so lovely to see you again, Liv, I'm just sorry it's under such difficult circumstances. Needless to say, I'll make damn sure you all have a dinner worthy of celebrating Clarence's life.'

While Fran had been speaking, Olivia had taken two mugs from a cupboard on the other side of the room. She held one up. 'I have no doubts about that, Fran, none at all. It's just that... Listen, can I get you a tea or a coffee and then explain? I expect you're wondering how I came to be here, apart from anything.'

'Tea would be lovely, thanks. Just milk, no sugar.'

A few minutes later, they were settled at the table with an enormous teapot between them. It was shaped like the Mad Hatter and had obviously seen good use.

Fran tapped its lid. 'Your boss sounds like quite a character,' she said.

'He was,' replied Olivia. 'Truly, one of a kind. I don't think I've ever met anyone quite like him. So much energy and boundless enthusiasm for life. But kind with it, and funny too, acerbic wit and a fine intellect.'

'Sounds like you were the perfect match for one another,' remarked Fran.

Olivia's smile was wistful. 'It's what makes all of this so much harder,' she confided. 'Not just losing him, but all the things he never got a chance to do...' She leaned forward. 'He and his family didn't get on, you see. It was his one regret in life and he was determined to try and put things right, with however much time he had left. That's why he'd planned a party for his next birthday – one last attempt to bring everyone back together again. Now that won't happen, of course, which is heart-breaking, but also... I'm a bit nervous about things.' She reached forward to touch Fran's arm. 'I'm so glad you're here, it's going to make this so much easier.' She sighed. 'I'm worried the family are going to be difficult, you see, and that the dinner might be... awkward.'

Fran smiled. 'Show me a family who isn't. But don't worry, difficult relatives are my bread and butter, no pun intended. I'm used to dealing with them and this is a difficult time for everyone involved, emotions are bound to be running high. I'm sure it will all be okay.'

Olivia sipped at her tea and then lowered her mug, her expression resigned. 'Are you okay for time?' she asked.

'Tell me all about it,' said Fran. 'You'll feel much better when you've got it off your chest. And I love a good story.' She leaned forward. 'Start with you, though. I want to know what you've been up to, and how you came to be here. Admittedly you were only nine at the time, but you were adamant you were going to be a famous explorer and if you couldn't be that, then an archaeologist at the very least. Most of us couldn't even pronounce it, let alone know what it was.'

'Oh my God, I did say that, didn't I?' Olivia grinned. 'Although for the life of me I can't remember why. As I recall, you wanted to be a vet.'

'Which went out the window as soon as I realised that you

had to be brainy and study for years and years. That's not really me, is it?'

'All those years ago,' mused Olivia. 'It's so weird looking back on our younger selves. Not surprisingly I didn't become a famous explorer – just as well given that I have a real thing about bugs and creepy crawlies. I wouldn't last five minutes in a jungle. Archaeologist was a bit more like it. The history part anyway. In fact, I'm an historian now – a writer, actually – that's really how I came to be here.' She took another sip of her tea. 'But before I tell you the rest, can I ask if you've heard of the book *Dungeons of Doom* or *Castle of Secrets*? Maybe even *Seas of Adventure*?'

Fran laughed. 'Who hasn't? I grew up reading those. There were games as well, weren't there? Blimey, the Christmases we had playing those, battling over who found the silver sceptre first. It was usually my brother, he was far more competitive than the rest of us.'

Olivia smiled. 'Well, the silver sceptre, the sword of Blackthorn, Goldring's dagger, all of those were Clarence's creations.'

'He was Ebenezer Doolittle?' asked Fran in surprise. 'No... but it's such a brilliant name. As a child I was convinced it was real, so I'm a little disappointed to find out it isn't.' She shrugged. 'Ah well...'

'He was the man behind the books, the games, everything. And hardly anyone knew who he was, or rather his real name. He took his inspiration from the character in *My Fair Lady* – Eliza Doolittle – it was his favourite film.'

Fran shook her head. 'I don't believe it, there go my childhood memories, shattered...'

'His publisher told him no one would ever buy books by someone called Clarence Lightman, so Ebenezer he became. He never imagined it would be a name he'd keep for so long. But when the books became successful, and then the games, he set up his company with Doolittles as the trading name. By then, of course, it was more to do with protecting his identity, for his family's sake. Not that they ever thanked him for it.' Olivia tutted. 'I'm getting ahead of myself, sorry. I came here just over eight years ago at the ripe old age of thirty-three. I'd got myself into a bit of a pickle. I'd married what my mother would have called a "ne'er-do-well". Although, obviously, when I married him, I didn't know he was a ne'er-do-well. I thought he was charming and clever and I really rather liked him. Until I found out that he had a gambling problem and had not only emptied our bank account but run up a huge pile of debt to boot.'

'Not sure that "ne'er-do-well" really covers it,' remarked Fran. 'I can think of several other words which might be more appropriate.'

Olivia shook her head. 'It was my own fault. I was too busy with work to notice what was going on around me and, by the time I had, it was too late. I was left with virtually nothing. It was my sister-in-law who saw the advert for a companion in *The Lady* magazine. In return for a few hours help around the house, a few hours playing chess with Clarence and a few more being scintillating company, I got free board and lodging and plenty of time to write. I was in the middle of writing a book so it seemed like the perfect solution. And it has been ever since. Absolutely.'

Fran smiled at the wistful expression on Olivia's face. 'I can tell how fond you were of him.'

She nodded. 'I was. And I can't really believe he's gone. I know he was eighty-two, but he seemed like he would go on forever. Sharp as a tack too, right until the end. Chess wasn't the only game we played, although it was his favourite, he loved anything that challenged him. And even though he'd stopped writing, he came up with new brain-teasers and puzzles all the time. He used to try them out on me to see if I could solve them, although I'm sad to report my success rate wasn't all that high.

His body might have been slowing down, but his brain certainly wasn't.'

'That's so sad,' said Fran. 'A friend of mine designs computer games and he's a bit of a character too. They're devious things, full of puzzles and problems to solve, much like Clarence's books, actually. He and Adam would have got on like a house on fire, he's always looking out for new ideas to tease people with.'

'Clarence leaves behind a massive legacy, and I'm going to find it very hard when that all goes up in smoke, probably quite literally. There's a room here, at the back of the house, which Clarence called his Inventing Room – very Willy Wonka – and it contains his life's work. It's a bit of a museum piece, admittedly, but then why shouldn't Clarence be proud of what he achieved? I can't bear to see it all go, but I have a horrible feeling that's exactly what will happen once his family get their hands on it. None of them are interested in it, apart from the money it makes – it's all too sad for words. Mind you, I probably won't be here by then, either, which will be a mercy under the circumstances.' She slurped at her tea. 'It makes me mad, actually. The way they treat him. *Treated him...*' She looked at Fran with an odd expression on her face.

'Isn't there anyone who could take it? Some of it, at least? A museum, or a private collector even?'

'Possibly,' replied Olivia. 'But sadly, I think even that decision will be down to his family. Clarence sold his company years ago, along with the rights to all his games, and his literary estate, such as it is, is managed by his agent. Now that Clarence is dead, however, the agent will look to the family for instruction. And I can imagine what their response will be. They won't do what's right, just what earns them the most.'

'You'll have done your best,' said Fran, even though she knew it would be of little solace. 'And that's all you can do.'

Olivia bit her lip. 'It's not just the estate though,' she said.

'That's bad enough but...' She shook her head. 'Clarence's family have only visited a couple of times in all the years I've been here, so I don't know them at all well, only what Clarence has told me. Yet despite the breakdown in their relationship, he still spoke so fondly of them. He was desperate to mend things and it's the only time I ever saw him looking sad – when he talked about it, I mean. I don't know the details of what went wrong between them, but it must have been something pretty bad for their falling-out to have lasted this long. And now Margaret's said something which really put the wind up me.'

'Margaret?' checked Fran. 'Who's that?'

'Oh... Clarence's solicitor. She was talking about the surprise Clarence had planned for everyone. It was meant to take place at his birthday party, but he left strict instructions with her that in the event he died beforehand, the surprise was still to go ahead, *after* the funeral. Bless him, it's like he's hoping he can bring the family together... even from beyond the grave.'

'Ooh, isn't that a bit spooky?' quipped Fran, her face falling when she realised how anxious Olivia looked. 'Sorry.' She frowned. 'But why has the surprise made you so worried? I don't understand.'

Olivia pulled a face. 'It's not the surprise as such – that's just a treasure hunt – apparently, Clarence used to set them for his children all the time when they were younger. But when Margaret was discussing it with me she said something so utterly ridiculous, I can't get it out of my head.'

'Go on...'

'She said she thought it was a very odd thing to do. But it isn't, not really, not if you knew Clarence like I did – he was as eccentric as they come. But she insisted that to make such a stipulation only a couple of months before his death struck her as rather out of the ordinary. As if it was foreshadowing, she said.'

Fran frowned. 'It sounds to me as if having the surprise take place was simply something Clarence cared about a great deal, particularly if his relationship with his family was his only regret in life. He was eighty-two, after all, and I imagine when you get to that age, the fact you might not have a huge amount of time left to live rather focuses your thoughts.'

'Exactly,' said Olivia, her face brightening. 'There's nothing sinister about it at all.'

'Is that what she said? That it was sinister?'

'She said he was particularly adamant that his surprise go ahead, party or no party. She admitted that she didn't know Clarence as well as me, but said she knew him well enough to know there must have been a very important reason why he was so anxious about it. When she queried it, he made some remark about suspecting foul play if he died from a heart attack.'

'And what did he die of?'

But Fran didn't need to hear Olivia's answer, her expression told her all she needed to know.

'But that was just a flippant comment, surely? You're not telling me she took him seriously?' said Fran.

Olivia shrugged. 'That's what it sounded like.'

'But that would mean...'

'That she suspects he might have been murdered. I know... it's absolutely crazy!'

2

'Oh God, listen to me. Melodramatic or what?' Olivia rolled her eyes. 'I'm having a hard enough time coming to terms with the fact that Clarence has actually gone, I can do without people putting stupid notions in my head.'

Fran studied her carefully. 'Which is exactly what this is: stupid. Pay it no mind, Olivia. Margaret obviously has a very vivid imagination. And it's not exactly tactful, is it, saying something like that? Not when people are grieving.'

Olivia nodded. 'I thought that too. Imagine what the family would think if they'd heard her? They might not have got on all that well, but...' She shook her head again. 'Anyway, there was never any question of Clarence's death being due to anything other than natural causes. Age-related heart failure. That's what it said on the death certificate and, given how old he was, it makes sense.'

'And there was nothing unusual about the day he died?'

Olivia shook her head. 'Nothing. He died in his sleep. I went in first thing, as I always do, to take him a cup of tea. He looked like he'd just slipped away.'

'There you are then,' Fran replied. 'Put the whole thing out of your head. I'm sure everything is absolutely fine.'

Fran sipped her tea, in part to hide her reaction. Her life had only just settled back to normal after the last set of shenanigans, and that was not even six months ago, in the summer, when she and Adam had solved another murder. They hadn't intended to, they never did, but catering for a weekend-long house party and having the host turn up dead one morning rather put them on the spot. Since then, she'd been enjoying the return of her days to their normal humdrum, and now here she was with murder on her mind again. Not on her mind exactly, but she couldn't pretend she hadn't felt a flicker of unease when Olivia mentioned the circumstances of Clarence's death. Despite what Adam said, solving murders wasn't cool, or exciting, and as long as she kept telling herself that, everything would be fine. Nothing would be wrong at all. She tried to focus on the job at hand.

'So, tell me about this surprise,' she said. 'You mentioned it was a treasure hunt, that sounds intriguing.'

Olivia nodded. 'But that's about all I do know,' she replied. 'Clarence wouldn't tell me any of the details. Wouldn't even let me help him with it. Just said it was something he wanted to do by himself. I could kind of understand that – I think it was important to him that his children should see him in a good light, so he wanted to prove that the surprise was solely of his making, something he'd done just for them. It was infuriating though, nonetheless. The party itself we *did* talk about, practical details like what I thought his family might like to eat and drink, although mostly we talked about whether they would actually turn up. He wrote each of them a letter, spent hours deliberating over what to say and how to say it. But if I mentioned the treasure hunt, he would simply smile and change the subject, telling me not to sound like a stuck record.

And the harder I tried to find out about it, the more evasive he became.' She smiled wistfully.

'So Margaret has all the details then?'

'Yes, along with all Clarence's other wishes. He was very well aware of his age and that, as he put it, he would be popping his clogs soon, so he said it would make things a lot easier on me if he made his own funeral arrangements. Even though he said he couldn't trust anyone apart from me to carry out those wishes and he'd end up with – his words – a right dog's dinner, he didn't want to burden me with the arrangements either, so he wrote everything down and sent it to Margaret for safekeeping. She's the daughter of an old family friend and so they were often in contact with one another. As soon as she was notified of his death, she started the ball rolling.'

'But that's a good thing, surely? When my mum died, I had no idea what her wishes were, and I really regret never talking to her about it. It sounds morbid, particularly given my mum was no age at all really, only sixty-three, but I really wished I had. My dad didn't want to think about it, not surprisingly, and my brother and I did what we thought best, but I always worried that we'd got it wrong. At the time it quite upset me.'

Olivia's face was full of empathy. 'I get that, completely. It isn't the funeral arrangements which are making me anxious, though, those are straightforward enough. But according to Margaret, Clarence's surprise is to be revealed during the family dinner afterwards. It's also when the will is being read, and knowing Clarence the way I did, and his love of the bizarre, I have a horrible feeling it's all going to backfire. I'm worried his family aren't going to take it very well at all, and I don't think I could bear that, for Clarence's sake. It was so important him.' She gave a tight smile.

'The guest list is also very specific, as is the order of events and even the seating arrangements. And although I refer to it as a family dinner, in fact the only three family members who will be there are his children, two sons and a daughter. There aren't many others, actually, a sister still alive, and a few on his wife's side of the family – she died a long while ago – but none of them will be attending.'

Fran frowned. 'So, apart from his children, who else *is* going to be there?'

'That's just it. There are a couple of people from the village, and one or two of his close friends who I have met, but the others... I don't know. I can only guess they must be old friends too, quite elderly I would imagine, but I've never met them. I don't know who they are and neither do his children.'

Fran gave her a wary look. 'Well, that is strange...' She thought a moment. 'Then who invited them?'

'Margaret. But she's being very tight-lipped, says Clarence didn't even tell her who they were, simply laid out the details during one of their meetings. It's all a little bit too mysterious for my liking.' She gave a wry smile. 'See what happens: you live with Clarence for any length of time and you start thinking like he does... did.'

Fran had no idea what to think. It was all very intriguing but, from the sound of it, Clarence's age may well have had more to do with things than Olivia realised. She was obviously very fond of the old man, but perhaps she was too close to the situation to see that Clarence's mind was no longer quite as sound as she thought it was.

'Perhaps you'd better tell me what the dinner arrangements are,' said Fran. 'And we can take it from there. That's the easy bit at least, and as far as everything else goes, let's just hope his family take the surprise treasure hunt with the good grace that Clarence obviously intended them to. I can leave a few sample menus as well if you like. Perhaps you and the family can have a look at them. As long as I have the final decision on choices over the next few days, everything will be fine.'

Olivia nodded. 'I'll give you Margaret's number too. She has some information about the guests, I believe, and one or two of them have special dietary requirements.' Olivia smiled. 'It really is good to see you, Fran. I've been so worried about all of this and just knowing you'll be around to talk to makes everything feel better.'

'We haven't seen each other for thirty-odd years, haven't spoken in...' Fran struggled to work out the numbers. 'Far too long. But you haven't changed a bit. It's good to see you too. And together, we'll make sure everything runs as smoothly as it should.'

Olivia smiled again, but she couldn't hide the doubt in her eyes and Fran could see she was really worried. She must make sure to have a good chat with the solicitor – maybe she could prise a few more details from her. Forewarned is forearmed...

'So, the dinner is to be served at six, although the funeral is at two, so I'm not really sure what we do between times. I imagine that the people coming to the dinner may well want to come back here, one or two have come quite a distance. It doesn't seem fair to make them hang around for several hours, does it?'

Fran shook her head. 'So Clarence's instructions didn't allow for any refreshments straight after the service, nothing elsewhere?'

'No. And I've no idea how many people will attend the service either. Clarence was quite well known locally and, aside from that, a couple of newspapers have also picked up on the story, so any number of folk could turn up.'

'Well, in that case, I think we have to limit things, otherwise you'll be incurring far more costs than were anticipated. I can certainly lay on tea and cakes for folks if you want me to, but that begs the question where we do it, and I wouldn't advise on that being here, you could have people hanging around for hours. I think it's better simply to stick to the dinner as Clarence wished and leave everyone else to their own devices, hard though that might sound. However, what I could do is make sure that there are refreshments here for those people coming back and then at least they can avail themselves. It might help bridge the gap before dinner. How does that sound?'

'Perfect. And we don't have to go overboard... I don't think Marcus would...'

'I can hide it in the cost of my original quote if that would help?' offered Fran. 'A couple of cakes and a plate of biscuits isn't going to be much.'

Olivia sighed. 'Thank you. Just that Marcus is, well, he...'

'I quite understand. Clarence may have provided for the cost of his funeral arrangements but what's left is very possibly part of his children's inheritance now. Marcus is one of his sons, I take it?'

'Yes. The eldest. I think he sees looking after the purse strings as his responsibility.'

Fran smiled. She was well used to this kind of thing. There was often one person in the family who liked to keep a wary eye on the budget.

'Right, so onto the dinner itself.' She leaned down to fish her planner from the bag at her feet. 'Let me make a couple of notes and then I can show you the menu options. Do you have confirmed numbers yet?'

'No, but Margaret does. The last time we spoke, which was the day before yesterday, there were eight guests, and then there will obviously be myself and Margaret, plus the children, so that's Marcus, Catherine – or Cate, as we call her – and Saul.'

Fran's pen stilled as she wrote the word 'thirteen' in her notes. She wondered whether Olivia had realised how many people would be seated around the table. She wasn't particularly superstitious herself, but...

'And you're certain you want three courses?'

Olivia nodded. 'That's what Clarence stipulated. It must be

three. We're to eat our starters and then each pull a cracker before the main course.'

'A cracker?'

'Hmm... I told you Clarence had his little eccentricities. And these aren't just any old crackers, they're ones he asked Margaret to order specially.'

'Okay... well, at least Christmas isn't too far away. I guess it won't have been too hard to get hold of some.'

'After that we'll eat our main course, at the end of which Margaret will read the will.' Olivia gave her an odd look. 'Apparently Clarence suggested that dessert is neither hot, in case it goes cold, nor something which could melt if left for any length of time.'

Fran frowned, her pencil scribbling across the page. 'Perhaps it's best if I plan to leave quite a large gap between the last two courses.' She looked up enquiringly. 'Is there anything else you think I need to know?'

Olivia shook her head. 'Other than to prepare for the fireworks, no.' She grimaced. 'And I don't mean pyrotechnics.'

Fran looked up. 'I'm sure it won't come to that. Clarence and his children may not have got on but they have still just lost their father. I'm sure that fact alone will temper their response. And you never know, they might find his surprise delightful, just as Clarence intended.'

'I hope you're right, Fran, but I—'

Her words were cut short by the back door banging open.

'Christ, it's cold out there!'

'Then put a coat on, Cate, like any normal person. And stop moaning. You've done nothing but bitch all morning—'

The two figures stopped dead as they entered the kitchen. One, the woman, was wearing nothing more than a jumper and jeans, and a thin jumper at that.

Olivia got to her feet and moved out from behind the table.

'Cate, Marcus, this is Fran who's going to be cooking dinner for us all on Friday night.'

Fran stared at the two people who stood in front of her. With all the talk of Clarence's children she had forgotten how old he was when he died. The 'children' were nothing of the sort, perhaps even a little older than herself and looking quite affronted to find her in their kitchen. But as she took in their appearance the woman broke into a warm smile.

'Hi... it's so lovely to meet you. I've heard great things about you.'

The woman was tall and gaunt, with such startling green eyes that Fran wondered if she was wearing contact lenses. By contrast, the man by her side was small and hulking, his thick jacket dwarfing him.

Fran stood up, tangling her feet in her bag as she did so. By the time she had extricated herself and managed to hold out her hand, another figure had joined them. He too stopped short when he saw her.

'Saul, this is Fran,' said Cate, reaching forward to take Fran's hand. 'She's the caterer for Friday's dinner.'

Fran shook hands with the others in turn.

Saul came forward with a welcoming smile. He was tall like his sister with soft brown eyes and warm hands. 'Please make us something nice,' he said. 'It's going to be a pig of a day.'

Fran dipped her head. 'I'm so sorry for your loss,' she said. 'And I will certainly do my best. In fact, I was just about to go through the menu options, if that's something you want to discuss now?'

Cate looked at her brothers. 'We've just come from the undertaker,' she said. 'It's been a bit of a horrible morning.'

'We should though, Cate,' said Saul, giving a tight smile. 'It isn't fair that everything gets left to Olivia.'

'I don't really care what we eat,' Cate replied. 'No offence,

Fran, I'm sure it will be lovely, but it's not really the occasion for enjoyment, is it?'

'Well, I bloody mind,' said Marcus. 'I don't want any fish. Can't stand the stuff.'

'There are lots of options,' replied Fran. 'Given the weather and other considerations, I've made some quite traditional suggestions. I can leave everything with you and you can let me know what you'd like in a day or two. And if there's nothing on my lists you like, just let me know, I can be flexible. The main thing here is that you're happy with the choices.'

'And that we don't spend a bloody fortune,' said Marcus, just as Olivia might have predicted. 'I don't even know half the people coming,' he added, as if that made a difference.

Fran took some sheets from her folder and spread them out on the table, standing back with a glance at Olivia. 'The suggestions are arranged according to price,' she said. 'Most families find this easier.'

Cate was the first to pick them up, squinting slightly as she scanned the contents. She shrugged, handing them to Marcus with eyebrows raised.

'Definitely no salmon,' he said. 'Or steak. Chicken's a better bet, isn't it?'

'Cheaper, certainly,' said Saul with a look at his brother. He made no move to study the options.

'What do we think about soup?' asked Marcus.

'It's lovely and warming,' said Fran. 'And doesn't have to be too heavy, or filling.'

'Then chicken of some sort and a... I was going to say cheesecake. But maybe a trifle?' He looked between Cate and Saul and back again.

Cate sighed, irritation flickering in her eyes. She reached out and took the sheets from Marcus, bunching them together and thrusting them at Olivia. 'That all sounds fine. Olivia, you make the final decision. You're better at this stuff than we are.'

She linked her arm through Marcus's. 'Come on, I need a drink before I go home. I don't want to hang around here any longer than I have to.'

Together they headed for the hallway, although Cate turned back at the last minute.

'Oh, nice to meet you, Fran.'

Olivia cleared her throat, looking down at the papers in her hand before flicking a glance at Fran.

'There's tea in the pot if you'd like some, Saul,' she said.

He nodded, staring at the table. 'I might...' He lifted his arm, pointing in the direction his siblings had taken. 'Thanks anyway. I should go, I'm leaving in a few minutes too. Is that okay? Can you decide for us?' His hesitant smile was directed at Fran this time.

She nodded. 'Yes, of course. It doesn't matter who makes the final choice, just as long as I know what I'm doing.'

Saul's smile changed to one of gratitude and he hurried away.

Olivia took a deep breath. 'Right then, where were we?'

3

Understandably, funerals were not Fran's favourite events to cater for. She was far too much of a softy and the sight of anyone crying usually provoked the same response in her within a matter of seconds. It was hard to remain focused and professional when she was blubbing alongside a client; more than one meeting had ended up with them both sharing a box of tissues. Funnily enough, no one had ever seemed to mind her becoming emotional. Jack said it made folks feel less awkward and maybe he was right.

Not that she would have that problem at Justice House. Here, it was stony faces all round. Apart from Olivia.

Fran knew she had been trying not to show her feelings the first time she and Fran met, and in part her tears had been kept at bay by the excitement of their reunion, but now, with the funeral service only hours away, she was white-faced and virtually silent. She felt guilty being so emotional, she'd said, which Fran thought odd. Why should she apologise for being fond of someone even though his own family seemed less so? So what if that appeared to highlight the contrast in their behaviour? That wasn't Olivia's fault, or her responsibility, and Fran had told her so. Only Saul had seemed to understand, but he appeared scared of putting a foot wrong with his siblings, so did nothing to help. Then again, he wasn't openly grieving for his father either. It wasn't the first time Fran had cause to reflect on how peculiarly complicated families could be.

'Things aren't always how they appear on the surface though, are they?' said Margaret, Clarence's solicitor.

She was sitting at the kitchen table nursing her fourth mug of coffee, while Fran attended to the prepping of the vegetables she would serve with dinner. Not that Fran minded plying the solicitor with drinks. Mrs Foster was a very pragmatic, down-to-earth sort, and had appeared in the kitchen at some point earlier in the morning and never left. She didn't quite know where to put herself, she'd told Fran, who understood perfectly.

'Not that I knew Clarence particularly well,' she continued. 'He was Dad's client, really. I sort of inherited *him*, which is slightly ironic under the circumstances. But he was always very pleasant when I met with him. He had a mischievous twinkle, though, I'll give you that.'

'I quite like a mischievous twinkle,' said Fran.

'Oh, so do I,' came the reply. 'But I'm not sure his family are quite so fond of his wily ways.'

Fran paused, potato peeler in hand. 'Hmm, Olivia mentioned there might be fireworks later. Maybe she shouldn't have said anything, but she and I were at primary school together and I think she wanted someone to talk to. It's obvious how fond of Clarence she was. I imagine she feels rather lost just now.'

'Sadly, I suspect it's rather more than that. Which is a shame as I rather like her too.'

'Oh?'

'Well, her position as Mr Lightman's companion is obviously no longer required. And given that this is also her home... well, you can imagine the situation. Clarence has stipulated that she be allowed to remain here for a month after his funeral so that she at least has time to find alternative accommodation and so on, but the request forms part of his funeral arrangements and, as such, there's nothing legally binding about it. I can't stop the family from ignoring Clarence's wishes.'

Fran was horrified. 'You mean she could get thrown out?'

Margaret pursed her lips. 'I believe there have already been one or two mutterings from certain family members, yes. Given what I know of her, I'm pretty sure Olivia can take care of herself, but it's not a nice situation to be in. Marcus is already talking about moving in.' She put down her mug. 'Are you sure I can't help you with that?'

Fran shook her head. 'I'm certain. But thank you. Have I got it right, though, that none of the family live here at present?'

'I don't think Clarence would have allowed it. There was a bit of a to-do when he decided he wanted to advertise for a companion. Saul is married, but Marcus and Cate are both divorced and the suggestion that either one of them should come back here to live instead caused quite an upset. But Clarence won out in the end.'

'But if Saul is married, where's his wife? Shouldn't she be here?'

Margaret shook her head, a slight smile playing on her lips. 'Clarence's wishes over who attends the dinner are very specific. I believe Saul's wife is staying in a hotel nearby and will attend the service but no more than that.'

Something had been playing on Fran's mind for a while now and she wasn't sure whether she should voice it or not. It certainly wasn't any of her business, but it intrigued her. Human behaviour was something she had had cause to mull over on quite a few occasions recently.

'You might not want to answer this,' she began, 'but from what I've heard about Clarence, both from you and Olivia, he was a lovely man, even if he did have certain eccentricities. Why were he and his family so at odds with one another?'

'I couldn't possibly comment,' said Margaret, her smile saying otherwise. 'But it's like I said, maybe things aren't always how they appear on the surface. All I know is that Mrs Lightman died when the children were still quite young, a tricky time for anyone to lose their mother, and indeed for Clarence to assume the role of sole parent. It was an incredibly busy time for him too. His books had already become hugely successful and the games he began to develop off the back of them were just beginning to take off.'

'So they felt neglected, is that what you mean?'

'Quite possibly, although I don't believe the real problems started until they were all much older, by which time Clarence had already set up Doolittles, a very successful company. When they were old enough, the children all followed him into the family business, and it's not unusual for that to cause problems, differences of opinions, that kind of thing. But in this case, it seems it was the very worst thing they could have done.'

Fran picked up a stray piece of potato peel and dropped it in the sink. 'How sad. I understand how things like that happen, but this is a family who had an opportunity to all pull together and become incredibly close. It seems such a waste that they let something like that come between them.'

Margaret gave her a knowing look. 'Unfortunately, it was rather more than simply sour grapes. Something happened, and I don't know what because Clarence would never talk about it to me, but all three children were summarily dismissed. Rumour had it that there had been fingers in the till, and after that relations broke down. Irretrievably, it would seem.'

'Didn't anyone ever try to mend the division between them?'

'I'd like to think so, but both parties have to be willing for that to happen and, in this case, I suspect that's where the problem lay. There are four very strong personalities in this family and in my experience that doesn't make for harmonious communication.' She caught Fran's eye. 'But what would I know?'

Fran nodded. 'And now it's too late for any kind of reconciliation.' She frowned. 'I just hope his family understand how much he regretted what happened between them. I certainly don't suppose they're going to have any qualms about accepting their inheritance, in any case. Sorry, but I'm not a fan of people who behave as if they're entitled... This house alone must be worth a fortune.'

'Oh yes, there's a fortune all right.' Margaret glanced at her watch. 'You'll have to excuse me, Fran, but I must just check on one or two things. I imagine the vicar will be here by now.' She paused. 'There is just one thing I'd like to ask you, however – that you remain in the dining room between the main course and dessert.'

Fran stilled her hand. 'Me? But isn't that when the will is being read?'

'Indeed. And the details of the surprise he planned. But it's something which Clarence stipulated in his list of arrangements for the day. I trust that's okay?'

'Yes, but I wasn't aware...' Fran wasn't sure how long before his death Clarence started making his funeral arrangements but she felt rather uneasy that she had seemingly become part of the equation long before she even knew about it. 'Sorry,' she continued, 'but I thought my presence here was down to Olivia, she—'

'Yes, that's right, it is.' Margaret smiled. 'Apologies, I didn't explain that as I should have done. I rather meant that Clarence had asked for *whomever* provided the catering to stay for the reading of the will. Olivia *was* charged with the task of engaging someone for the job and obviously that someone is you.' She got to her feet. 'So can I take it that's okay?'

'Yes, of course. As long as folks won't mind there being a

longer than usual gap before dessert can be served. People will have to bear with me, I—'

'I can assure you that will be absolutely fine, Fran.'

Fran studied Margaret's face, deliberately impassive. 'So, what's this surprise all about then? Some kind of treasure hunt, Olivia said.'

Margaret collected her handbag from the table and held it clasped in front of her. 'Now *that* I really can't comment on.'

The remainder of the morning passed by in the usual blur of industry, for which Fran was immensely grateful. She didn't want to think about the ramifications of her conversation with Margaret any more than she had to. There was something very 'off' about this whole job, and the sooner it was over, the better. Apart from meeting up with Olivia again, it didn't have much to recommend it and she didn't even have the bonus of cooking anything particularly interesting for the guests. The choices the family had made were distinctly lacking in imagination. Cheap though, as Marcus had commented.

The only thing about today which was even remotely pleasing was the setting, and that was simply stunning. Fran hadn't yet had an opportunity to see that much of it, but the dining room alone was worth a visit. A large oak table and regal chairs provided the centrepiece to the room, while the walls were covered in ornate tapestries which overlaid rich oak panels. Fran had a ridiculous impulse to start tapping on them. Clarence had written about secret passages enough times through the years, and if anyone was likely to have a house filled with them, it was him.

Olivia had told her that the dresser on the far wall would hold everything she needed to set the table and, given its size, she didn't doubt it – it filled nearly one whole wall. In places the old oak was so dark, it was almost black. Pulling open the doors she bent down to see what was available.

'Can I help you with anything?'

Fran shot upright, the voice from directly behind her making her jump. It was Marcus, and she knew from his tone his words were not the offer of assistance they suggested, but rather a brusque demand to know what she was doing. She ignored it.

'Yes, thank you, that would be really helpful.' She smiled. 'What china would be best, do you think? Is there a family favourite?'

Marcus glared at her. He was wearing a dark-navy suit, but the trousers were far too long for his short stature and he looked very uncomfortable.

'Or one that shouldn't be used?' She waited patiently for his response.

'There are plates and things in the kitchen that might be better suited,' he replied. 'The things in there have been in the family for a considerable time.'

'Oh, Marcus, at least play the game,' said Cate, coming into the room. 'We have to use the posh stuff, it's expected. Heaven only knows who's coming. Haven't you managed to find out anything?'

'No. I told you, she won't budge an inch. Everything is in that damned handbag of hers and she keeps it clutched to her as if someone's going to pinch it at any moment.'

Cate smiled. 'Be fair, Marcus. That's exactly what you had planned to do.'

'And I might have succeeded if Saul hadn't had an attack of conscience. He never changes. Says it doesn't matter anyway. Maybe not to him, but—'

'Marcus, it doesn't matter, not really. We'll find out who they are soon enough and what difference does it make? I told you, my lawyer is the best there is. If there's a problem then we'll... solve it.' She moved towards him and fished in the front pocket of his shirt, pulling out a lighter. 'I'm going for a ciggie. Are you coming?'

'In a minute. I need to get changed.'

Cate studied him. 'Why? What you have on is perfectly acceptable.' Like her brother, she too was wearing a suit. Hers fitted, at least, but did nothing to hide the sharp angles of her body.

'I don't like this shirt. It's new and creased to buggery.'

'Then iron it, darling brother.' She gave Fran a complicit smile. 'What are they like?'

On other occasions, on other jobs, Fran had undertaken tasks which, strictly speaking, were not in her remit as the caterer. Like the time when a very nervous bride had spilled wine down her future mother-in-law's jacket, which had been hanging on the back of a chair, an hour before they were due to leave for the church. Fran had whipped it away, sponged it, dried it with a hairdryer and pressed it, all without the mother-in-law in question being aware that anything was amiss. But on this occasion, Marcus could iron his own shirt. Or change it. It wouldn't make a tap of difference to the way his suit looked.

She smiled at Cate. 'Is there a dinner service you'd like me to use?'

'Oh, heavens... whatever you think. I'm not really sure what's in there any more. There used to be a blue thing with flowers on it when Mum was alive. Use that if it's still there. You're a star.'

'Thank you,' Fran replied, bending back to her task. From what she could see, the 'blue thing' was a beautiful duck-egg Royal Worcester service. And it would look perfect in this room. She drew a stack of plates towards her and carefully began to remove them. She was under no illusion that any help would be forthcoming.

Cate pulled at her brother's arm. 'Go and get changed if

you're going to, we haven't got that long. And for God's sake, Marcus, have something to calm your nerves while you're at it, it will be hours before this is all over.'

Holding her precious cargo firmly, Fran straightened and watched the siblings leave. She shook her head and carried the plates back to the kitchen. Justice House was a good name for this place, she'd certainly like to see some.

She was still midway through the washing of the crockery when Olivia and Margaret appeared in the kitchen.

'We're off in a moment,' said Olivia. 'I just wanted to check you have everything you need before we go.'

Fran smiled. 'All under control, but thank you. I'll lay the refreshments in the drawing room, ready for when you get back, and then people can help themselves if they wish. I'll have pots of tea and coffee on standby too. This is going to be hard enough for you, Olivia, without having to worry about anything else. So don't, I'll take care of things here.'

Margaret nodded. 'Excellent. Now just one last thing before we go, Fran.' She opened the clasp of her bag and fished inside, withdrawing an envelope. 'Inside here are cards with the guests' names printed on them. They're to go on the table, please, and there's a layout so you know where to place each. It's important that this is done exactly as specified.'

Fran stared at the package in her hand as if it were an unexploded bomb. She had the feeling that's exactly what it was. She nodded. 'Understood. I think Marcus was rather keen to get his hands on these earlier.'

'I don't doubt he was. He's been pestering me all morning for information about who will be in attendance at the dinner.'

'Maybe he was planning to have a google of the names and see if he could work out who they are,' added Olivia.

'Quite probably. In any event it wouldn't have helped him. The guests are simply ordinary people, just like me and you, but it's been rather satisfying withholding the information.' She gave a small smile.

'Margaret, I like your style,' replied Olivia. 'But did Clarence really ask for the names to be kept secret?'

'Oh yes, for reasons which will become apparent later on.' She touched Olivia's arm. 'Come on, my dear, time we weren't here.'

Fran moved forward to draw Olivia into a hug. 'Don't be afraid to cry,' she said as she released her. 'This is your moment to say goodbye to Clarence. Make sure you take it for yourself.'

Margaret nodded at her. 'Very wise words. Thank you, Fran. We'll see you later.'

And with that, they were gone and Fran was left contemplating the vast kitchen, suddenly conscious that the whole house would very soon be empty of everyone except for her. She picked up another plate, thoughtfully. It was supremely tempting to go exploring but this was still Clarence's house and she couldn't betray his trust like that, or Olivia's for that matter.

There was, however, one room she would permit herself a little peek inside and as soon as she had finished washing the dinner service and laid it out on the table ready, she took the short flight of three steps that led from the great hall into the room which Clarence had made his more than any other in the house – what Olivia had called his Inventing Room.

It was certainly striking. An impressive space, lined with bookcases and shelving, a vibrant tartan carpet adding to the feeling of grandeur. A kneehole desk stood to one side of the room beneath a window, and to its side, in front of another imposing fireplace, were two armchairs. Battered and worn, one might think that they didn't quite fit with the elegant furniture elsewhere, but if you thought about the room's function, it was obvious that they were, in fact, the focal point. Between them stood a smallish table, round, with a polished surface, on which a game of chess had been laid ready to play. A lump immediately formed in Fran's throat. Clarence had played his last game, but she could picture Olivia sitting there with the old man locked in a battle of wits. She must find the sight of this terribly hard.

Olivia was right, there was a museum-like quality to certain aspects of the room. Several of the shelves and a couple of display cases held various items of merchandise which Clarence's books had spawned. A series of framed pictures along one wall held awards he had won, as well as several news-paper clippings, including one showing the Queen being presented with a game by Clarence himself. But it was evidently also a room where he had enjoyed writing, and devising puzzles and brain-teasers before settling down to play a game of chess. There were scribbled notes on his desk, and what looked like prototypes for a possible new game, cut from card-board. How long they had sat there, Fran had no idea.

Her tour of the room hadn't taken long, but it felt fitting that she should make a final tribute to the man who had spent his life bringing so much joy to people. If Olivia was right, it was doubtful the room would ever appear like this again once Marcus and his siblings got their hands on it... She shook her head. It was just too sad to contemplate. That a person's life's work could be all but eradicated by—

Her reverie was interrupted by a loud ping from her pocket and she pulled out her phone, expecting to see a text from Olivia. Instead, Adam's name lit up the screen and her mouth automatically curved into a smile.

She hadn't seen Adam for weeks. Not that there was anything unusual about that. He was the son of a friend of hers, only twenty-four years old to her forty-one, and if it hadn't been for the murders they'd managed to solve together they wouldn't have a great deal in common. In fact, the very first murder they solved had been one where his mum had been in the frame and Fran had stepped in to help when he'd had no one else to turn to. It was an odd friendship, but it worked. She opened the message.

You'll never guess where I am.

Fran thought for a moment and then typed back.

Rhetorical question?

It was something of an in-joke between them. Adam had a very literal way of navigating the world and didn't always understanding the subtle nuances behind things people said. Or, at least, he hadn't when they'd first met. Now he was much better at figuring out things, but it was still a question he posed with regularity... mainly to check he wasn't about to make an idiot of himself.

No! I want you to guess.

Adam, I'm working... we could be here a very long time.

Fair point. I'm at a funeral.

Oh God, Adam, whose? Your mum didn't mention anything.

No, she doesn't know. Who it is, I mean. But he's one of my heroes, Fran. I couldn't believe it when I read he'd died. I wasn't sure if I should come, but the paper didn't say you couldn't. There are many people here th

The message stopped abruptly.

Is everything okay?

Yes, I'm not sure if I should be here though and some woman has just given me the evils. But Clarence is the man behind Dungeons of Doom, you must have heard of that?

Fran nearly dropped her phone. Her fingers paused over the keyboard. She typed carefully.

I know it. I bought it for Martha when she was younger.

I took inspiration from that for some of my early games. It's awesome! He's awesome! How could I not come and say good-bye? Shame you didn't know about it tho, you could have done the funeral tea, wouldn't that be incredible?

Wouldn't it?

Fran paused again, adding a laughing emoji.

Quite a coincidence. Listen I'd better go, I have stuff in the oven. Speak soon though?

Okay, BFN

She sent a thumbs up by way of reply, forcibly resisting the urge to add 'xx' as she did to all her friends. She'd forgotten once and had totally freaked out Adam.

And then she sighed and looked around the room.

Oh, Adam you'll never guess where I am, she thought.

4

Fran nodded with satisfaction as she took one final look at the table. The beautiful china glowed under the room's lights and the sparkle from the heavy crystal glasses provided the perfect accent. She straightened a soup spoon and picked up one of the place cards, moving it fractionally. Francine Collins... The name meant nothing to her. Neither did any of the others: William Butler, Paul Iveson, Mary Duggan, Stephen Forrester, Sheila Blacksmith, Sidney Barnard, Neil Pope. Who were these people? And why were they attending a dinner in honour of Clarence's life?

Fran shook her head and hurried from the room. The longer she stared at the names, the more her sense of unease grew. There was something inauspicious having strangers at the table, and she couldn't dispel the notion that they would be here as some kind of jury. But there was no point speculating any longer, she would find out soon enough and she had far too much still to do. People would be arriving from the funeral service soon and although preparations for dinner were well in hand, she still needed to put the finishing touches to the cakes she had made for the afternoon refreshments.

Whatever job Fran undertook, there was always a point when it seemed that things would never be finished on time. Everything could go according to plan for the entire day, and then suddenly the sheer number of things to attend to would gang up on her and a familiar feeling of panic would threaten to overwhelm her. She knew from experience, however, that ten minutes later, everything would suddenly fall into place and come together, and today was no exception. The only issue was that whereas Fran's nerves would normally begin to ease at this point, today they were still fraying at the edges.

As she carried the first tray of soup through to the dining room, the sound of Cate's querulous voice did nothing to allay them.

'I don't wish to be rude, but why does it matter where we sit?'

'Because your father wished it so, Ms Lightman,' replied Margaret with a swift glance to Olivia beside her. 'He was very particular about the seating plan.'

'Yeah, I got that. But... look, I know you're only doing what you've been told, but surely we don't have to? I don't know about anyone else but this day has been difficult enough as it is, and I'd like to sit with my brothers.' She raised a hand to her cheek, holding it there a moment. 'I need their support just now.' She turned to the woman beside her. 'No offence,' she murmured.

Margaret pursed her lips. 'I'm sure. But the intention behind the seating plan was not to make things difficult, it was simply – now you've been introduced to everyone – an opportunity to get to know your father's friends a little better.'

'Even so,' said Cate again, 'we're unlikely to ever see any of you again after today.'

Margaret held up her hand. 'Naturally, I can't stop you from sitting wherever you like, Ms Lightman, but... Does anyone else have any objections?'

Heads turned, clothing rustled, chairs creaked, but no one said a word. Fran hovered on the threshold of the room, head slightly downturned. The last thing she wanted to do was catch anyone's eye. But if Cate was aware how rude she'd been, she made no show of it. Her head was held high.

A man at the far end of the room cleared his throat. Sidney, his name was if Fran had remembered correctly. 'I think your father hoped you would honour his wishes one last time, and I'm sure he had good reason for it. He never did anything without good reason.'

Marcus drew in a sharp breath. 'Just come and sit here, Cate, or the soup will be stone cold.' He turned to his neighbour, an elderly woman. 'Perhaps you wouldn't mind swapping places?'

Fran automatically glanced across to the other side of the table where Saul was sitting. Predictably, he half rose with an apologetic look on his face. 'Perhaps I might also... sorry.' His apology was directed to the gentleman on Marcus's left, who slowly got to his feet, giving Sidney a pointed look. He held onto the table edge for balance and shuffled his way around the table.

Waiting until everyone was seated once more, Fran wasted no time in serving the guests their soup. She'd be damned if anyone should find it cold through no fault of her own. That done, she scuttled back to the kitchen to make her final preparation for the main course.

Ten minutes or so later, the staccato snap of Christmas crackers being simultaneously pulled was Fran's signal that the guests had finished their soup, and she hurried back to the dining room to collect the – hopefully – empty bowls. The rather unusual adornments had been carefully added to the table at the last minute by Margaret, something else about which she would say little, only that it was Clarence's wish that they be pulled just before the entrée.

'Hey, aren't these just like the ones we always had at Christmas?' asked Marcus as Fran entered, waving his cracker in the air.

Fran couldn't see if his question was directed at anyone in particular, but it was Margaret who answered.

'Indeed they are,' she replied. 'Your father thought it might be fun for you to have these one last time. They're just the same as he always made.'

'Which means there'll be no novelty inside, just some silly riddle and a hat.'

'Now, now, Marcus,' said Cate. 'Don't be so ungrateful.' She tossed the end of a cracker to one side and peered inside the cylindrical body, pulling out a bright-red slip of tissue paper. 'Do we really have to wear these?' she asked. 'Christmas is one thing, but...'

'Your father left no specific instruction over the wearing of them or not,' replied Margaret. 'So the decision is yours.'

Beside Cate, Olivia's eyes were still downcast, and Fran felt for her. If the three children were making this much fuss about seating arrangements and crackers, goodness only knows what they would make of the treasure hunt.

Cate was still fishing for her riddle when Saul held up his. 'Okay, listen... Oh...' He stopped, turning the paper over and then back again. 'Well, that's daft. It only has one word on it. Look. It just says "rain".'

'Mine's the same,' said Cate. 'Only I've got "looks".'

All eyes turned to Marcus.

'"Like",' he said, tossing the slip of paper back on the table. 'It's just rubbish, ignore it. And I'm not wearing the hat.'

Around the table, the other guests were also fiddling with their crackers, one or two of them resolutely pulling out the hats and slipping them on their heads. Whatever Clarence's intention had been, it would appear to have fallen flat. The conversation, such as it was, dried up completely, the cheery paper hats distinctly at odds with the atmosphere. It was all rather surreal, and Fran's stomach twisted with nerves again. Whatever was going on here was beginning to feel very unpleasant.

By the time Fran served the main course her heart was beating uncomfortably fast. Margaret had reminded her that she should remain present for the reading of the will, a remark which had earned Fran a sharp look from Marcus.

Apart from paying their last respects to Clarence, whatever else he had invited his guests here to do was evidently playing on their minds; their enthusiasm for their food was already dwindling and despite the heartening comments she had received for the fare, from her point of view it was looking like a disaster. She had served lacklustre, unimaginative food, and now it looked as if there was going to be quite an amount left over. For a chef that was never a nice thing to see.

After a few more minutes of near-silent eating, Cate pushed away her plate. 'Can we bring this ridiculous charade to an end and just get on with it, please?' she asked. 'No one wants to eat and I can't see the point of stretching this out any longer.' Her lips were pursed, highlighting a series of tell-tale lines around her drawn lips. Cate had been a smoker for many years.

'I agree,' said Marcus, laying down his knife and fork.

Olivia looked just as anxious as Fran felt as she quietly removed the napkin from her lap, and laid it on the table.

Margaret looked up, her fork loaded with chicken, which she gently lowered. 'If that's what everyone wishes,' she said, turning her attention to the other guests.

One by one there were answering nods.

Margaret laid her knife and fork on her plate, signalling to Fran that she should clear the dishes. Every eye in the room was on her as she did so and Fran had never felt more uncomfortable. No one spoke and every scrape of cutlery, every chink of china sounded extraordinarily loud.

Just when Fran could bear it no longer, Olivia sprang to her feet. She rushed to help Fran, and together they shuttled every-thing back to the kitchen as fast as they could. The room was still silent, however, when they returned. Fran managed to give Olivia's hand a quick squeeze before she returned to her seat, leaving Fran, once again, hovering like a spare part.

Margaret looked up, giving a warm smile. 'Thank you, Fran,' she said. 'The food was absolutely delicious, I'm sure you'll all agree. Rather a shame not to fully enjoy it, but under the circumstances...'

The murmurs of 'hear, hear' did little to improve Fran's mood.

Margaret cleared her throat and bent to pick up her handbag from under her feet. Fran wouldn't have been at all surprised if she'd had it chained to her wrist. Drawing out an envelope from its depths, Margaret removed from it a letter on paper so thick it was almost parchment. She laid it on the table in front of her.

'Fran, could I ask you to observe this?' She looked expec-tantly around the table. 'I have in front of me the last will and testament of Clarence Edward Lightman. As you can see, the will is sealed with wax. Fran, as a truly independent witness, could I ask to you to look at this document and ascertain if it has been tampered with in any way.'

Fran swallowed and duly took the letter, peering closer at the wax seal. She turned the letter over, not because she was expecting to see anything but more to make a show of exam-ining it more fully. She passed it back with a hand that she hoped wasn't visibly shaking. 'Everything looks fine,' she said.

'Excellent,' replied Margaret. 'Then I will commence with the reading of the will.' She cleared her throat. '"I, Clarence Edward Lightman, of Justice House, Shrewsbury, Shropshire, and being of sound mind, do hereby revoke all former wills and testaments made by me and declare this to be my last will and testament."' Margaret paused. 'There follow two paragraphs:

the first naming myself as the executor of Clarence's estate, and the second, rather more lengthy paragraph, contains the details of Clarence's wishes for his funeral arrangements, a copy of which was sent to me under separate cover prior to Mr Lightman's death. I have this here should anyone wish to check the detail, though suffice to say we are now almost through the arrangements he left for today. There is only one other stipulation before we come to the legacies themselves and that is that Ms Olivia Turner be allowed to remain at Justice House for the duration of one calendar month from today.'

Saul took up his glass of water and sipped at it.

'So on to the bequests themselves, which are very straightforward. "Firstly, to my dear friends: Francine Collins, William Butler, Paul Iveson, Mary Duggan, Stephen Forrester, Sheila Blacksmith, Sidney Barnard and Neil Pope I leave the sum of five thousand pounds each, in gratitude for all that you have brought to my life, and for services rendered following my death."'

Fran looked at the faces of those sitting expectantly round the table. If anyone else had found Clarence's last statement odd, they didn't show it. All three siblings sat wearing expressions of polite interest. Margaret continued.

'"Secondly... to Olivia Turner I leave my rosewood chess set and the sum of twenty thousand pounds. And thirdly, to my nearest and dearest, I bequeath the entire residue of my estate in equal shares."'

There was an audible sigh of relief. Olivia's eyes closed as she drew in a slow breath, whereas Cate grinned. Whether she meant to or not, Fran wasn't sure, but she had evidently given up trying to look demure.

'"However..."' Margaret's voice was louder than it had been before. She held up a hand. '"There are certain conditions attached to my final bequest and these conditions must be met if the estate is not to become liable for forfeit."'

'Forfeit?' queried Saul. 'What does that mean?'

Marcus leaned forward. 'Shut up and listen!'

'"In the event of the estate being forfeit, then it shall pass in full to the Shropshire Wildlife Sanctuary."'

'What?' Marcus looked around him.

'It means it goes to someone else,' said Cate.

'Yes, I know that,' he snapped back. 'What I meant is, what conditions? What's he said?'

'Your father made the following statement,' replied Margaret calmly. '"As you will all know, I have been very fortunate in my life. I have been able to follow my dreams and write adventure books which have captured the imagination of children and adults alike. That these books subsequently went on to become board games and puzzles gave them a longevity I could never have dreamed of, and brought me immeasurable pleasure too. I am also extremely grateful that the years have been equally as kind to my mind, so that I have been able to enjoy my passion for these games and other brain-teasers throughout my life. My work has also afforded me an extremely comfortable living. My only regret in life, therefore, is that none of my children ever truly shared or understood this passion—"'

'What the hell?' Marcus's voice was harsh, and dark with anger. 'He chooses his death to stand us all on the naughty step again.'

He half rose to his feet, only to be pulled back down again by Cate.

'Shut up,' she hissed.

'Thank you, Cate,' replied Margaret. 'I do understand that this is a difficult day for you, but I would advise you to listen carefully.' She pinned Marcus with a fierce stare. 'I shall continue your father's words... "My only regret in life, therefore, is that none of my children ever truly shared or understood this passion... *or so I believed.* Many years ago I allowed this hurt to fester, forgetting that each of them is their own person, and consequently must have their own opinions and be able to live their own lives. In forgetting that their choices were as valid as mine, I condemned them simply for wanting different things. I have, however, come to realise over the years that it is these stubborn beliefs that have caused the difficulties between us, lying in the heart of our family, rotting it from within.

"'On the 26th January next I would have reached the ripe old age of eighty-three and as my dearest wish is to right some of the past wrongs, I had planned a birthday celebration to which you would all have been invited. As part of the celebration I had also planned a little surprise and I sincerely hoped it would be the occasion when our wounds began to heal. Now, sadly, time has robbed us of this opportunity. However, all is not lost. I still believe that we may yet be able to put our differences aside and so I invite you all to join in one last game with me, a surprise treasure hunt, just like we used to play before our idiotic pride and arrogance got in the way. We used to play for chocolate, if you remember, but this time you'll be playing for something far greater than that: my legacy, an equal share for each of you, *provided* you play by the rules of the game.'"

Margaret swallowed and looked up, scanning the faces around her. 'In fact, there is only one rule, or rather one choice. Would you like me to read it out?'

Marcus still looked angry, an ugly flush colouring his cheeks. 'I think you better had, don't you? So we can get this stupid charade over and done with.'

'Very well.' Margaret dipped her head. "'I have given the rules of the hunt a very great deal of thought, and, as I have already mentioned, it is my greatest wish to see our family reunited. So I am giving you an opportunity, and I believe it is the best opportunity you will have, to put aside your differences with each other, and with me, and work together towards a common goal. Something that, sadly, we were never able to do. Therefore, to take part in the treasure hunt, you simply have to choose. Play as one team, all of you together, and you each receive an equal share of the estate upon completion. However, decide to play individually, or in any other combination against one another, and any losers get nothing.

"'I trust you will allow me this one final wish, and let me end my time with a cracker of a game for you.'"

There was a stunned silence which swelled almost unbearably until Marcus's chair shot backwards.

'I don't believe this! That we're expected to just sit here and listen to this... rubbish. And in front of all of you. People who don't even know us, sitting there, making judgements, making...'

Beside him, Cate was white-faced with shock. Saul looked as if he was about to cry, his body seemingly taking up half the space it had before.

Marcus stared at first one end of the table and then the other. 'Well, go on then, someone say something,' he shouted, even though his tone warned them not to. He stood for a moment more, and then sank back into his chair. 'This is ridiculous,' he muttered.

Fran risked a glance down the table at Olivia as the beats of silence stretched out once more. She sat motionless with her head bent and Fran didn't blame her. She had a horrible feeling that Olivia was about to be given the blame for Clarence's words. Fran could hear Marcus in her head as clearly as if he'd spoken out loud – how Olivia had wormed her way into their family, how she had colluded with their father to cook up this stupid game. None of it would have been true but that scarcely mattered to people like Marcus.

He was still muttering under his breath when Cate spoke softly, green eyes flashing in the overhead light.

'I suppose you knew all about this.' She directed a venomous look towards Margaret. 'What did you do, egg him on? Yes, Mr Lightman; no, Mr Lightman; why don't you make a point, Mr Lightman? Well, you don't know what it was like when we were children, how he was after Mother died. You don't know anything about what happened.' She all but snarled at the solicitor. 'I hope his fee was worth it.'

Margaret blanched. 'I can assure you that it was nothing of the sort. Your father has been a client of ours for years, and his affairs passed to me when my own father died. What you imply would be completely improper and I resent the accusation that —' She stopped and swallowed. 'I understand that you must all be extremely upset, having to cope with your father's death and now learning that there are conditions to your inheritance, but I cannot comment on the content of your father's will, I can only do what has been asked of me and that is to discharge my duty regarding Mr Lightman's final wishes. I do, however, feel that his actions were taken with your best interests at heart, as he has made very clear. He has also left each of you a letter, his personal farewell if you like. All he asked is that you read it with an open mind, and heart.'

'So, let me get this straight,' said Marcus. 'Ignoring all the other crap for a moment, am I right in understanding that we have to play some sort of stupid game before we get his money?'

'That is correct,' replied Margaret. 'A "treasure hunt" is how it was described.'

Marcus placed both hands on the table, palms down, and levered himself upright, leaning forward to thrust his face closer to Margaret's. 'Well, I will not be treated like a child,' he hissed. 'Dad can shove his bloody game, I'm not standing for it a moment longer and—'

'Sit down!'

Marcus looked as if he'd been shot.

It was Saul who spoke, twin red blotches burning his cheeks. He glared at his brother. 'Don't you see what this is all about?'

'Of course, I bloody see! That's exactly my point. This is all about Dad teaching us a lesson for having the audacity to disagree with him, and I am *not* having our inheritance reduced to some pathetic parlour game.'

'You haven't listened to a word that's been said, have you?' argued Saul. 'Haven't you ever thought how much nicer life would have been if we had got on with Dad? With each other? Even hoped that things could change?'

'You're living in cloud cuckoo land if you really think that's what this is all about, Saul. This isn't about redemption, or forgiveness. It hasn't been done out of any largess on Dad's part, it's just another way of showing us he'll always have the last word. Well, I'm not having any of it.'

'I'm not sure we have any choice, brother dear,' drawled Cate. 'This is so like him. Unbelievable...'

'At least give Margaret a chance to tell us what we have to do before you go off on one, Marcus. We don't even know what it is yet.'

'Thank you, Saul,' said Margaret. 'The instructions for the game are quite straightforward, and in essence require the solving of various clues, each of which will lead to a specific location where the next clue is to be found, and so on. Once the final clue has been solved, your father's estate will be divided accordingly.' She looked at Marcus. 'Now, if you're ready to hear the instructions, I shall read them out.'

Marcus shrugged.

'Very well.' Margaret smoothed out the papers and began to read. '"Firstly, my will cannot be challenged. If none of you wish to take part in the treasure hunt under the conditions I have described, then the entirety of my estate, minus the afore-mentioned bequests, will go the Shropshire Wildlife Sanctuary. Secondly, in order to safeguard the rules and the spirit of the game, there is a strict method for its playing.

'"Save for the last, each of the clues has been devised with the help of one of my friends around the table today and, when solved, will lead to a specific location. At that location will be a telephone number belonging to them and once called, they will provide you with the next clue, and so on. They do not know what the answers to the other clues are, nor do they know which clue in the series they have. They do not have any other information than the clue they have been given. Do not, therefore, use coercion to try to gain anything else from them. Calls to these numbers will also be logged, so if you elect to play individually and the game is unable to progress because someone has jeopardised it by removing the telephone number at any clue location then it will be obvious who has done so and that person will be disqualified. Likewise, should anyone ring a number only to find it does not exist then you are to call Mrs Foster immediately and it will be known that the numbers themselves have been tampered with. Similarly, if you elect to play individually and anyone is found to have cheated by any means, they will be disqualified."'

'So, when do we get the first clue?' asked Cate.

'I believe that information has already been given to you,' Margaret replied.

Cate stared at her. 'Well, it hasn't, obviously, otherwise I wouldn't be asking.'

Margaret raised her eyebrows but remained silent.

Cate looked ready to explode and stared at Marcus with an expression which clearly implied he should do something. All she got in return was a muttered expletive.

'So, what is it then?' Cate demanded when Marcus seemed unable to help. 'What's the clue? We're not going to get very far if you don't even tell us what it is.'

Margaret dipped her head a fraction. 'As I said, the information you need has already been given to you.'

For a moment it looked as if the battle of wills was set to escalate, but then Saul laid a hand on Cate's arm.

'Cate, wait a minute.' He wiggled his fingers. 'Let's think about this. If we already have the clue, then it's something which is either physically here, or something which has been said.' He looked back at Margaret. 'What did Dad say?' He turned his head, staring across the room as he tried to recall the words Margaret had already read out.

Cate simply stared at him, nonplussed.

Saul's brow furrowed as his eyes swivelled to take in the table and everything on it. Suddenly his expression cleared. 'Dad said that he'd devised a cracker of a game for us...' His hand rested lightly on one of the pieces of cardboard which still littered the table. He pulled it towards him. 'That's it, the crackers...' He turned the cardboard aside, scrabbling for the slip of paper that had fallen from it. A slip of paper with a single word printed on it.

'I don't bloody believe it,' he exclaimed. 'The clue is *here*, in these words.' He jumped to his feet. 'You two, find the words!' He seized his neighbour's cracker, peering inside it before tossing the carcass to the floor. Then he snatched up another piece of paper from where it had been tossed, resting against a glass. 'Look, here!'

Cate got to her feet. 'God, he's right, Marcus, quick! Find your word.'

Fran watched in horror as the three siblings dashed around the table from place to place, snatching up the papers with neither care nor heed for anyone else sitting there.

Marcus spread out the slips of paper on the table, shoving his glass sideways in the process. 'Right, let's look at what we've got...' He picked up each slip of paper and laid them in a line. '*Is*,' he intoned. '*Where... it... standing... bright... from... rain... I'm...* None of this makes any sense.'

'That's because they're in the wrong order, dummy!' said Cate, elbowing her brother to get a better look.

'But they could go in any order. How the hell do we know when we've got it right?'

Fran bit her lip. It was so obvious. Adam would be proud of

her. She dared a look at Margaret, only to find the solicitor studying her, a slight smile playing across her mouth.

Marcus continued to lay out the slips. '*Sun... the... like... but... looks...* That's it, that's all of them.'

'This could take forever,' muttered Saul. 'It's obviously a sentence, so what would come first? *The?*'

'Try it,' said Cate. '*The sun is... bright?* But what comes after that?' She tutted in frustration. 'How will we even know when we have it right? There must be something else.' Her eyes raked the table. 'What word did you have, Marcus?'

He hunted for his slip. 'Like,' he said. 'This one here.'

'And mine was "looks",' said Cate, picking up the appropriate paper. 'Yours has your name on the back of it though,' she added, looking at Marcus. 'Mine doesn't. It's someone else's.' She paused a moment. 'Hang on, which one does have my name?' She sifted through the other words until she found the one she was looking for. 'This one says "standing".'

Saul held out his hand. 'Give it to me a minute.' He looked towards the head of the table, his head nodding imperceptibly as he counted each chair around it.

Fran smiled. He had worked it out.

'But originally, you were sitting over there, and I was four down from you...' He turned over all the pieces of paper so that the names were showing instead of the words. Then with a glance towards the occupant of each chair, he began to rearrange them. Once done, he turned them back over, one by one. "Each of the crackers was in a specific place so that, when opened in turn, the words spelled out the sentence. That's why there was a seating plan, so that we would know when the words were in the correct order. Putting them back in that order we now have: *From where I'm standing the sun is bright but it looks like rain.* Is that right?' He looked enquiringly at Margaret. 'Is that it?' said Marcus. 'You've known all along?' He rolled his eyes. 'Of course you did.'

Margaret ignored him, and simply straightened out the piece of paper in front of her. 'Well done, that is indeed the first clue. And now that you have it, I'm obliged to read you the following. I suggest you listen carefully.' She drew in a steadying breath. *"'From where I'm standing the sun is bright but it looks like rain* is indeed the first clue and you are now on your way to claiming your inheritance. There are a further five clues, but the path ahead will be determined by you alone.'"

Margaret held up her hand to stave off any further comments. She continued reading. "'You now have a decision to make. All Mrs Foster requires to settle the inheritance is the answer to the final clue, however, as I've already described, you may elect to play the game together and share the inheritance equally or play individually, or in any combination, and risk losing the lot. Equally, you may decide not to take part at all, in which case you forfeit your share, but the game must be played to its conclusion or no one will win. It must also be concluded within one calendar month from today. The time has come to make your choice and you must inform Mrs Foster of your decision at nine o'clock tomorrow morning, when the game will begin. Good luck.'"

Margaret gently laid down the paper and looked up. 'I trust that's clear?' she asked.

No one spoke. The three siblings were staring at each other, a conflicting mixture of expressions on their faces. Fran was almost certain she knew which way this was going to go and it would be very interesting to see which of the three spoke first.

'You don't have to tell me now,' reminded Margaret. 'But I must hear from each player at nine tomorrow.' She reached into her handbag and pulled out three envelopes. 'Meanwhile, here are the letters your father wrote, one for each of you. Marcus... Cate... and Saul. Perhaps you might like to have a read of them this evening?' She handed them over, a gentle query on her face.

None of the siblings spoke; Marcus took his letter as if it were an unexploded bomb.

Fran swallowed. Now didn't seem quite the right moment to mention that there were still thirteen portions of trifle sitting in the kitchen.

5

The dinner party broke up not long after that. Cate was the first to leave, getting up and stalking from the room without a word. Marcus was hot on her heels; Fran imagined so that he could talk his sister into forming an alliance. Admittedly, Fran didn't know Cate at all, but she wished him luck. Something told her that Cate wasn't about to entertain any ideas of sharing Clarence's estate, not when there was a chance she could claim it all. That left Saul, sitting alone with a stunned expression on his face. Fran still wasn't decided whether she felt sorry for him. Eventually, he too got to his feet, muttering a general apology and at least had the decency to excuse himself from the table.

Margaret cleared her throat. 'I do apologise, everyone. I think we all knew that wasn't going to be easy but, for Clarence's sake, I want to thank you all for sticking with it.'

'It's quite all right, Margaret,' said Sidney. 'You have performed your duties admirably and our role in all this was made very clear right from the start. Clarence hoped for a better response from his family but he was equally realistic about how they might take the news of his surprise. He warned us what we might expect, and I'm sad to say his hunch was right. As they say, you can lead a horse to water but you can't make them drink.' He paused to look around the table at his fellow diners. 'The time has now come, however, for us to fulfil our part in proceedings and I think I'm speaking for everyone when I say that the sooner we leave Justice House, the better.'

Several heads nodded their agreement, they all looked mightily relieved at the opportunity to escape.

Margaret got to her feet. 'In that case, then, it simply remains for me to thank you all for coming. Your presence and your ongoing help meant a great deal to Clarence. I shall obviously be in touch with you all, but if there's anything else I can do for you now, then please let me know.'

Sidney gave a small bow. 'Perhaps our coats? As earlier, those of us with cars can ensure that everyone is ferried safely to the hotel where we're staying. I'm sure we shall spend the remainder of the evening very pleasantly, reminiscing about our dear and much-missed friend.'

As Margaret bustled off to fetch everyone's outdoor things, Fran took the opportunity of a vacated chair to sink down next to Olivia, who hadn't spoken for quite some time. She leaned in and nudged her shoulder gently. 'You okay, Liv?' she asked.

Olivia stared at her. 'I don't know what to think. About any of it. This is crazy. It's...' Her eyes filled with tears. 'It's just the sort of thing Clarence *would* do. The game part of it, I mean, but the rest... I might have known his family would react badly. But he was such a wonderful man and so kind, for his sake I'd hoped for more. And I can't help thinking about what he said to Margaret, about *if* he died from a heart attack.'

'You don't really believe there was anything in it, though, do you? It was just a flippant comment, like you said, and there was no reason to suspect his death wasn't natural.'

'I know,' replied Olivia. 'I just don't know what to think. It's all so...'

'Surreal?' suggested Fran.

'Yes!' Her eyes widened. 'I can't imagine how people must be feeling.'

'Me neither, although with the possible exception of Saul, I can't bring myself to care all that much. You, however, are a different case entirely. What are you going to do, Liv?' she whispered.

'I don't know. Get out of here for one. Staying was going to be difficult before all this, but now... I don't think I can stand it. It was very good of Clarence to insist that I be allowed to stay for a month if I need it, but imagine what it's going to be like.' Her lip trembled a little. 'Cate and Marcus will be vile.'

'Yes, though Cate and Marcus may well be a little busy hunting for clues,' replied Fran. 'Hopefully, they won't have time to make your life a misery.'

'That's just it though. I know what they'll be thinking – that I knew all about this – that it was my idea even and I know where all the clues are. But I don't. I told you, I knew Clarence was up to something but I never imagined it would be anything like this.'

Fran nodded, suspecting that Olivia's summing up of the situation was very accurate. 'Do you have anywhere you can go?' she asked.

Olivia was about to answer when she paused, her eyes flicking up over Fran's shoulder. It was Sidney, a scarf well wrapped around his neck and overcoat in hand.

'I'd like to thank you both for your hospitality,' he said. 'Although, alas, I suspect we never got the opportunity to sample any of your finest work, Francesca. I've never met anyone who could equal my wife's Victoria sponge, but you may even have pipped her to the post.' He held out his hand. 'It's been very nice to meet you both.'

Fran shook his hand, leaning back so that Olivia could do the same. She moved to stand but Sidney shook his head.

'No, don't get up. Mrs Foster will show us out.' He paused,

a soft smile on his face. 'Clarence was inordinately fond of you, my dear. Take care, won't you... and good luck.' He smiled, dipped his head and with that, he was gone.

Olivia looked up at the milling group of people out in the hallway. 'I'd still better...'

Fran smiled. 'Of course. Go on, and I'll have the kettle boiled by the time you've said goodbye.'

She turned her attention to the debris on the table and the stack of serving dishes still on the sideboard. Washing and clearing up at the end of an event was actually a part of her job she enjoyed. She found the returning of things to normal calming and quite therapeutic, but more so perhaps because it was usually during this time she felt her deepest sense of satisfaction. Her food had been enjoyed, and appreciated, and whatever the event there was a real sense of achievement for her part in it. Tonight, however, none of those things had happened. It all felt like a massive waste of time, and although she was looking forward to feeling calmer and somewhat restored, that was about it. The task still had to be done, however, and she got wearily to her feet.

At the sight of the uneaten trifle, Fran's spirits sank even further. *Where was Adam when she needed him?* He'd polish off several portions of dessert without seemingly stopping to breathe, and she hadn't found much yet he didn't like. Except for anchovies... She smiled at the memory of their first encounter when he had complained bitterly about some tiny fish-laden canapés. Canapés he'd pinched, she might add, so it was his own fault. One thing was sure, she'd damned well have some trifle herself; she could do with something sweet.

She emptied the tray of dishes she was carrying and then flicked on the kettle, returning to the dining room to fetch the glasses and remaining crockery. By the time Olivia returned to the kitchen with Margaret in tow, Fran had already run the sink full of hot soapy water. She crossed to the kettle.

'Now,' she said, 'sit down and I'll make us all a drink.' She was about to offer them tea or coffee when another thought occurred. 'I spied some hot chocolate in one of the cupboards earlier,' she said. 'And in the absence of a stiff brandy, I think it might be just what we all need. What do you reckon?'

Olivia groaned. 'Oh, that sounds like heaven.'

'Margaret?'

The solicitor paused for a moment. 'I haven't had one of those in forever, I normally live off coffee. Go on though, I will.' She eyed the row of bowls on the work surface. 'Are those the trifles?'

Fran nodded and then smiled. 'I was thinking that too.'

'Do you suppose we should offer some to the others?' asked Olivia. 'I suspect they're in their rooms.'

'Presumably they know where the kitchen is,' replied Fran. 'I will gladly offer pudding and drinks if they appear, but until that time...'

Ten minutes later, they were sitting around the table, tucking in.

'I've never thought of frothing the milk first when I make hot chocolate,' said Olivia, 'but the difference is incredible.'

'My daughter adores them like this,' said Fran. 'And it's much cheaper than going out for a treat. Just use one of those handheld blenders, I'd be lost without mine.'

Olivia dipped her spoon into the rich froth and sighed. 'What do you suppose they're thinking?' she asked, plugging the spoon into her mouth.

Fran knew immediately who she was referring to. 'I can't begin to imagine,' she said. 'Because it isn't just the fact that Clarence has set them all a treasure hunt, is it? From a personal point of view, he's perhaps set them an even bigger challenge. Admitting to their shortcomings as a family and taking on board what Clarence said probably doesn't come that easily to them.

The only way ahead is for them to work together, but whether they see it like that is another matter.'

'He's making them choose the outcome,' said Olivia. 'If they don't play, no one inherits. Similarly, if they play on their own, while they all presumably have an equal chance of winning, it's a big risk to take. Yet, if they do what Clarence wished and play together, they increase their chance of inheriting, but at the same time *decrease* their actual inheritance. That's a lot to mull over, when what Clarence could have done is simply split his estate between them equally. They could still have played the game for a bit of fun, but to make their inheritance dependent on it...'

'Course there might be another reason why he's done it,' said Margaret with a look over the top of her spoon.

Olivia sighed. 'You're thinking about what he told you again, aren't you?' she asked.

'I can't help it.' Margaret shook her head. 'Are you sure Clarence never mentioned any fears to you that he might not die from natural causes?'

'No, of course, he didn't. I think I'd have remembered. Margaret, he was eighty-two.' Her eyebrows all but disappeared under her fringe. 'Are you honestly suggesting what I think you're suggesting? Besides, who on earth kills someone in their eighties?'

'Why does anyone commit murder?' replied Margaret. 'I'm not sure what age has got to do with it. Surely the motives are the same whatever the age of the victim?'

'Fear, anger, envy and desire,' said Fran before blushing slightly as both women stared at her. 'The four motives for murder. I read that somewhere,' she finished with a lame smile. She hadn't, it had been told to her by Nell Bradley, the head police detective she'd worked with on a few occasions. Perhaps now wasn't the best time to mention this.

'Exactly,' said Olivia. 'And clearly none of those apply in

Clarence's case. And the medical professionals would have flagged up anything amiss, surely?'

'Yes, I know,' Margaret replied. 'And there was never any suggestion of that.'

'You've also got to look at means and opportunity,' said Fran, the words beginning to sound far too familiar to some of those she'd used in the past.

'I know. You're right, it's a crazy idea,' said Margaret. She shook her head. 'He must have been joking,' she added, giving Olivia an apologetic look. 'Sorry, I'm being melodramatic. And far too emotional.'

Olivia gave her a warm smile. 'Which you're entirely entitled to be. It's been a tough day, and worse for you, having to say everything you have.'

'Emotional for us all,' replied Margaret with a gentle nod at Olivia.

Olivia pressed her lips together and drew in a deep breath. Fran could see she was close to tears again. 'Do you think they'll all want to play?' she asked, changing the subject. 'Saul looked like he was going to be sick.'

'Of course they will,' said Margaret without hesitation. 'Saul might not wear his air of entitlement quite as loudly as his brother and sister but there's a lot of money at stake here. Obviously, there are various disbursements still to make from the estate before everything is finalised, but we're talking six figures here, and some. He wouldn't give up the chance to inherit. What interests me, though, is whether any alliances will be formed, or whether they will all elect to play individually.'

'I know what I think,' said Fran.

'Me too, but let's just wait and see, shall we? They have a lot to consider. Not least the first clue itself, which doesn't sound at all easy, does it?'

Olivia was toying with her spoon, but looked up. 'Don't you know the solution?'

Margaret shook her head. 'No, and I'm glad I don't. The fewer people who know the solutions to the clues, the better. That way no one can cheat. Clarence was pretty canny in that regard.'

Fran nodded. 'Makes sense. But what was that clue again? "From where I'm standing the sun is bright but it looks like rain". What even does that mean?'

She looked at Olivia, who shrugged.

'I haven't the foggiest. I was never that good at his brain-teasers. Give me a game of chess any day. I have a more tactical mind, I think. But whatever it is, let's hope someone works it out, because I for one do not want to be around if Clarence's inheritance ends up going to a wildlife sanctuary. Not that I have any objection to that per se, but his family would go mad.'

'Can you imagine what Marcus's reaction would be?' said Fran.

'I *can* imagine,' replied Olivia. 'Which is entirely my point.' She sighed. 'Hopefully, I'll be long gone by then.'

'We got interrupted earlier,' said Fran. 'But do you have somewhere in mind to go? Even if it's just in the short term?'

Olivia pulled a face. 'Not exactly... There are plenty of places available to rent, but my issue is not so much where to stay, but how to fund it. Living here has given me a buffer against the vagaries of earning a living through writing. It's my fault, I should have given these things far more thought than I have, but you don't, do you, when things are settled? And somehow the years just slip on by.'

'Your bequest from Clarence can be paid immediately probate is granted,' replied Margaret. 'And I will do all I can to speed that along.'

Olivia bowed her head. 'Thank you. I sound ungracious, don't I? I'm not...' She ate another quick mouthful of trifle. 'Sorry, this is all beginning to catch up with me. It's just that ever since Clarence died, I haven't been able to think about the future. Didn't want to, I suppose. And his gift is amazing... truly... I'd just rather he were here instead.' She sniffed. 'I do have some savings to tide me over, enough to find a place to live, and see me right for a little while, but longer term I'm going to have to seriously think about finding some other paid work too. What I earn from writing simply isn't sufficient.'

Fran pulled a face, then gave Olivia her best reassuring smile. 'Listen, it isn't very big, but we have a spare room if you get stuck. You'd have to put up with Martha dancing around the place, and Jack shouting whenever Manchester City score a goal, but you'd be very welcome.'

'Thank you.' Olivia's smile seemed heartfelt as she laid her hand on Fran's arm, giving it a squeeze. 'Really, thank you.'

Margaret lifted her mug of hot chocolate, blowing gently across its surface. 'There is one other option open to you,' she said.

'Don't tell me... I could run away and join the circus,' joked Olivia, but then she checked herself. 'That's a very mysterious expression, Margaret,' she added.

Fran had noticed it too; the rather playful smile on Margaret's face that was trying to make itself known.

'Not so mysterious, really, I just wanted to point something out, that's all. You see, Clarence's will was very carefully worded, Olivia. No one else will have noticed the way it was phrased, which was entirely the point. More importantly, if its meaning was challenged, from a legal standpoint, there'd be no justification.'

Olivia frowned. 'I'm sorry, I'm not following you.'

'See, you missed it too,' said Margaret, smiling. 'Think back to when the details for the bequests were being read out. Firstly, there was the money left to Clarence's friends, then the provision for you—' She held up her hand. 'No, don't interrupt, I know how much it means to you. Because thirdly, what Clarence actually said was "I bequeath the entire residue of my estate to my nearest and dearest..." At which point, if you recall, Cate started grinning like the Cheshire cat. What she failed to grasp, alongside her brothers, was that Clarence wasn't just talking to his children at that point. He was also talking to you, Olivia. Perhaps more than any of them, *you* are Clarence's nearest and dearest.' She laid a hand on Olivia's shoulder. 'Which is all a roundabout way of saying that, if you would like to, you are also very eligible to take part in the treasure hunt.'

'What? No, I couldn't! I...' Olivia sat back in her chair with a bump. 'Are you trying to tell me that Clarence hoped I would?'

'That's exactly what I'm trying to tell you.'

'But that's... that's... crazy!'

'Perhaps,' replied Margaret. 'But perhaps also incredibly astute. We know what Clarence hoped would be the outcome of all this. It really was his deepest wish that he and his children's differences be resolved, but he was also no fool. I think he suspected all along that they would behave as they always have. We don't know that, of course. We won't find out how they're choosing to play until tomorrow. But by giving you a separate bequest, he ensured that you would have something, even if you didn't wish to take part in the hunt yourself.'

Margaret's words hung in the air as Olivia looked first at Fran and then back at Margaret, the stunned expression on her face turning slowly through incredulity to excitement as she realised the implications of what Margaret had said.

'Could I really do that?' she asked eventually. 'I mean, actually take part and have any chance of winning?'

'You have the same odds as any of the others separately,' replied Margaret. 'Or, you play together and help each other solve the clues to the final solution. I can be of no further help in the matter, but I *was* asked to make you aware of the situation. And that, I have done. The rest is up to you.'

Olivia thought for a moment, her face falling. 'No, I

couldn't, it wouldn't be right. This is a family matter and whatever the relationship between Clarence and his children, this place, everything, it's their birth right, I couldn't interfere.'

'I agree that they're not going to be bowled over by the idea of you joining them, but let's cross that bridge when we get to it.' Margaret raised her eyebrows. 'As for whether you should even consider taking part, I'll remind you that you've given the last eight years of your life to Clarence and, by all accounts from those who knew him well, during that time, he was happier than he'd been since his wife died all those years ago. You gave him a purpose again, Olivia, made him believe that what he spent his life trying to achieve had been worthwhile, was still worthwhile. His relationship with his children broke down through no fault of yours, indeed you were not even here during that time. They are all responsible adults, capable of making their own decisions and, had they wanted to, they could have tried to change that situation at any point over the last twenty years or so, longer probably. Instead, they stayed away. You are well aware how often they called or visited.'

Olivia dropped her head.

'Exactly. Clarence told me it was so infrequently you could literally count the occasions on one hand. And yet they still seem to persist with a view I gather they have held all their lives, that simply being a son or daughter entitles them to everything that Clarence has or held dear. Well, it doesn't. Not in my book anyway.'

'Not in mine either,' said Fran. 'My mum always used to say to me what you sow, you reap, and while I didn't agree with everything she said, I do agree with that.'

'So, what do we do now?' whispered Olivia. 'I can't think straight.'

But Fran's thoughts were already racing ahead. 'Margaret, would I be right in thinking that if Olivia did want to take part in the game that she doesn't have to do so on her own?'

Margaret nodded. 'That's correct. She has the same options open to her as the other siblings – play together and share the inheritance, or play singly and, if she wins, keep it in its entirety.'

'And if it's the latter, does she have to play strictly on her own, or can she enlist help from someone outside the family?'

'I don't believe any stipulation was made,' Margaret said, an amused smile on her face.

Olivia leaned forward. 'Why, what are you thinking?'

Fran grinned at her. 'That we finish our trifle, and while we're doing that I'll just message a friend.'

She pulled her phone from her pocket, called up her last message and typed:

Adam, what are you up to at the moment?

6

Adam arrived forty minutes later, ushered quickly into the hallway by Fran, who pulled him into the kitchen, shushing his incredulous noises as they went.

'But...' he protested.

'I know,' whispered Fran. 'They're trompe l'oeils, and you can have a look in a minute. For now, come with me and don't announce your presence. I'll explain shortly. Did you leave your car out on the road?'

He nodded and was about to speak again when Fran held a finger to her lips.

They appeared in the kitchen just as Olivia was leaving via the other door. Margaret still sat at the table, looking almost as surprised as Adam.

'Weren't you at the funeral?' she asked.

Adam nodded and slid his beanie from his dark curls, holding it in front of him as if it were a shield. He looked at Fran for an introduction.

'Margaret, this is my friend, Adam. Adam, this is Margaret Foster, who was Clarence Lightman's solicitor.'

Adam stood stock-still, cheeks pink from the cold.

Margaret smiled. 'I almost introduced myself earlier,' she replied. 'But then the vicar wanted a word and, when I looked again, you seemed to have gone.'

Adam looked a little embarrassed. 'I was hiding,' he said. 'Behind a pillar in the church. I thought you were going to ask me to leave.'

Fran smiled. That was *so* like Adam.

'On the contrary, it was nice to see a few extra people there,' said Margaret. 'I worried that no one else would turn up.'

'I saw the funeral details in the paper,' Adam replied. 'I couldn't not go... I mean, this is Ebenezer Doolittle we're talking about. Mr Lightman, I mean.' He stopped himself. 'Sorry,' he added unnecessarily. 'I'm a big fan. I get a little excited.'

Margaret wasn't the least bit offended. 'Fran has told us all about you,' she said, which made Adam look even more uncomfortable.

He turned to Fran. 'You weren't kidding when you said you hadn't been entirely honest with me, were you?'

She smiled. 'Adam texted me from the funeral,' she explained to Margaret. 'And joked that it was a shame I wasn't doing the catering. I might not have mentioned that I was.'

He raised his eyebrows. 'She thinks I'd have gate-crashed and then bounced all over the place, rambling on about my childhood hero.'

Fran pursed her lips. 'I was trying...' She trailed off. How could she put her feelings into words without hurting Adam's?

'She's quite right, that's more or less exactly what I would have done,' he replied, not upset in the slightest. 'I can be really annoying,' he added. 'Mind you, it didn't look much like anyone else was all that sorry he'd died. What's with his family? They weren't exactly grief-stricken at the funeral.' He dropped his head. 'Sorry, I probably shouldn't have said that.'

'Not at all,' replied Olivia, coming back into the room, 'I'd say that was a pretty accurate assessment.' She smiled. 'Hi, I'm Olivia – Liv. Fran's told me all about you.'

She hadn't, actually. Neither was Olivia completely up to date with all of Fran's recent sleuthing activities. But that was a story for another day. Possibly...

'And it's okay,' Olivia added. 'The others were in the drawing room when Adam arrived, bickering like crazy, so they've no idea he's here. They've also just gone to the pub, so we've the house to ourselves for a while. Cate was desperate for a "proper" drink.' She looked at Adam. 'Would you like to see what Clarence called his Inventing Room?'

Adam looked back at Fran and she could tell he was having a very hard time keeping his excitement under control.

'You're going to love it,' she said.

Olivia led them back into the hallway, pausing so that Adam could finally have a look at the amazing scenes painted between the arches on the hallway walls. 'This part of the house dates back to the fourteenth century,' she said. 'So these were here long before Clarence moved in. They depict the view as it would have looked back then.'

Adam moved nearer. 'They look as if they were painted yesterday.'

'They have been restored,' said Olivia. 'The previous owners clearly didn't rate them as highly as Clarence. They'd all but disappeared by the time he bought the house, but he managed to find someone who specialises in this kind of thing and after a lot of painstaking research, the artist was able to reproduce them as they would have been. This is my favourite,' she added, pointing to the one she was standing beside. 'I love how there's the shadow of a figure standing in the doorway, as if they're just gazing at the view, lost in wonder.'

Adam studied the painting for a while longer, captivated. 'So why Justice House?' he asked after a few moments. 'How did it get its name?'

'The house was built for the head of the local church, which is next door, albeit quite some distance away. He also happened, as was common at the time, to be the local magistrate. The name was changed at some point to Mulberry Cottage, which doesn't really make any sense at all, and one of the first things Clarence did when he moved here was to give her her old name back again. He said it was far more suitable. As an historian I have to agree.'

'And he would want it to be called Justice House, wouldn't he? That's what he did,' said Adam.

Olivia gave Fran a quick glance. 'Sorry, I'm not sure I follow.'

'In his books – Clarence made sure the wrongdoer was always brought to justice.

Whatever happened, you always knew the baddie would get their just deserts.'

Olivia stared at him. 'I've never thought about that, but yes, you're right.'

Adam nodded, smiling broadly. 'I think it makes perfect sense, him living here. And, wow, the things this house must have seen over the years.'

Fran shuddered. Adam looked perfectly cheerful, but she could well imagine the type of justice that was metered out in the fourteenth century.

'And the Inventing Room...' said Olivia, stepping back so that Adam could go first, 'is through there.'

He paused, one hand lightly touching the wall as if he couldn't believe he was actually allowed in the room. Fran smiled at the reverence on his face. Adam may not be like a lot of people, but she was very glad he wasn't.

She followed him up the short flight of steps.

'Oh my God,' he said slowly, turning through one-eighty degrees. 'This is so incredible. I can't believe I'm standing here. Look, there's all his books and... Is that the actual castle from

Aquilla? It is! Oh God...' He turned to face Olivia. 'You've no idea how long Clarence has been a hero of mine. I've read everything he's written, and I used to get his magazine when I was little too. Honestly, it was the highlight of my week. We'd buy it on the way home from school on a Friday night and I'd spend the whole weekend poring over it, trying to work out his clues. And then I'd have to wait a whole week until the next edition to see if I was right.'

'There are some copies of it over on the bookcase there,' said Olivia. 'Sadly, not all of them. He never thought to keep them.'

Adam took two steps and then stopped, as if torn between looking at them and something else which had caught his eye. *Kid in the proverbial sweetshop*, came to Fran's mind. It was lovely, but she was very aware of the reason why she had asked him here. Almost as she thought it, Adam turned around.

'So why the cloak and dagger?' he asked her. 'I never thought I'd get to be standing somewhere like this, but you hinted at something I might be able to help with. I don't quite understand.'

'Shall we sit down?' said Margaret, who had brought up the rear. 'And perhaps I can explain.' She very quickly and concisely brought Adam up to speed.

'So you see,' said Fran, 'if Olivia does want to go ahead and take part in Clarence's challenge, you could be just the person to help her.' She flicked an apologetic glance at Olivia. 'If she wants help, that is.'

'If she wants help,' echoed Olivia, snorting with suppressed amusement. 'Of course I want help. I don't have the foggiest how to go about any of this.'

'And that would be okay, would it?' asked Adam.

Margaret tilted her head to one side. 'Well, the rules don't say otherwise.'

'You'd have to be a part of it too, Fran,' said Olivia. 'After all these years, it's like fate bringing us back together again. It will be just like being back at school.'

'Don't,' said Fran. 'We got into far too much trouble back then.' She paused, the corners of her lips twitching. 'It was fun though, wasn't it?'

Adam looked as if he were fit to burst.

'We'll only do it on one condition though,' added Fran. 'If we win, we want none of that nonsense about sharing the inheritance. We forfeit our right to it, here and now. It's your money, Olivia. Isn't that right, Adam?'

'Wait... what?' But then he smiled. 'My condition is that you promise me when this is your house, I can come for a visit and have a proper look around.'

'We've got to win first, but it's a deal on visiting the house. The rest is open for discussion.' Olivia put her palms flat against her cheeks. 'Oh God, what have I done? I still can't get my head around all this.'

'Me neither,' said Adam. 'Ebenezer Doolittle...' He shook his head in wonder. 'Who'd have thought it? Still, a treasure hunt will make a nice change from solving a murder, won't it?'

Fran watched as both Olivia and Margaret's heads swivelled first towards her and then back to Adam.

'What?' he said. 'What did I say?'

'Um... I haven't exactly told everyone how we got to be friends,' said Fran.

'Ah...' Adam dropped his head.

Olivia wriggled forward in her seat. 'Francesca Eve, you dark horse, you. You blame me for all the scrapes we got up to at school when you're just as capable of getting into them all by yourself. Come on, explain.'

Fran could feel her cheeks beginning to burn. 'There's not really much to tell,' she said. 'Just that I met Adam at a party, his mum's party. It was her birthday and she thought a murder-mystery game would be a great way to celebrate with her friends... and then the friend who was the victim at the party actually died in real life a few weeks later. Murdered. And Adam's mum was one of the suspects. So Adam and I might have worked out whodunnit, so she didn't go to prison.'

'And then there was our second case,' said Adam. 'Back in the summer when Fran catered for a weekend house party. Only one of the hosts turned up in the morning with his head bashed in.'

'And you solved the crime?' asked Margaret.

'None of us could leave the house and Nell, she was the chief detective on the case, was looking at the wrong person, so... But it was Adam who actually worked out how the murder had been committed. It was very clever.'

He tutted. 'Which was all well and good, except we had no proof, until you realised the slip-up the murderer had made.'

Olivia's eyes were wide. 'Sounds as if the pair of you are very good at solving puzzles,' she said, looking at Margaret. 'I think we may have ourselves a team.'

'Nine o'clock tomorrow morning,' she replied. 'Don't tell me before then.'

'Is that when the first clue will be read out?' asked Adam.

Fran shook her head. 'No, that was given during the reading of the will. Very clever. The clue words were hidden inside Christmas crackers and had to be fitted together in the right order to give a sentence: *From where I'm standing the sun is bright but it looks like rain.* What do you think to that?'

Adam narrowed his eyes. 'Sounds like Clarence all right.' His brow furrowed. 'Do either of you have any idea what it means?'

Olivia looked to Fran for confirmation. 'Not a sausage,' she replied.

'Hmm...' Adam looked around the room. 'So the hunt starts officially in the morning...' He checked his watch. 'Which doesn't give us that long to think about it, unless you want to stay up half the night. It's nine o'clock now.' He looked at Fran. 'And you'll be going home soon, won't you?'

Fran gave a coy smile. 'Not necessarily.'

'But what about Jack and Martha?'

'Martha went straight to her dance class after school today, where she was whisked away for a weekend-long masterclass at a rather posh performing arts school. And Jack... will have just about arrived in Amsterdam for a weekend of drunken debauchery. Otherwise known as a stag party. I therefore seem to have the whole weekend to myself.'

'Oh...' Adam's mouth was round with surprise. 'Well, that's handy.' He grinned at her.

'Isn't it?'

Olivia looked between them. 'You'll be wanting a bed for the night then,' she said. 'And, fortunately, even with Margaret, Cate, Marcus and Saul staying, there are still two spare rooms. I had better go and make them up. Then maybe we should try to figure out the first clue.'

'Oh, but I don't have anything with me,' said Fran. 'I don't need much but I'm still in my work clothes and I'm—'

'Still the same size as me, luckily,' replied Olivia, grinning. 'We spent several years swapping our clothes, as I recall. Admittedly that was for school discos but I can sort you out something that isn't covered in sequins, I promise. How about you, Adam? Can you make do for tonight? I'm not sure I have much that will fit you.'

He blushed furiously. 'I'm good,' he managed. 'I travel pretty light.'

'Excellent,' said Olivia. 'So that's that sorted.'

Margaret cleared her throat. 'Which is my cue to leave. It wouldn't do for me to be party to your discussions,' she said in response to their surprised expressions. 'In the interest of fairness, it's better if I keep out of it. And I brought a very good book with me which I'm quite keen to get back to.'

Olivia nodded. 'That's a good point,' she said. 'But...' She smiled at the solicitor. 'I can't thank you enough, for everything.'

Margaret dipped her head. 'You are so welcome. Now, don't stay up too late, any of you, you're going to need fresh brains come the morning.' She smiled at Fran. 'And thank you for a delightful dinner. It's a shame it wasn't under better circumstances, but perhaps another time.'

The three of them waited until Margaret had left the room.

'Come on,' said Fran, 'I'll help you with the beds. The quicker we get them sorted, the quicker we can start thinking about this puzzle.' She looked at Adam. 'Will you be all right down here?'

'Oh yes, I...' He made an expansive gesture around the room. 'I have plenty to keep me occupied. And I promise I'll be careful.' He wrinkled his nose. 'Although I don't suppose...'

Fran knew immediately what he was going to say. 'I have a large quantity of trifle which needs eating,' she said. 'Will that do?'

Adam's eyes lit up. 'Perfectly. Fran always says I have hollow legs,' he explained for Olivia's benefit. 'I think better on a full stomach.'

Adam carried his bowl full of pudding back down the hallway to stand in front of the paintings. There was something extremely compelling about them, and a level of detail that wasn't immediately apparent on first glance. But the longer he looked, the more he saw and, in Adam's experience, that was the case with a lot of things. He'd read something once which had always stayed with him – life, like art, is all about perspective, and sometimes it just depends on your point of view. It was a sentence which had stood him in good stead, a reminder not to take everything at face value, or to believe what was immediately obvious; that sometimes the message was more subtle, or required a slight shift in perspective to truly appreciate it. He had a feeling that Clarence had understood that concept extremely well.

Adam spooned in another mouthful of trifle, giving the paintings one final look before returning to the Inventing Room. He couldn't believe he was standing there. That, if he wanted, he could sit in the same seat where Clarence had once written his books. Reading them as a child had provided Adam with some of his happiest memories, before life became too complicated and everything went wrong. Because adventure games and solving puzzles were fine when you were young but not when you were at school and trying to figure out things far beyond the boundaries of what was being taught. Adam had thought his thirst to understand anything and everything would be welcomed, but it made him different from his classmates, and unable to fit into the boxes his teachers wished to tick. So he and education had had a rather acrimonious parting of the ways. It wasn't until Adam was much older and began to understand that his intelligence was a good thing all over again that he stumbled upon a talent for designing computer games, and the weirder and more complex the better. And now he was standing in a room where he would have felt truly at home. If only Clarence were still alive.

Except that if he were, of course, it was highly unlikely that Adam would be standing where he was. Nor would he be about to embark on the last adventure that Clarence ever devised, one that no one else would get the chance to puzzle their way through. The thought left him almost breathless with excitement.

His next made his heart thump. He hurried to the desk and put down his bowl. Was this where Clarence had been sitting when he devised this last game? Was it here where he'd conjured up the clues? And if he had, had he written them down? Made notes? Left behind the thoughts in his head like a trail of breadcrumbs for someone to find?

Adam paused. He wasn't at all sure he should rifle through the things on Clarence's desk, pull open drawers and fish inside. It felt a little as if he were walking on his grave. But, then again, Clarence had set out a series of clues for them to follow, and if there were clues to *those* clues, wouldn't Clarence expect them to follow them also?

Inhaling deeply, Adam pulled open the top drawer and peered inside. It was full of the normal paraphernalia: pens, paperclips, elastic bands, Post-it notes, all jumbled together in an untidy and disordered heap. It made Adam's fingers itch. On top of it all was a large, folded rectangle of paper. Carefully, Adam withdrew it, and with a quick check to make sure he was still alone, he opened it.

In the centre of the paper, someone, presumably Clarence, had drawn a big smiley face. And that was all. Adam sat back and laughed. It was tantamount to a finger being wagged in admonishment. *Oh no you don't...* Adam could almost hear Clarence's voice. He slid the paper back in the drawer, still smiling. *One nil to you, Clarence,* he thought. There was nothing else to be gleaned there. Nothing at all. Clarence had taken care to ensure there wouldn't be, his note was mocking proof of that. Adam picked up his bowl of trifle and began to eat it with relish.

He was just finishing off a second bowl, deep in thought, when Fran and Olivia reappeared.

'You should see the rooms, Adam,' said Fran. 'I might have to move in. And I see you made yourself comfortable.'

'I couldn't resist sitting here, you know, where he used to sit.' He flicked a glance at Olivia. 'I hope that's okay?'

'Of course it is. If Clarence were alive he would have invited you to. He loved talking to people, not just about his books and games, all sorts of things.' She smiled wistfully. 'Actually, mostly about his books and games, but he loved anyone who liked to play.' She paused. 'He was terribly lonely when I first arrived. That's why the attitude of his children angers me so much. All he wanted was someone to share his world with. It wasn't about being smart, or being the best at what he did. He wasn't about the money either, or the success. He only did it because he wanted people to enjoy themselves. It seems so little to ask.'

'There's one thing I don't understand,' said Adam. 'Especially given what you've just said. And that's why his family is in the pub. I would have thought, given the hour, that they'd be here, trying to figure out the first clue. The more I think about it, the more certain I am that the first clue must be close by. Not necessarily in the house itself, but the grounds must be pretty big. Are they?'

'Oh yes,' replied Olivia. 'But why do you think the clue is here?' She looked around the room as if she should be searching for something.

Adam shrugged. 'A hunch, maybe... A feeling that's what Clarence would do. His books always had such a huge sense of place. Some of them were world-building on an epic scale, but for whoever was sent on a quest, there was always something very important about home – they journeyed from it and they always returned to it. I can't explain it all that well but I got the feeling it was important to him.'

Fran looked at Olivia. 'See?' she said, as if that explained everything.

Adam didn't have a clue what she was talking about. And now Olivia was giving him a knowing smile and that just made things worse.

'The answer to your question, however, is that Cate and her brothers will be in the pub because they're trying very hard to make the point that they will not be told what to do. They're also acting, trying to convince one another they don't care, as if the last thing they want to do is play some silly treasure hunt.

But don't let what you might see on the surface fool you. Cate is the one who plays games the best, psychological ones that is. And Marcus... he's the most competitive, but he also won't want to share the inheritance with anyone, so his mind will be very firmly on the task, even if it doesn't look like it. He could already think he knows what the clue means.'

'And Saul?' said Fran. 'What about him?'

Olivia thought for a minute. 'Saul will be pretending resignation. That he already knows he's beaten before he even starts, when really, behind their backs, what he wants more than anything is to come out on top for once, to finally be noticed. It's curious, because out of them all, I'd say that Saul has the most chance of winning at the things which matter in life. Like being a decent person, being true to yourself, having some semblance of integrity. The trouble is, Cate and Marcus don't value those things, and so, because he wants to be liked and shape himself to fit their mould, he often turns those things aside and pretends they don't matter to him.'

'And don't forget that none of them are aware you'll be playing yet,' said Fran.

'Exactly. They think they're only up against each other, so while they're together, no one can get the upper hand. I reckon they're trying to psych each other out. Pretending nonchalance, when I doubt they're feeling anything of the sort.'

'Wow,' said Fran. 'I've said it before, and I'll say it again, but I'm very glad my life is so much less complicated compared to other people's.'

'Oh, me too,' said Olivia. 'What you see is what you get.' She looked at Adam. 'So, what do we do now?'

'We think,' he said. '*From where I'm standing the sun is bright but it looks like rain.* What on earth does that mean?'

7

Fran squinted at her phone, groaning when she saw the time. She laid it back down on the bedside table and stared at the ceiling. Not that she could see much, the room was pitch-black, the hour far too early for the winter sun to have braved the horizon yet. But Fran had already spent the night tossing and turning; there was little chance of her catching any more sleep. It was such a shame as the bed was one of the most comfortable she had ever slept in. The room was decorated in just the style she would pick if she had the space, or rather had the money... which was the irony in all of this. For money was precisely what she had spent the night thinking about. Or, more specifically, that someone's fortune rested on the outcome of a game.

She swung her legs over the edge of the bed and stood up, crossing to the window. She had stood in the exact same place the night before, looking down into the darkness of the garden below as if all manner of truths might be found there. What she had actually been doing was checking for the moon. It was something she'd done since she was a child, away from home, nervous and anxious about being apart from the things and people she loved. 'Look for the moon,' her mum had always told her, 'and wherever you are, know that I'll be watching it too. We'll share the night sky.' Last night though, her moon-gazing hadn't been because she missed being at home. In fact, had she been there she would have been relishing the prospect of a little solitude. But something about this weekend was making her feel very uneasy, and she didn't altogether know why.

A flicker of a shadow out the window caught her eye. In reality, no more than a darker shade of night that thickened for a moment before thinning again. She peered closer, and as her eyes grew accustomed to the night's tones and gradients of colour, a paler strip revealed itself. Just for a second it darkened as if something had crossed it... or someone. She stood back a little, deep in thought, turning away just as another movement caught her eye. She swung back, but the darkness was still. Whoever she had seen was gone.

Wearily, she sat down on the edge of the bed, looking at her clock and trying to convince herself there was still time to climb back under the covers and sleep. But she knew she wouldn't; she was restless, with too many thoughts running through her head. She reached for the chair beside the bed and the leggings Olivia had lent her, pulling them on.

The kitchen floor was freezing and she cursed under her breath. She hadn't thought of that when she'd crept barefoot down the stairs. The wooden boards in the hallway were cool, but didn't have the same bone-numbing chilliness of the kitchen's ceramic tiles. She wrapped her arms around herself and went to fill the kettle.

Perhaps it was a mum thing, but having a child had given Fran the ability to move around almost silently, and in the dark. Martha was well on her way to being a teenager, but when she was small it had felt as if she was the lightest sleeper on the planet. Six years of tiptoeing around had honed these skills to the point that when someone else crept into the kitchen and carefully closed the back door behind them, Fran was confident she had not been heard. Or seen.

Either way, she pressed her back against the darkness of the wooden cabinets and held her breath, certain that her thumping heart would give her away. But Marcus wasn't looking for anyone else, he was simply wishing to get from one place to another as quickly as he could. And in seconds he was gone.

Fran drew in a huge breath, drawing the air deep into her lungs as she waited for her pulse to slow and return to normal. And then, with all thoughts of tea forgotten, she crept silently back upstairs, praying that she wouldn't bump into any other nocturnal wanderers.

Which is why, with relief flooding through her as she pushed open her bedroom door, the sight of a figure standing by the window almost gave her heart failure all over again.

'Adam,' she hissed. 'What on earth are you doing here?'

'I couldn't sleep either,' he said. 'Where have you been?'

She narrowed her eyes. 'Never mind me. Have you just been in the garden?' she asked, thinking of what she had seen from the window earlier.

'I might have been.' He moved back into the room. 'I've been thinking and I—'

'Adam, I'm not doing this now. You need to go back to bed.'

'Yes, but something just occurred to me and—'

'And I've just seen Marcus. For God's sake, Adam, you need to be careful. Clarence's family don't even know we're here. Their reaction on finding we are isn't one I'm looking forward to, but imagine what it would have been if he'd caught you outside.'

'I thought you didn't want to talk about this?'

'I don't. So, go on, shoo. Go back to bed and I'll see you in the morning... you can tell me then.'

'But it might be too late then...' He paused, looking back

towards the window. 'Although I do need to wait until it's light to be certain.'

Fran sighed. This was exactly what she hadn't wanted to happen. Adam had piqued her interest and if she sent him away, she'd only wonder endlessly what it was he had found. She switched on a lamp which sat on a table beside the bed. As she suspected, Adam was fully dressed. She gave a shiver, realising just how cold her toes were.

'Right, come on then,' she said, climbing back into bed and thrusting her feet under the still-warm sheets. 'Sit down and tell me what you've discovered, or I'll never get any peace.'

He looked at her a moment, hesitating, and eyeing the end of the bed which might as well have been on fire. He looked around the room. 'I'll just sit here,' he said, settling himself cross-legged in the middle of the floor.

Fran bit back a smile.

'So, I was thinking about the clue...' he began. 'The first bit, *from where I'm standing*. Do you suppose that refers to Clarence, or to someone else?'

'It could be either.' She pulled a face. 'But I suspect you've already worked that out.'

Adam nodded. 'See, I took it to mean Clarence when I first heard it, but now I'm not so sure. I need to ask Olivia, though, in case there *is* somewhere Clarence had a habit of standing.'

'But it could be anywhere.'

'Well, no, it couldn't. Otherwise it wouldn't work as a clue. To be in there at all, it has to refer to something which has meaning, something which stands a chance of being worked out, and therefore it makes sense that it would be somewhere habitual, or a fixed point. The same is true for the rest of the clue. That refers to the sun and rain. *From where I'm standing the sun is bright but it looks like rain*, so it has to be somewhere where both those things are visible at the same time.'

Fran hugged the covers closer. 'That makes sense, but how

can you have sun and rain together? Although I suppose that does happen at odd times... Oh, a rainbow perhaps?'

Adam wrinkled his nose. 'Possibly... But I don't think so in this case. I think it's more likely to be what you said, actually the sun and rain together, or rather what *looks* like rain... Clarence was always very particular about the words he chose for his puzzles. Think back to the will, the same was true.'

Fran had to admit that he was right. And she was even more convinced she had made the right decision in asking Adam here. They needed his brain, one that worked in a very particular way; without him she wouldn't have the first idea how to begin solving Clarence's clues. She *didn't* have the first idea about solving Clarence's clues.

'So what is it?' she asked.

'I don't know yet... but I'm sure I'm on the right track.'

'Is that why you were in the garden?'

He nodded. 'Mmm, I thought I might spot something which made sense. I didn't though.'

Fran studied his dejected face. 'Which is probably just as well. Come nine this morning, there are going to be three other people hunting for the solution to that clue, and just suppose you had found something, you could have led Marcus right to it.'

Adam looked up sharply. 'Do you suppose he followed me? Or did he have the same thought I had?' He sighed. 'I'm not sure which is worse.'

'I don't think he could have followed you,' replied Fran, thinking for a minute. 'Because everything I've learned about Marcus so far points to him raising an alarm if he'd spotted you. In fact, he would have raised merry hell. No, I think it's far more likely that he was trying to work things out for himself.'

'Then we need to come up with a plan,' said Adam. 'So that once we've worked out what the clue means we don't unwittingly lead the others to it.'

'All assuming we work it out first, of course...'

Adam rolled his eyes. 'Oh ye of little faith.' He got to his feet. 'I'm going now – to have a think and see what I can come up with. But remember, sun and rain, or what looks like rain. Where would you get that in the same place?'

An hour and a half later, Adam was back again, tapping softly on Fran's door. She had her head resolutely in a book, her circular thoughts driving her mad.

His voice was no more than a whisper as he shut the door silently behind him. 'Good, you're awake. Listen, I think I've found something. I didn't want to wake Olivia, and it's still too dark outside to see anything properly, and too cold.' He shivered. 'So I wondered if there was a way to find out more about the house itself without leaving the comfort of my room.'

'Well, obviously you found one, or you wouldn't be here,' replied Fran, laying down her book.

Adam had taken up his position in the middle of the floor again. 'To start with, I began looking online for anything relating to the history of the house. And there's quite a bit, as you might expect with a property of this age and historical importance. I didn't really know what I was looking for so jumped around a bit and, really by chance, stumbled across the website of an artist who specialises in renovation, the very same artist who restored the incredible trompe l'oeil paintings downstairs to their former glory. Not surprisingly, he was pretty proud of his work and his website not only detailed the restoration, but showed the research he'd had to undertake to do it. There were loads of photos, both before and after shots of the paintings themselves, and also internal and external views of the house and gardens.'

'So what did you find? What do the paintings have to do with anything?'

'I didn't really have any idea of their importance when I started reading, I carried on more because I was interested in them than anything else, but then I spotted something. Remember what Olivia said about the scene which is her favourite, it's the one where you can just see the outline of a person at the edge of the painting, as if they've opened a door and are standing on the doorstep gazing out at the view?'

'Oh...' Fran leaned forward. 'And you found something? In the painting?'

'Not quite. But I think I might have found somewhere to start looking.' He pulled out his phone and began scrolling. 'When the artist began the restoration he had virtually no source material to start from because the scene the painting depicts dates back to when the house was first built and, obviously, it looks very different now. Imagine standing in the hallway downstairs and, instead of looking at the painting, pretend the wall isn't there so you're looking at the view itself. Because that's exactly what the chap doing the restoration did. He went outside, put his back against the outside wall which corresponds to the locations of the paintings in the hallway and took a series of photos. Look...' He handed over his phone. 'This is the first of them, and you can see why they'd be useful because the hills are clearly visible in the distance, as is the corner of the church. The immediate area surrounding the house is obviously now laid to garden, but check this one...' He tapped the image that Fran was looking at.

She looked at him, frowning. 'I think I'm supposed to know what I'm looking at, but you're going to have to give me a clue.'

Adam smiled. 'But that's just it, think about our first clue. *From where I'm standing...* I think the person the clue refers to is the one you can see standing at the edge of the painting. *The sun is bright...* again, think of the scene shown in the painting, *but it looks like rain...* What can you see in the photo?' he tapped his phone screen again.

'Lawns, hedges, a swimming pool—' Fran caught the change in Adam's expression. 'The swimming pool?' she said. 'That's what you want me to look at?' She peered closer, but she still couldn't see what had got Adam so excited. 'Okay, I get that it's water, but how does it look like rain?'

'Zoom in.' Adam took back the phone and, using two fingers, enlarged the photo. 'The image is very grainy, which makes it hard to see clearly, but I think that' – he pointed to a dark spot on the wall at the rear of the pool – 'might be a shower.' He looked at Fran triumphantly. 'Which, if it's running, from the right vantage point, might possibly look like rain.'

Fran darted a look at the bedroom door, keeping her voice low. 'God, Adam, that has to be it!'

Adam pulled a face. 'Well, it doesn't have to be, it's just one possible solution that seems to fit. I like it though because if you think about it, when would you swim in an outdoor pool? Answer, when the weather is good, when the sun is bright, so it makes sense on more than one level.'

Things were beginning to fall into place for Fran. 'That's why you were in the garden earlier.'

He nodded. 'But it was too dark and I didn't want to use my torch and risk being seen, so there's nothing for it, I'm going to have to check in daylight.'

Fran thought for a moment, one detail about all of this niggling her. 'But what about Marcus?' she asked. 'If he *was* in the garden, he either followed you, or was there because he'd come to the same conclusion you had. So how do we allow you to take a closer look at the pool area without giving the game away?'

'Leave it to me,' replied Adam, tapping the side of his nose.

Which was why a few hours later, Fran was in the middle of helping to create a diversion. Making breakfast for everyone had been a good idea. It not only gave Fran something to do, helping to keep her nerves under control in the process, but it also provided a suitable setting for Margaret to announce that, under the terms of Clarence's will, it was his intention that Olivia take part in the hunt. She might not be family, but he still very much regarded her as one of his 'nearest and dearest' and, therefore, after much consideration, Olivia had decided to participate. Fran would have been very pleased had Margaret felt able to remind Marcus that, given this fact, he should stop referring to Olivia as the hired help, but perhaps this was pushing things a little too far.

Giving a reason for Fran's continued presence in the house had been the first part of the plan, and that had been easily explained. She was an old friend of Olivia's so it was natural for her to want to stick around and offer a consoling shoulder. Besides, as Olivia had informed Cate, she and Fran had got talking the night before and hadn't realised the time until it was very late, so Olivia had offered Fran a bed. And since she was here it seemed the most natural thing in the world for her to make breakfast for everyone. It was, after all, what she did for a living.

There was, of course, one other reason why breakfast had been laid on, although Fran tried not to think about it. It was as if the very presence of it in her mind was enough to broadcast it to anyone in the vicinity. But she still smiled as the thought popped into her head – she couldn't help it.

Apart from Margaret and Olivia, no one else was aware that Adam was even in the house, a fact they could use to their advantage. But first they had needed to make sure he had time to slip out to the garden unobserved. This was why Fran making breakfast was so important. Not only did it give her a reason for being there but serving it in the dining hall also ensured that everyone was well away from any windows that overlooked the rear gardens.

The second part of the plan was almost as easy, given that the siblings' reaction on learning about Olivia's inclusion in the hunt was all too predictable. Judging by the noise coming from the dining hall, the commotion looked set to continue for quite some time.

'And we're to take your word for that, are we?' said Cate harshly.

'It's not my word, Ms Lightman, it's the word of law,' replied Margaret. 'Your father's will is a legal document and decisions over the dispersal of his estate were his alone. My function, as his solicitor, is to ensure that those wishes are carried out as he specified them, not to sway his judgement in the first place, and I find your insinuations that I might have somehow influenced him extremely distasteful. The will is watertight, I assure you, but should you wish to challenge it, I will also point out that there is a timescale under which the treasure hunt must be conducted. Any challenge to the validity of the will would result in a significant delay, perhaps even one which renders the hunt obsolete. In which case, as I'm sure I don't need to point out, none of you will inherit. You might not agree with your father's wishes, but my advice is to accept them and move forward.'

'Even when this is all clearly a set-up?' replied Cate. 'Did Dad really think we're so stupid? For God's sake, Olivia obviously knows all the clues and their solutions. She probably helped work out the damn things. I don't know why Dad didn't just leave his estate to her in the first place, instead of playing silly games.'

Fran couldn't hear under the swell of several voices all talking at once whether Olivia made any reply.

'That's enough!' Margaret's voice cut through them all. 'May I cast your minds back to last night's dinner where several of your father's friends were also sitting around the table. They were there, not only as his friends, or because a bequest had been made to each of them, but, as was pointed out to you, because they had each helped your father with one of the clues for the treasure hunt. Neither I, nor Olivia, had any hand in them and that is the end of the matter.' There was a moment's silence and then Margaret's voice came again. 'Now, having cleared up that unpleasantness, Cate, Marcus and Saul, would you please inform me how you wish to play? Provided, of course, that you still wish to?'

'Cate and I are playing together,' said Marcus.

'What?' gasped Saul. 'No, you're not! Last night we agreed we would all take part separately.'

'Yeah, well, Cate and I had a rethink.'

Fran couldn't hear what came next but she could guess. Poor Olivia, having to stand and listen to all this.

'You're mad, Marcus, if you really think Cate will split the money with you.'

'I like your thinking, Saul – assuming we're going to win. You're really not that confident of your chances, are you? Which is, of course, exactly why we elected to play together. Why carry dead wood if we don't have to?'

Fran closed her eyes against a particularly vehement turn of phrase as Saul let go a volley of insults and expletives. Whatever Margaret was saying to try to instil order was being drowned out. Fran certainly didn't envy Margaret her job.

Fran picked up another plate and lowered it into the sink full of soapy water. It sounded as if the argument might continue for quite some time, every moment of which gave Adam a better chance of succeeding. And once everyone turned their attention back to the treasure hunt, Fran would be perfectly positioned and ready to alert Adam to anyone leaving the house via the back door, the most obvious route into the gardens. She just had to hope that the time they had given him was long enough. And, of course, that he found whatever he was looking for.

8

Adam kept a careful eye on the house as he skirted the hedges lining the lawned area. Once he got to the pool he'd be shielded from view, but he had to get there first and walking across the grass would be far too risky. Thankfully, the night had been cloudy so the lawn was free from frost, but he was still wary of laying an obvious trail through it. Breathing a sigh of relief, he slipped between the gap in the hedge and out onto the path beyond. This was as far as he had got in the night, realising that if he went any further, he was in danger of doing himself an injury.

Reaching an intersection in the path, he turned left, heading for the pool, though he still didn't really know what he was looking for. But when he got there he realised just how clever Clarence's clue actually was. If he stood with his back to the water, Adam could see the side wall of the house, behind which was the hallway with its beautiful trompe l'oeil paintings. So, if the reverse were true and he was in the hallway, pretending the wall wasn't there and looking out, what would he see? The answer was obvious.

It wasn't a shower at all. The pool was bordered by a high

wall at the rear, at least eight-foot tall, and what Adam had seen in the grainy photo on his phone had simply been an arched recess, halfway down it. Checking the photo again, however, revealed that at some point in its history, the recess had been enlarged and the area in front dug out to create another small pool. Purely ornamental, it was now full of somewhat slimy-looking water, but in its centre was a large carved fish made from stone. A fountain.

Poised as if in mid leap, the fish's 'lips' faced uppermost, providing the main water spout, while, by its side, two smaller fish were similarly posed. Adam peered closer before straightening again to look around him, spying what he was looking for at the base of the wall. Curiosity was calling, and although switching on the fountain was risky, he wanted to see the full effect of Clarence's clue and there was really no other way to check. Bending, he lifted the cover on the electrical box and, praying that it still worked, flipped the switch.

After a short pause, small jets of water leapt from the fishes' mouths, cascading into the pool below. Adam almost laughed out loud. If you were sitting on the poolside on a hot summer's day, with the sun beating down, and just happened to glance across at the fountain, it would indeed look like rain falling.

He quickly shut off the water again and, excitement mounting, began to examine the stone statues. Adam had often been described as a square peg in a round hole, never quite fitting with others' expectations of him. But this, this was something he felt he'd been born to do. He had designed so many games where hunting for treasure had been a feature, he'd often wondered what it would be like to do it for real. And now here he was, rooting around a fountain looking for clues. It felt like coming home.

Margaret had explained that they would be looking for a telephone number which, when rung, would put them through to the person who could give them the next clue. So, most likely,

Adam was looking for a slip of paper. And one thing was certain – paper and water didn't mix – so he was almost certainly looking for some kind of container and a waterproof one at that. Where on the fountain could you hide such a thing?

Grimacing, he sank to his knees, wincing at the cold, hard ground beneath them. The only possible hiding place on the stone fish was inside the mouths, but to reach them Adam would have to climb into the fountain itself, with its freezing, slimy water. He would, if he had to, but he'd exhaust any other possibilities first.

He poked a finger reluctantly at the scummy surface of the pool. Green with algae, it was even colder than he envisaged and he withdrew his finger abruptly. The water wasn't deep, but by his calculations it would come almost to his elbow, so it was a toss-up between sinking his arm into it, or his legs. He took off his jacket, flinching at the cold air which hit his body, and began to roll up one sleeve.

The water was too murky to allow him to see the bottom, but if he was to search it at all, he must do so systematically, otherwise he'd simply be going around in circles. He fished a coin from his pocket and laid it on the fountain's stone rim so that it could act as a reference point. Then he plunged his hand to the bottom of the pool and, ignoring everything utterly yucky he could feel with his fingers, began to sweep his arm back and forth in a line, from the outside in.

After no time at all however, he withdrew it, shaking off the water and rubbing it briskly against the leg of his jeans. The water was truly freezing and the pain of keeping his arm submerged had built quickly to intolerable proportions. Yet how else was he supposed to do this?

He could try to find some waterproof gloves, like the kind Fran did her washing up with, but the water was too deep and would only slosh over the top of them. He sat back on his haunches, rubbing his hands together, then sticking them under his armpits for warmth. He was shivering now. *Think, Adam, come on...*

It was as he was idly watching a snail crawl along the rim on the far side of the pool that it came to him. Eyes following the shiny trail left in its wake, Adam could see that it had crawled upwards to reach its current position, but that would mean climbing up from the water's edge, not a very clever thing for a snail to be doing unless it was very good at front crawl.

He almost groaned out loud when he realised where, in fact, the snail had appeared from. Underneath the pool's stone rim was a quite substantial lip, where the top of the rim bevelled out and over. The dark-green reflection of the water and the weathered stone itself had made it almost impossible to see. Adam scrabbled forward, leaning on the rim, and began to sweep the area underneath with his fingers. Whatever he was looking for had to be here, surely? It was a far better hiding place, and dry for one.

Fighting the urge to pull his fingers away from the gunk they were encountering, he stuck to his task and two-thirds of the way around the pool, he was finally rewarded. There was something there, something hard. He probed it, trying to gauge its size and shape and, importantly, how he could detach it from its hiding place. Whatever it was, it wasn't very big.

In the end, Adam resorted to brute force to pull it free, sitting back on his heels to examine what he had found. It was a black plastic container of the sort used to store spools of film away from the light, back before digital cameras and smartphones removed the necessity for such things. He wiped his frozen fingers down his jeans and prised the lid free. He had no idea how long it had been since Clarence had hidden it, but he prayed that whatever was inside was still legible.

With a careful look round him first, Adam tipped out a roll of papers into his hand and carefully unfurled them. Each was five centimetres by two and held a string of digits immediately recognisable as a phone number. Carefully removing one from the bunch, he turned it over, peering closely to examine anything he had missed. Satisfied there was nothing, he was about to slip it into his pocket when he had another thought. Quickly counting the numbers of slips, he realised there was one for each potential player, four in total, and he imagined that Clarence had provided this many in the belief that people would take the number away with them. Which was fine, except that in doing so it would be very easy for the other players to work out how many people had beaten them to the clue. Adam pulled out his phone and took a quick snap of the number. Checking first that he had captured the image clearly, he refolded the bundle of slips and popped them back in the canister. He didn't want to give anyone more knowledge than was absolutely necessary.

Carefully replacing the lid and pushing it on good and tight, Adam ran his fingers back under the rim of the pool until he located the clump of putty the canister had been clinging to. He'd been aware you could buy glues which worked under-water but he hadn't appreciated just how good they were. He made a mental note to investigate them at a later date – he was always on the lookout for things to add to his arsenal of gadgetry.

Retracing his steps to the house, Adam had one hand on the kitchen door when he suddenly stopped. Raised voices were coming from inside and he stepped back onto the path, flattening himself against the wall. He quickly checked his phone but there was no message from Fran. Either she hadn't felt the need to send anything, or she wasn't in any position to. Either way, he was stuck. He could be there for ages and, worse, he was in open space. If anyone came out the door he'd be seen in an instant. Now what did he do?

Pulling his coat tighter, he jammed his hands back inside his pockets. He was trying to think but his fingers were so cold, they were beginning to throb. He could go back to his car and wait there, but to do so he'd have to walk around the side of the house and down the main drive – it was far too risky. He was still eyeing up the possibility of hiding behind a hedge when a shout sounded on the other side of the door. He had the presence of mind to step away from the wall but, as the door was yanked open, he came face to face with a man who could only be Marcus Lightman. Fortunately, he was just as surprised to see Adam and it took him a moment to work out what was going on.

'Who the hell are you?'

Adam looked genuinely astonished. 'Erm... sorry, is this the back door?' He stared into Marcus's flushed face. 'I'm looking for my mum.' It was the only thing he could think of to say. Fran was going to kill him. That's if he didn't die of embarrassment first.

'Your mum?'

'She's working here,' he replied. 'She's a cook.' Adam was doing his best to look about ten years younger than he was. Thankfully, his black, slightly long curly hair and colourful beanie often worked in his favour. That and the fact that he didn't look at all like a responsible adult.

A woman appeared behind Marcus. 'What's going on?' she said. She didn't look any more welcoming.

'I'm looking for my mum,' said Adam with slightly more conviction as he warmed to his theme. 'She said to come to the back door.' He slid his beanie from his head and held it in both hands, plucking at the woollen folds.

'Well, I don't see why she would be here, do you?'

'It's the cook woman, Cate,' said Marcus. 'Hang on a minute and I'll—'

'Sorry, sorry...' said Fran, bustling through the door. She was holding her purse. 'Here, love, is twenty quid enough?'

'Oh yeah... thanks, Mum.' He smiled at Marcus and Cate.

'Sorry...' He waited until Fran had extracted the note from her purse, taking it with a sheepish smile.

'And next time, make sure you think first and go to the cashpoint, okay?' Fran gave him the sort of smile his real mum used all the time. Fond, but slightly admonitory too. They must go somewhere to learn it.

'Yeah, I will. Thanks... see you later.' He flashed another smile, tucked the money in his pocket, and pulled his beanie back on his head. Then he sauntered down the path with as much of a rolling swagger as he could manage, his heart threatening to leap through his ribs with every step.

He had to wait another ten minutes before Fran messaged to tell him he could come back to the house, but via the front door this time so he wouldn't be seen by the others who were in the back garden. Her message ended with a rolling eye emoji. He sent one back with a row of gritted teeth, none of this was doing his nerves any good.

'You enjoyed that far too much,' he said as she ushered him through the front door, moments later.

She grinned at him. 'You have to admit it was funny,' she replied. 'Although I'm not sure which is worse, me being old enough to be your mum, or you being young enough to be my son. On second thoughts, the first one is definitely worse. Good thinking, though.'

'I didn't have much time *to* think,' said Adam. 'But what are we going to do, Fran? We can't keep skulking around like this.'

She grimaced. 'After today I don't think we'll need to. But never mind about that for a minute, did you find anything?'

His face glowed with pride. 'I did. Sometimes a misspent youth comes in very handy indeed.'

She put up a hand. 'Don't tell me yet, wait until we're in the kitchen. The others have all taken off into the garden and Margaret is about to leave.' She pursed her lips. 'That woman is a marvel. This morning hasn't been what you'd call easy.'

Judging by his first impressions of Marcus and Cate, Adam wasn't in the least surprised.

Olivia looked quite tearful as they both entered the kitchen. She was drawing Margaret into a warm hug. 'I don't know what I'm going to do,' she said, as she pulled away. 'I can't thank you enough.'

'You are going to be fine, Olivia. I know that without a shadow of a doubt. Have faith,' she said. 'It's all you'll need. I may not be an expert in such matters but I think Clarence will be watching over you.' She gave Olivia one last, long look, before turning to smile at Fran and Adam. 'Now, I must go before either of you say something I mustn't hear. But it's been lovely meeting you both.' She picked up her handbag from the table. 'I'll see myself out,' she said. 'And I'll look forward to hearing from you again... soon.'

Olivia sat down at the table with a bump. 'Have we got time for a stiff drink?' she said. 'I don't care what time it is.'

Fran pulled a face at Adam. 'As you might have imagined, Marcus didn't take the news of Olivia joining in the hunt particularly well. Neither did Cate. She wasn't quite as vocal as her brother but I'm afraid Olivia rather took the brunt of it, despite Margaret doing her best to slap them both down.'

'I'd like to actually slap them,' remarked Olivia, holding her palms to her cheeks, which were both flaming.

'However,' said Fran, 'due process was eventually recorded, and there are now three groups playing to inherit Clarence's estate.'

'Three?' queried Adam. 'But I thought—'

Fran raised her eyebrows. 'Marcus and Cate elected to play together,' she said. 'I know, that was a bit of a surprise to us, too. And Saul, who didn't like it one little bit. Seems last night they all agreed to play individually, but Cate and Marcus obviously went behind his back.'

'Poor Saul,' said Olivia. 'It's one thing having to play against your siblings, but another having two of them effectively gang up on you.'

'Don't feel sorry for him, Liv. He might be quieter than the other two, but you didn't see his face later on – if looks could kill. He's just as determined as the other two, take my word for it. Plus, if he were to win, which he isn't of course, but if he did, then he'd get the estate in its entirety, whereas Cate and Marcus will have to share it. In any case, you are not to worry about them. The way they treated you this morning... the only thing you have to think about now is winning. And we're already one up.'

Olivia gave a sudden shiver. 'Did you find something?'

Adam nodded. 'I found the clue. We have ourselves a phone number, we just need to get somewhere private to ring it.'

Olivia's face lit up. 'You actually found it?' she exclaimed, and then flinched, repeating her words at half the volume. 'Where was it?' she whispered, even though there was no sign of the others. 'Was it where you told Fran?'

He nodded. 'Hidden in the fountain by the pool.'

'I told you he was good,' said Fran.

Adam beamed.

'So, what do we do now?' asked Olivia. 'I don't know if any of the others have worked out the first clue, but they're all somewhere in the garden and who knows how long they'll be. I really don't want to be around when they get back.'

'No, and I don't think we should be either,' said Adam. 'If we hang around, we're going to keep tripping over one another, and we'll lose any advantage we might have gained. We can't afford to give away any locations, or clues.'

'But what if the clues are all here? At the house, I mean,' said Fran.

Adam shook his head. 'I don't think they will be. Clarence was very clever, he'd have thought about the difficulties of everyone searching for clues at the same time. I think he'd have scattered the locations, although I'm guessing they'll most probably be around the local area. And, don't forget, this is the way he always wrote his stories – sending his characters out on a quest, away from home – so in all likelihood we'll be following a similar pattern. The more I think about it, the more I'm convinced this game isn't simply to test our abilities to solve puzzles and work out clues. I also think it's about Clarence making a point. Fran, you said that Clarence made mention in his will of his family seemingly never appreciating his work, so he devised one last game for them, not only to bring them together, but in the hope that they'd change their minds. I think it's a test to see just how much they *did* appreciate his work... because it's only those who did who can possibly win.'

'So, the clues will all be ones he's set before, do you mean? The ones in his books?'

'I don't think they'll be exactly the same,' said Adam. 'That would be too easy. But I think they'll be similar in style. I think they'll have Clarence's trademark stamp all over them.' He smiled. 'Or should I say, Ebenezer Doolittle's?'

Fran looked at her watch. 'Then we have to get going as quick as we can. We can't lose this advantage.'

'But where do we go?' asked Olivia. 'Who knows how long this is going to take.'

Fran gave Adam an amused look. 'Liv, can you pack an overnight bag and anything else you think we might need, quick as you can. I suggest we relocate our HQ to somewhere less obvious.'

Adam frowned. 'And where's that?'

'Well, Jack and Martha are away all weekend,' said Fran, eyebrows raised. 'Why don't we use my house?'

9

Ten minutes later, they were on their way to Fran's house, Olivia sharing Fran's car and Adam following in his close behind. They had no way of knowing how long it would take any of the others to solve the first clue and Olivia wasted no time in getting on the phone.

Balancing a notebook on her lap, Olivia dialled the number Adam had given her and put the call on loudspeaker. It was answered almost immediately.

'Hello, this is Olivia Turner—' She broke off, clearly not knowing what else she should say.

But the voice from the other end was warm and reassuring. 'Hello, Olivia. This is Mary Duggan. It's a pleasure to be hearing from you. Now, you'll need a pen and paper for this, there's a little bit to take down. Do you need me to wait a moment?'

Fran flicked a glance at Olivia, who had pen tip poised against paper.

'No, I have one here, go ahead.'

'So there are three parts to this clue and each has a one-word answer. Here's the first.' She paused. '*What disappears as soon as you say its name?*'

Olivia bent to write quickly on the pad. 'Okay...'

'The second part is this: *This belongs to you, but everyone else uses it.* Got that? *This belongs to you, but everyone else uses it.*'

'Yep, I've got that too.'

'And the last part... *If two's company, and three's a crowd, what are four and five?*'

Olivia scribbled one last time. 'Okay.'

Mary cleared her throat. 'When you have worked out the riddles, you will have three, single-word answers, and those words are the clue to the next location. Do you understand?'

Olivia flashed Fran a quick look. 'I think so,' she said. 'Yes, I mean. That makes sense.'

'Then that's all I can tell you. I have to go now, Olivia, but good luck.'

'Thanks, Mary, I—'

But the line was already dead.

Fran risked a look at Olivia. 'Short but sweet,' she said.

Olivia sighed. 'She couldn't be anything else, could she? And I can't say I blame her. Would you want to engage in conversation with Cate or Marcus any more than was strictly necessary? No, say what you need to, then get off the phone as quick as you can.'

'Fair point,' replied Fran. 'If Clarence had a better relationship with his family, none of us would be doing this at all.'

'No, we wouldn't. Says a lot, doesn't it? The way this whole game has been set up, all the fail-safes, the checks and balances so that no one can cheat. Clarence might have wanted things to be better between them, but he also knew them very well.'

Fran nodded. 'Makes you wonder why he's giving them the chance to inherit at all. Why not simply leave his money to charity the way he threatened?'

'I suppose... That's what makes me so sad on his behalf. Whatever reason their relationship broke down, it really hurt him and yet he still hoped they would enjoy playing one last game with him, just like they did when they were little, before everything went wrong. It's so awful that despite his hopes and best intentions, his family aren't going to change one little bit.'

'It is sad,' replied Fran. But she wasn't altogether convinced. Something about this whole thing felt off to her and she couldn't get what Margaret had said out of her mind. Was Clarence's comment about his death being suspicious just an innocent quip? Or was there more to it than that? With two solved murders under her belt, however, perhaps she was simply getting a suspicious mind. Then again...

She pushed her thoughts to one side, they had other, far more urgent matters to think about and surely if there were anything suspicious about Clarence's death it would have been investigated? She turned her attention back to the road, checking that Adam was still behind her. They were almost home.

'So these are simple riddles,' said Adam a little while later.

They were sitting around the island unit in Fran's kitchen, Olivia's notebook between them.

'The what am I sort... where you have a single word as the answer,' he clarified.

Olivia nodded. 'Yes, that's what Mary said.'

Fran peered at the first part of the clue. 'And presumably when we put the answers together, it will spell out where we need to look for the next clue. So maybe a place name?'

'It could be,' said Adam. He wrinkled his nose. 'The last one is easy, anyway. The answer's *nine*.'

'What?' exclaimed Fran, staring at him. 'How did you get that?'

'*If two's company, and three's a crowd, what are four and five?*' intoned Adam. 'The answer's nine. Four plus five equals *nine*. You have to look at the clues in a literal way, not follow the path that the riddle would have you take.' He pulled a face. 'Which, given that I have a tendency to do that anyway, puts me at a slight advantage.'

'Okay then... how about the first part?' she replied. '*What disappears as soon as you say its name?* What's the answer to that one?'

Adam stared at the notebook for a moment. 'Nope, nothing's coming immediately.' He gave Fran a coy smile. 'You know what the problem is?' he asked.

Fran slid off her chair with a sigh. 'Fine, yes, I'll get some biscuits.'

She returned a minute later with a Tupperware tub and cranked off the lid, placing it beside Adam. He immediately took two fingers of shortbread and bit the first clean in half. He beamed at her.

'Perfect,' he said, chewing. 'So come on then, shout out some answers.'

Fran helped herself to a biscuit, then slid the tub across to Olivia, thinking. She couldn't even come up with anything that disappeared, much less when you said its name. Maybe it was something magical, like a witch or a wizard... or...

'A spell,' she said. 'Obviously a disappearing spell but... no, that can't be right.'

'The sun?' suggested Olivia. 'Seeing as whenever you say how beautiful the day is, it usually starts to rain.' She looked at Adam. 'You know the answer, don't you? You're just trying to give us a chance.'

Adam held his hands in the air. 'I don't, I swear.'

'Maybe it's a naming thing?' said Fran. 'Like in the fairy tale, Rapunzel, where knowing the name is what's important, and saying the name unlocks the power.'

'Yes, but it can't be an actual name,' said Adam, shaking his head. 'Because that would *reveal* an identity, not make it disappear.'

'A secret identity then. If you uncover the real one then the fake one disappears,' suggested Fran. She frowned. 'Except that I don't know what a word for that would be.' Her eyes widened. 'Or, maybe, it's just a secret... If you tell a secret, then the secret itself is the thing that disappears.'

'There's something in that,' said Adam, tapping his fingers on the table. 'But I don't think it's quite right. The secret doesn't exactly disappear, it becomes something else. I like your thinking though, keep going...'

Fran cast about for another word which would fit the clue, but every time she set a train of thought in motion, something derailed it. 'Is anyone else finding it hard to concentrate?' she asked. 'I'm really struggling because I'm constantly wondering how Cate and co are doing – whether they've found the fountain clue and if they've already worked out these riddles.'

'I know what you mean,' said Olivia. 'But if we worry what everyone else is doing, we'll never focus ourselves. We obviously have to work as quickly as possible, but...' She took a biscuit and stared at it thoughtfully. 'That was a clever thing you did, Adam, not taking the slip of paper when you found that first clue. The one with Mary's number on it.'

'It was,' replied Fran. 'That's just the way his brain works.'

'It's simple logic,' replied Adam. 'Think about those times when you were at school and everyone was working on the same task at the same time. If you thought you were behind you worked as quickly as you could to catch up because you didn't want to be the idiot who came last. But if you knew you were in the lead you took your foot off the gas a little, not intentionally, you probably wouldn't have even realised you were doing it.' He paused. 'That doesn't mean my little act of subterfuge will work. Half the time people don't behave the way I think they should at all, they're completely illogical. That's what trips me up.'

'But you think like Clarence at least. I often asked him how he came up with the ideas for his books. Some of the puzzles seemed so difficult to me, particularly for children, but he always replied that that was my problem, that I was being far too adult about it and that I should look at them the way a child does. I'm not sure I really understood that, but you— Oh God... that didn't come out at all the way I intended, sorry,' said Olivia, blushing furiously. 'I didn't mean you were like a child, not at all. Just that—'

'I'd take it as a compliment, actually,' said Adam. 'Adults have a habit of making things far more difficult than they need to be at times. Perhaps it's their experience of life, I don't know, but because they often expect things to be complicated, they look for a complicated solution when a simple one is staring them in the face.'

'Well, let's just hope in this case, you're right,' said Fran. 'Because for the life of me I cannot work out the answer to this next riddle.' She put her fingers on her temples as if she was thinking hard. 'Think logically,' she said. '*What disappears as soon as you say its name?* It's obviously the saying of the thing which is important here. What *actually* happens when you say something?' She looked up at the other two.

Olivia's brow wrinkled. 'You make a sound?'

'Yes...' said Fran, picking up on her thought. 'And if you make a sound, what... Oh—' Her mouth curved upwards. '*Silence*,' she pronounced, extremely pleased with herself. 'If you say its name, the thing itself disappears.'

'Yes!' said Adam. 'That's it, brilliant. So, come on then, last riddle... *This belongs to you, but everyone else uses it.*'

Olivia laughed. 'Oh, that's clever...' she said. 'And you've just given us an extra clue, Fran.'

'Why? What did I say?' She looked back and forth between Adam and Olivia.

'It's *name*,' said Olivia, grinning. 'That's it, that's the answer. *Name* – the thing which belongs to you, but everyone else uses.'

Adam chewed, staring into space. 'So, we have silence, and name and the word nine, the number nine I guess, which means...' He looked back at both of them. 'What does it mean? I haven't the foggiest.'

Fran sighed. 'Me neither. But Mary said these three words are the clue to the next location, so they must relate to a place somehow. Does that mean we're looking for somewhere those things are relevant? So somewhere there *is* silence, for example. But then if that were true then the word name and the number nine would have to be relevant as well.' She screwed up her face. 'Maybe it's simpler.'

'Have you got a map?' asked Olivia. 'Perhaps if we have a look at one, we might spot something which leaps out at us.'

Fran got out her laptop and, opening an internet tab, pulled up a map of the local area. 'So, what radius do we need to look in?'

Olivia stared at her, anxiety looming in her eyes. 'How on earth would we know that? It could be anywhere.'

'It could,' replied Fran. 'But we need to think like Clarence. Was there anywhere he was particularly fond of? Somewhere he liked to go, or a place that had particular meaning for him?'

Olivia frowned, staring across the kitchen as she ransacked her brain for ideas. 'I can't think of anywhere. He used to talk a lot about his work, as you might expect, or things he achieved, like the time he met the Queen, but I don't remember him ever speaking about a favourite place.' She paused. 'Occasionally, he would talk about the time when his wife was alive and the children were little. They used to holiday in Pembrokeshire a lot.

There were a couple of beaches he mentioned, but... surely those are too far away?'

'Who knows?' said Adam. 'I've been assuming we're looking for somewhere pretty local but that doesn't have to be the case.'

'It is more likely, though. After all, Clarence lived a large part of his life at Justice House, so when he was thinking up his clues it would make sense to use locations he was more recently familiar with.' Her eyes began to search the map on the screen in front of her. 'So, we're looking for a place, the name of which relates to silence and name and the number nine...'

The kitchen fell silent as all three of them pored over the map. Every now and then an intake of breath would herald the appearance of an idea, but then a tongue would click or a sigh would be expelled and they would be back to looking all over again.

'This is crazy,' said Olivia. 'It's like looking for a needle in a haystack.'

'And we don't even know if we're looking in the right haystack,' added Fran. 'It might not be the name of a place we're looking for, but instead a local landmark, Carding Mill Valley maybe, or the Quarry park in Shrewsbury, Acton Scott Farm...'

'But even then...' mused Adam. 'It's not specific enough, is it? If it were somewhere like the Quarry, how would we know where to look when we got there? It's huge.' He shook his head. 'No, there must be something else to this, something we're missing. Think about the first clue – the fountain – that was a specific thing, small enough to search. I can't believe Clarence would have us work out the clues only to be left searching a huge area with no idea what we're looking for. The words themselves must mean something.'

Fran screwed up her face. 'God, this is impossible. I'm going to make a cup of tea.' She got up and crossed to the sink, automatically running water to wash up the few things which had been left beside it by Jack and Martha. She'd only been gone from her house for just over a day, but it felt like she'd been away for years. Restoring order always calmed her, and she did some of her best thinking while washing up or peeling potatoes, the mundanity of the task allowing her brain to slip its gears and freewheel.

Ten minutes later, however, with the dishes washed and a cup of tea made for everyone, she was still no further forward with her thoughts. It was as if her brain was stuck repeating the same ideas over and over and, even though she knew they were wrong, she couldn't exorcise them from her head. 'I've got Dorothy L. Sayers' *Nine Tailors* stuck in my noggin,' she said, turning around. 'And the film *Silence of the Lambs*. And I know both of these have absolutely nothing to do with anything, but I can't shift them.' She leaned up against the sink and practically growled with frustration. 'Okay...' She closed her eyes and tried to empty everything from her mind. 'So what are our clues again? What three words?'

When she opened them, Adam was staring at her, a slow smile spreading across his face.

'What did you say?' It was a casual enough question, but the tone in Adam's voice was anything but.

'Why do I get the feeling that's a rhetorical question?' Fran said. She was beginning to recognise the expression on his face.

'*What Three Words*,' said Adam, a broad grin on his face. 'Oh my God, that's genius!' He jumped up from his chair and paced the floor, first one way and then the other, whirling around as he came to a standstill. 'Don't you get it?'

Fran looked at Olivia. 'Do you know what he's talking about?'

'Nope,' she answered.

Adam moved around the island again to look at Fran's laptop. 'May I?' he asked. When she nodded, he opened another tab, quickly typing into the search field.

'What3words is a mapping system,' he explained. 'A bit like

postcodes, only much more specific. There's a what3words location for every three-metre-squared area in the world.' He waved a hand around the room. 'Your house will have several, as will your garden... combinations of words which relate to a specific area and nowhere else.'

As they watched, another web page loaded, a prominent search box at its top.

'So all we have to do,' said Adam, typing, 'is find out where our combination of words takes us and we'll know exactly where we need to search for our next clue. Silence. Name. Nine.' He hit the return key.

As they watched, the map on the screen revolved, shifted, and settled itself once more, a line pointing to a tiny box highlighted among a page filled with identical boxes. Adam clicked on the zoom out function. They peered closer, mouths open, eyes wide. He tapped the screen.

'That's it. That's the location of our next clue.'

10

Fran drew her car to a halt. 'So this is it?' she asked Adam. 'You're sure?' She stared out the driver's side window at the trees, which seemed to stretch for miles on end. 'Talk about not being able to see the wood for the trees.'

They were somewhere in a swathe of woodland about a mile or so away from the rear of Justice House. Navigating to the what3words location had seemed easy until they realised that what looked like the best route to take according to their road map didn't account for the geography of the area and ease of access. Fran had ended up driving around almost in circles while they looked for the best way to get to where they needed to go.

'It's not exactly it,' replied Adam from the passenger seat. 'But we're as close as I can get us by road. I think the rest of our journey may have to be on foot.' He peered at his phone and then showed the screen to Fran. 'We're the blue dot... and we need to get to the red dot, which is through there somewhere, not far.'

Fran glanced in her rear-view mirror. 'Okay, well, I can't stop here, the road is too narrow. Let me see if I can find a place to pull in. I haven't got a clue where we are.' She moved off again, scouring the road ahead for somewhere to park.

Spotting what looked like a clearing up ahead on her right, she slowed once more, realising as she drew nearer that it was the driveway for a small cottage. But the road was wider there and by tucking herself into one side of it she reckoned neither the lane nor the driveway were blocked. It meant Adam would have to slide out of the passenger seat at a very peculiar angle, but he was young, his body would cope with it. She glanced up at the grey and gloomy sky, already lowering, the sort which would rapidly turn to night as soon as half past three came around. It was almost one in the afternoon and time could fast disappear if they weren't careful.

Pulling her gloves from the pocket in the door, she climbed out, feeling the dank air bite after the heat of the car. She gave a shiver and pulled her coat tighter. 'Right, which way?' She looked at Adam, who was also hurriedly buttoning up his coat.

He frowned at the hedge opposite and then at his phone. 'Let's head back the way we've come, and then cut across the field.' He glanced at Olivia, who was busy winding a scarf around her neck.

'I shall have a word with Clarence when all this is over. Bloody treasure hunt in the middle of November, honestly.'

Fran smiled. 'In his defence he didn't know when he was going to die, it could just as easily have been in the middle of su —' She stopped. 'That's actually a good point,' she said, brows drawing together. 'Who planted the treasure-hunt clues?'

Olivia shrugged. 'I have no idea. I assumed Clarence did, but...' She looked at the road ahead and the distant woodland which ran along it. 'I'm not sure he would have come out here, not by himself anyway. In which case, who came with him? It must have been one of his friends.'

'Could it have been Margaret?' suggested Fran.

'She said she didn't know where any of the clues were. She

only has the answer to the final one, so that she knows when someone has got it right.'

There was something which didn't quite add up about all this, but Fran wasn't at all sure what. She flicked a quick glance at Adam. Clarence presumably *didn't* know when he would die, so when would he have planted the clues? His birthday party, when the hunt was originally planned to take place, wasn't for a couple of months yet. And if he did know when he'd meet his end, it rather begged the question: *How?*

Adam pointed at the road. 'One to ponder about later,' he said, gleaning Fran's concerns. 'Come on, we should get going.'

Finding the location of *silence.name.nine* was easy enough with a phone to navigate by. But even so, it took them about twenty minutes to get there, having first crossed a couple of fields and then jumped a water-filled ditch. Even Fran managed it with relative ease and, after a few more minutes' walk, they were standing in the middle of a three-metre-squared space which was completely filled with trees. And the odd bush. And a lot of damp undergrowth.

Adam turned slowly on the spot. 'I guess we start looking,' he said. 'Because this is as specific as it gets. And I reckon we're looking for something small and, given where it is, probably waterproof too. It could even be the same type of film canister I found by the fountain, or some other small container which could hold another batch of slips with phone numbers on them.'

Fran nodded. 'Which could be absolutely anywhere. I was joking earlier when I said you couldn't see the wood for the trees, but...'

'It will be hidden,' said Adam. 'But not impossible to find, otherwise what would be the point? So, nothing buried, for example.'

Olivia took a few steps backwards. 'We should spread out,' she said. 'Three metres square isn't huge, but it's big enough.' Her eyes were already scouring the ground.

Fran selected a tree and began to walk around it slowly, looking up and down as she walked, scuffing at the undergrowth with her foot. The others began to do the same as the minutes ticked by.

Fran's heartbeat quickened as she came upon a tree with a hollow at its base. Surely this was a perfect spot to hide something? She dropped to her haunches and began to probe inside, grateful that her gloves were protecting her fingers from whatever else had crept in there. But everything she touched was soft and yielding and although she pulled out several handfuls of decayed mulch, the hollow was empty of clues. She was about to move on to the next tree when Olivia gave a shout.

'Here!' she said. 'Does this look like something?'

Fran hurried over.

Olivia was standing beside a tree where a green plastic pipe seemed to be growing out of the ground. 'Could something be in here?'

Fran dropped to her haunches again and followed the line of the pipe into the undergrowth. It was only about thirty centimetres high and tethered to the tree. She slid her hand down it, pulling at the mass of ivy which was also snaking its way around the trunk. 'Whatever this is, it's been here a while,' she said.

Pushing further down, she felt a hard edge and slid her fingers underneath the pipe to search for the other end. She quickly pulled off her gloves and tried again, but to her dismay realised that the pipe wasn't hollow at all, but sealed off at the bottom.

'Well, if there is anything in there, I don't see how we're going to get it out,' she said.

Adam switched on his phone's torch and shone it into the top of the pipe. 'Hard to tell because of the angle,' he said. 'I can't really see anything.' He pushed his fingers in the gap between the pipe and the tree, wiggling it as much as the tether would allow. A distinct rattling noise could be heard. He looked up, eyes full of excitement. 'There *is* something in there!' He shook the pipe again. 'Dammit, we need something long to draw it out, or...' He broke off to move around the side of the tree. 'Or something to break these ties. But they're metal, so it won't be easy. Why is this pipe even here?' he added in frustration. 'What's it doing tied to a tree?'

But none of them had any answers and it didn't much matter.

Fran stood up, thinking. 'What else can we do other than maybe get a long twig and winkle it out? Everyone start looking. It needs to be straight, and if you can find one with a forked end that would be a miracle.'

'Hang on a minute,' said Adam, still staring at the pipe. 'I did this in one of my games once, it was part of the solution to a locked-room escape.' A slow smile spread up his face. 'Ebenezer Doolittle, you old devil, you. In my game, the key to the room was tied to a piece of cork which had been dropped into the bottom of a jar whose neck was too narrow to get your hand through. You weren't allowed to break the jar, because it rested on a pressure plate and removing it would trigger a deadly boobytrap.'

'So what did you have to do?' asked Fran.

Adam grinned. 'Float out the key. There was a goldfish tank standing on a table in the corner of the room. Transferring water from the tank to the jar made the cork rise up, bringing the key with it. It's the same principle here – if the pipe is sealed at the bottom and we *are* looking for another one of those film canisters, it's plastic, it should float.' He half turned around, checking the direction in which they'd walked. 'The ditch between the last two fields we crossed had water in it, could we get some of it here?'

Fran's eyes lit up. 'Adam, that's brilliant!' Her hand went to her coat pocket. 'What could we use though? Does anyone have anything? I've got my car keys in my pocket, but that's it.'

'We need something plastic,' said Adam. 'Or waterproof, obviously. Maybe there's something in all this undergrowth we could use. Someone may have dropped some litter, a crisp packet or a bottle...' He broke off at the sight of Olivia's face, who was staring at him open-mouthed. 'Are you okay?'

'Yes... but I remember Clarence telling me about that. It was ages ago, it was...' Her eyes widened even further. 'Are you the guy who has the weird fox thing as his game logo, the one with loads of tails?'

Now it was Fran's turn to stare. If he was, this was news to her as well.

Adam's cheeks were already pink with cold, but there was no mistaking the blush which rose up his neck. 'It's a kitsune,' he replied. 'In Japanese folklore they're foxes who possess paranormal abilities, and the more tails they have, the older and wiser they are. It's the symbolism I like though, foxes in folklore are usually seen as tricksters and cunning. It seemed a good fit for my games.'

'I never knew that,' said Fran.

'No real reason why you should,' he replied. 'It's just a thing game designers do, and it's handy because if, like me, you work for different companies, it's a way for your fans to be able to recognise a game as one of yours. It's a bit geeky really, I...' He trailed off, embarrassed.

'But Clarence knew about it, did he?' asked Fran. She wasn't sure that Adam had fully grasped the implication of what Olivia had said.

Olivia nodded. 'We spoke about it once. I don't really remember how the subject came up, it was a long time ago. Clarence didn't like computer games – in fact, he had some very strong opinions about them – but that didn't stop him from keeping up with developments. He mentioned the thing with the key and the escape room one time, that *was* a concept he loved. There was another one he mentioned as well, he thought it was very clever. Something about a statue with lots of arms...' She frowned. 'Sorry, I can't remember the details.'

Adam broke into a broad grin and Fran saw he had realised what Olivia's words meant. 'Clarence actually knew that game?' he asked. 'He liked it?'

Olivia smiled back, not really sure what she was talking about, but pleased by Adam's reaction nonetheless. 'He did. He said it showed a quite brilliant mind. I don't think he would have played the game though, more likely he read about it some-where. Would that have been possible?'

Adam nodded eagerly. 'The example you mentioned was often one quoted in game reviews, maybe that's where he saw it.'

'It must have been. Blimey, talk about a small world...'

Adam looked several inches taller, a fact which pleased Fran no end. That Adam's childhood hero had not only seen his work but thought highly of it as well.

She leaned into him, nudging him with her arm. 'Get you,' she said, grinning. 'But come on, tell us what it was, I'm intrigued now.'

'It was only a tiny detail,' he replied.

'Which I still want to hear about.'

He dipped his head. '*Okay...* it was just a part in a game where players had to pass through a particular room to progress any further. Yet every time they did so they found the room was pitch-black. They couldn't see anything, and they got eaten by a voracious monster. There was seemingly no way around it. No time to search for a light switch, or flick on a torch, so players got killed over and over again. But, if you've played these games before, you'll know there are a number of objects you can collect along the way, and in this case there was a small statuette of the goddess Shiva in another room, way back, which seemingly had no purpose.'

'Shiva...' murmured Fran. 'Is she the one with lots of arms?'

'One of them, yes,' replied Adam. 'And the trick was that if you happened to be carrying the statuette when you entered the room with the monster in it, miraculously the lights came on and you could slay the monster before it got you.'

Fran frowned. 'I don't understand.'

'It's a bit of a corny pun,' said Adam, wincing. 'Many hands make light work...'

Olivia groaned. 'That's it, I remember now.'

'God, that's genius,' exclaimed Fran. 'No wonder Clarence was impressed. I had no idea your games were that tricky.'

'Not all of them are,' said Adam, blushing again.

'This is incredible,' said Olivia, staring back at the pipe. She swung her bag around to the front, pulling it over her head. 'Bloody well done, Adam. Now, something waterproof...' she said.

She upended the bag, unceremoniously dumping its contents on the ground and scattering them. Disregarding several items which were obviously of no use, she popped them back in. 'I thought I might have had...' She picked up a purse, hairbrush and biro, holding them in one hand as she peered closer at something in the other. It was a small bottle of eau de cologne with a spray top. 'I might be able to get the lid off this,' she said. But then she stopped and picked up something else, something folded into a smallish square. 'Aha!' she said triumphantly. 'This is what I was looking for.' She quickly threw the rest of her things back in her bag and opened out the square. It was a plastic carrier bag.

'Oh, that's perfect,' exclaimed Fran. 'Come on, I'll help you get some water.' She flashed a broad grin at Adam. 'Wait here,' she said.

The trek back to the ditch seemed to take far longer than

the outward journey, but once there, Olivia wasted no time. She sank to her knees, leaning over the side of the ditch with the bag in her hands. 'Shit, it's cold.'

'Hold on,' said Fran, assuming a similar position, the wet from the grass seeping through the leg of her jeans. The ditch wasn't very full but with Fran 'encouraging' water into the bag with both hands, they were able to fill it with several inches of the dirty brown stuff. 'Do you think this will be enough?' she asked.

'We can always come back,' said Olivia. 'And the pipe isn't very big.' She gingerly lifted the bag, checking there were no holes in it, and then cradled it to her as the pair of them set off in search of Adam.

They'd been walking for several minutes when Fran realised she had no idea where they had joined the woodland, one patch of trees looked very much like another. And she couldn't risk calling out, what if one of the Lightmans were around and heard her?

She stopped, looking at Olivia, who was also peering anxiously through the treeline ahead. 'I think it's this way,' Fran said. 'Although Adam's wearing a blue coat which isn't going to make him that easy to spot.' She tutted and pulled out her phone, checking for signal. To her relief, several bars were showing.

'How will ringing him help?' asked Olivia. 'If he doesn't know where *we* are.'

'I'm not ringing him,' Fran replied, fingers tapping the phone screen. 'I should have brought his phone with us but, in its absence, I'm hoping I can download the what3words app and find him ourselves.' She paused, muttering encouragement under her breath.

Olivia smiled. 'I remember you used to do that at school – talking to inanimate objects. Does it help?'

'Oh yes, I'm on very friendly terms with my food mixer,'

replied Fran, rolling her eyes. 'Come on, let's keep walking until this thing sorts itself out.'

With her eyes glued to the screen, they carried on until, a moment later, Fran was forced to stop by Olivia's hand on her arm.

'Shh,' she whispered. 'I saw something.'

Fran followed her line of sight, seeing nothing beyond another line of trees.

'A flash of red, over there... but it's gone now.' She looked at Fran. 'Never mind, it could have been anything.'

Fran grimaced. 'This is almost there... Oh, hang on.' She typed quickly and held her phone out so Olivia could see it too.

It was immediately obvious where they'd gone wrong, walking forward too far instead of at an angle. Adam was behind them and way off to the right. They turned around, Olivia holding the bag protectively to her chest. Fran's still wet hands were beginning to throb with cold.

'This is it,' she said after another couple of minutes, frowning at her phone. 'But where the bloody hell is Adam?'

A sheepish face appeared around a tree a little distance away. 'I heard you coming,' he said. 'At least, I heard *someone* coming, I wasn't sure if it was you. I've been hearing all kinds of noises.' He pulled a face. 'Although I do have rather an overactive imagination.'

Fran smiled. She'd probably be just the same. 'Olivia thought she saw someone too. We couldn't remember where you were when we started walking back, we've been on a bit of a detour.' She shivered. 'Come on, let's just get this done and get out of here.'

Olivia held out the bag. 'There wasn't that much water in the ditch, mud more than anything, but it should be enough.'

Adam took it, resting it carefully on the ground for a moment, so that he could turn down the top of the bag a little to make the water easier to pour. 'Fingers crossed,' he said.

All three of them held their breath as they crouched around the pipe. With Fran guiding the spout that Adam had fashioned, he began to slowly tilt the bag, encouraged as a trickle of water ran out.

'Can you see anything?' he asked Olivia.

She shook her head. 'No, but keep going.'

Fran shifted her position a little, grimacing at the feeling of wet jeans on her knees. It was cold too... She looked down.

'Wait! Stop a minute,' she said, suddenly aware that the wetness was increasing. 'Shit... there's a hole in the pipe.' She slid her hand down the pipe and pressed her fingers against it, staunching the little spout of water which was flowing out. 'Okay, try again.'

Adam was about to pour for a second time when a loud crack sounded a little way behind them. He froze, hunching down further. The others followed suit, heads swivelling to see what had made the noise.

'It came from over there,' whispered Olivia. 'And the same flash of red I saw earlier. I think it might be one of the others.' She nodded at the pipe. 'You keep going, I'll see if I can spot who it is. I might be able to distract them a minute.'

Fran nodded. 'Okay,' she whispered back. 'Carry on,' she added to Adam. 'We need to get this done quickly.' He held her look for a moment, neither of them wishing to mention they had no idea if there was even anything in the pipe.

Adam tilted the bag downwards to slow the flow, and then dropped it even further so that it stopped. He lowered it to the ground as a slow smile spread across his face. A trickle of water had overflowed the top of the pipe and there, bobbing on the surface, was a black plastic canister. He quickly fished it out, only just managing to hook his index finger under it in the tight space.

Fran watched as Adam pulled at the lid of the canister, cold, wet fingers hampering his task. He wiped his hand on his jeans and tipped the contents into his palm. It was another bundle of papers, just like the one he had taken a photo of before, a phone number scribbled across its centre. Only then did she release the pressure on the pipe. Water immediately spurted from the hole on the side.

'Coincidence... or by design?' she said.

'Knowing Clarence, I'd say by design. I don't think he would have left anything to chance. And why make the first person who finds the clue do all the work? That would be far too easy for everyone who comes after. No, I reckon he designed this little puzzle to reset itself after each use.' He carefully separated the little slips of paper in his hand.

'How many are there?' she whispered.

'Four,' he said.

Fran's eyes lit up. 'So we're the first,' she said.

'Unless no one else has been taking the slips either.' Adam wrinkled his nose as he pulled out his phone to take another snap. 'But let's assume we are the first,' he said. 'Obviously.'

He rolled the slips back up again and popped them in the canister, snapping the lid back on and making sure it was sealed good and tight. Then he dropped the canister back into the pipe, where it fell with a satisfying clunk.

'You'd never know we were here,' he said. 'And just to be on the safe side...' He took his gloves from his pocket and dried off the top and sides of the pipe. 'Don't want to give anyone any clues.'

'Speaking of which,' replied Fran. 'Now we can get on and obtain the next one.' She looked up. 'Once Olivia gets back, that is.' Getting to her feet, she cocked her head to one side. She'd been so intent on filling the pipe with water she hadn't given a thought to where Olivia was. 'Where on earth has she gone?'

11

————

Adam turned a slow circle. 'I can't see her anywhere. Can't see anyone... What do we do now?'

'Wait for her, I guess,' replied Fran. 'I hope she's okay. This is exactly the same problem she and I had earlier when we were trying to find you. You think you're going the right way, but everywhere looks the same and you end up walking in completely the wrong direction. I should have given her my phone and then at least she'd have been able to find her way back.' She took it out and began to compose a message. 'You don't suppose she did find any of the others, do you?'

'It's possible.' Adam held her look. 'Why, what are you thinking?'

Fran shook her head. 'I'm just being melodramatic,' she replied. 'I'm sure nothing's wrong. But I don't trust Marcus an inch, or Cate, for that matter. If it was either of them we saw, then I—'

'What do you think they've done? Tied her to a tree?'

'It's silly, I know but—' She stopped as she caught sight of the expression on Adam's face. 'You don't think I'm being silly, do you?'

'I'm hoping you are, but I also can't forget the reason why we're doing all this in the first place: because Clarence didn't get on with his family and they don't seem to have got on with each other either. And I'm not forgetting what Margaret said, that Clarence had suspicions about the manner in which he would die. Just because there's no dagger or gunshot wound, no obvious sign of poisoning or blunt instrument lying around, it doesn't mean this is any different from our other cases. Clarence was a very astute man by all accounts.'

'Cases? You're surely not thinking this is... Oh.' Fran's mouth closed abruptly as she took in the possibility of Adam's words. She looked at his raised eyebrows and blew out a puff of air. 'How have we managed to wind up in the middle of yet another suspicious death? If that's what it was. I don't believe it.'

'Just lucky, I guess.'

She threw him a dark look. 'You can stop that. This isn't funny at all, or exciting, it's...' But she didn't trust herself to reply. She wouldn't admit it to anyone but Adam, but there was a teeny bit of herself that had found their past adventures really quite thrilling.

She cleared her throat. 'Whatever is happening, we need to find Olivia, and fast. We have another clue to collect, and we're never going to get to the bottom of all this until we finish the treasure hunt. That has to be our priority.'

'Agreed,' replied Adam, nodding. 'I also think we need to find out what we can about Clarence's family, and the reason why their relationships broke down. Olivia has to be the best person to help us with that.'

Fran finished typing her text message and pressed send. 'So what do we do now? The obvious answer is to stay here and wait for Olivia, but I'm not sure that's particularly wise. If the others have worked out the clue – *when* the others work out the clue – they're going to be headed to this very spot. Odds are that sooner or later we'll bump into them and I really don't want to if we can help it.'

'Then let's go back to the car and wait for Olivia there. Maybe that's an easier place for her to navigate to.'

'I'll tell her.'

Fran sent another text winging on its way, praying that Olivia would pick them up, and soon. They couldn't move on to the next clue without her.

As it happened, they all arrived back at the car more or less together some twenty minutes later. Olivia was a few seconds behind them, crashing out of the undergrowth a little further along the road, panting as she ran to catch up with them.

'Sorry,' she called. 'My sense of direction is hopeless at the best of times. I think I've been going around in circles. Did you get the clue?'

Adam grinned and held up his phone. 'We did. The water worked a charm. Floated the little film canister right up to the top. And the best thing was that when Fran took her fingers off the hole in the pipe, it emptied itself of water. Whoever finds it next is going to have to go through the whole process again. But I have the next number to ring, so when you're ready…'

'That's brilliant! Do you think we might have got to it first?'

'Who knows?' Adam shrugged. 'Did you see anyone?'

Olivia shook her head. 'Not exactly… the same flash of red clothing once or twice, but whoever it was was moving pretty fast and I never caught up with them. I'd gone some distance before I realised I'd lost them, which was when I began to panic.'

Adam flashed Fran a pointed look and said to Olivia, 'I wonder if someone was running deliberately, trying to lure you away.'

Olivia stared at him. 'Do you really think so?' She shivered, through cold or anxiety Fran wasn't sure. 'I hadn't thought of that.'

'It's probably nothing,' said Fran, trying to reassure herself as much as Olivia. 'It could have been anyone. Even an animal perhaps.'

'Either way, it's a good thing you sent your message, Fran. I could have been blundering around in there for hours looking for you two. Come on, let's get on with the next clue. We should—'

Fran followed Olivia's line of sight, heart rapidly sinking as she stared at her car, one tyre of which seemed to be puddled on the road.

'Dammit!' She kicked the tyre in frustration. 'I should have parked the car somewhere less conspicuous. I didn't think.'

'Fran, you weren't to know,' said Adam, turning to look down the road.

'No, but I still should have thought about it. I've cost us valuable time. My car was parked at Justice House the whole time I was there, it stands to reason the others know what it looks like. We've got to be more careful.'

'You think someone did this?' asked Olivia, obviously surprised.

Adam crouched down beside the car. 'The tyre hasn't been slashed and there's nothing obvious that I can see. It could just be one of those things.'

'But you don't think it was,' put in Olivia.

Fran shook her head. 'I'm probably just seeing shadows where there are none, but isn't it a little bit too much of a coincidence?'

'Perhaps...' replied Olivia. 'But you obviously think it is.' She looked at Adam. 'Do you think so too?'

He pursed his lips, eyebrows raised.

'Let's just keep focused on what we need to do,' said Fran. 'And at the moment that means changing the tyre. Good job I've got a spare, isn't it?' She looked down at her hands. 'Oh well, I'm already cold, wet and muddy. Rolling about on the road isn't going to make much difference. Unless you're volunteering of course.' She looked pointedly at Adam, only to see his gaze drop to the floor.

'Um...' He gave Fran a sheepish look. 'I would, except that...'

She rolled her eyes. 'Right then. I'll roll around on the road and you can metaphorically mop my fevered brow,' she said. 'And provide some muscle because I can never get the wheel nuts off. Liv, why don't you ring for the next clue, we can still get on with working it out while I'm doing this.'

She nodded, pulling out her phone. 'Good idea.'

Fran stared down at her sodden jeans, feeling suddenly very cold and sorry for herself. There were occasions in her life when, much as she normally loved her job, the thrill of icing one hundred and thirty identical cupcakes wore a little thin and solving murders seemed far more exciting. Today, however, she'd much rather be sitting in her neat, ordered kitchen where things were under control. She gritted her teeth and opened the car boot to collect her jack and tools.

Fran had only had occasion to change a tyre twice in her life before, and the first occasion, when Martha had been six months old, had scared the life out of her. It had suddenly dawned on her how responsible she was for her daughter, a tiny bundle of love and joy who depended on her utterly for everything her small life required. And the potential disasters that could arise from being stranded with her miles from home were extremely thought provoking. On that occasion she'd been lucky and Jack had been at home, only five minutes away. He'd come to her rescue, but she'd given him Martha to hold and, under his instruction, changed the tyre herself, vowing never to get caught out again.

Olivia made the call while Fran worked and, although changing the tyre was tedious and Fran's hands were so cold they throbbed, at least hearing the details of the new clue helped to take her mind off the task. William Butler had been on the end of the phone this time, and Fran struggled to recall his face from the party of mourners who had sat around the dining table at Justice House only the day before. It felt as if ten years had passed since then. At least. But William had duly delivered Clarence's next clue, which Olivia carefully transcribed into her notebook.

'So we have some words,' she said. 'Which, not surprisingly, make no sense at all.'

'Go on,' said Adam.

'All it says is: *who now shifted death.*'

Fran heaved in a deep breath. 'Nope, means absolutely nothing to me either.'

'*Who now shifted death...*' murmured Adam. '*Who now shifted death...* The only thing I can think of is an undertaker,' he said. 'Or a gravedigger maybe – someone who literally shifts death, from one place to another, but that can't be right.'

'Can't it?' asked Fran, beginning to jack up the car.

'No. It doesn't quite work. It's not clever enough for Clarence because the wording is wrong, it doesn't scan.'

'I agree,' said Olivia. 'Clarence loved puns and playing with words, but only if it was a really clever puzzle. He might say "one who shifted death" perhaps, but why say "who now"? That doesn't seem right, it isn't a natural way of saying things.'

'Hmm,' Adam replied. 'I wonder if it's actually a question.'

'Oh, I didn't think of that,' replied Olivia. 'But William didn't specifically mention any punctuation, so either there isn't, or if there is, it's not particularly relevant.'

'But it could make a difference to the answer,' said Fran. '*Who now shifted death* might not make sense as a question, but it could work as part of a longer sentence. So you could say: "After a recent career change, Jim the gravedigger was a man who now shifted death on a frequent basis".'

Adam studied her for a moment. 'That does makes sense,'

he said. 'It sounds a more natural way of saying things. In which case, if those words *are* part of a sentence, then how and where would we find it?'

'A graveyard,' suggested Fran. 'Might it be written somewhere? Olivia, isn't there a church next door to Justice House? Could it be written there?' She paused, trying to catch her breath. 'To me, that phrase also sounds as if it could mean cheating death... If you shifted death somewhere else or onto someone else, might you cheat it yourself?'

'That makes sense,' replied Olivia. 'But Clarence wasn't a churchgoer. In fact, I'm not sure he ever set foot in the place. So if the words were written somewhere there, I'm not sure how Clarence would know about them.'

Adam looked down at Fran. 'Shall I take over for a bit?'

She nodded. 'Please, we're almost there.' She got to her feet as Adam swapped places with her. 'So if those words *are* part of a longer sentence, it must be from something Clarence knew well, or at least had to hand. Could they have come from a favourite poem, or a book maybe, even one of his own?'

Olivia nodded. 'It's possible. And he obviously loved to read. Not surprisingly, murder mysteries were what he liked best – anything with a good puzzle in it.'

'Any that were particular favourites?'

She thought for a few seconds. 'There were loads. He didn't read poetry, fiction was more his thing. Not sure I could pick out one absolute favourite, however.'

'It's a good idea, though,' said Adam, straightening.

The car's wheel was now just clear of the ground.

'Okay,' said Fran. 'Let's get this tyre off before we do anything else.' She picked up the wrench and began to undo the wheel nuts, which Adam had already loosened for her. The phrase ran repeatedly through her head like words on a scrolling screen. She motioned to Adam. 'We can take the wheel off now. Can you give me a hand? You hold that side, I'll take this. Just pull straight towards you, jiggle a bit if it doesn't want to come.'

Fifteen minutes later, after quite a lot of swearing (Adam) and puffing (Fran) the spare wheel was in place and they were finally ready to concentrate on the clue. Adam gave the wheel nuts one last tighten and stood up.

'Let's see that sentence again, as you've written it down. Sometimes I think better that way.' He took the notebook, wiping his hands down his jeans before he did so.

For a few moments all three of them stood staring at the words. And then Adam groaned. 'Of course... It isn't part of a phrase at all, it's an anagram. That's why the word order looks odd.' He banged the heel of his hand against his forehead. 'God, I'm so slow.'

'An anagram,' repeated Fran. 'Is it? But what of? Okay, assuming it is, we need to work this out quickly... what words can you find from what we've got? *Who now shifted death...* Shout them out.'

There was silence for a moment as each of them grappled with the letters, rearranging them, trawling their heads for something which made sense.

'*With...*' said Olivia.

'*Sand...*' added Adam. 'Or *shed?*'

Fran rolled her eyes. 'Oh God, no more sheds, please.'

He smiled at her, clearly remembering the time when Fran had been locked in a garden shed by a potential suspect in a murder case. Adam had had to rescue her.

'Still could be part of something,' he replied, eyes twinkling. 'We need to know what though or we could be here for a very long time. Are we looking for a place name? Or... I don't think it will be another what3words location, but it could be a landmark or something similar, something well known.'

'Could it be a title?' asked Fran. 'A book title? I've got the idea of it being part of a sentence stuck in my head.' She looked again at the letters. 'Not *shed* but *sh... show...*'

'Wind...' said Olivia, intent on her task.

Something in Fran's chest flipped, a quickening. She stared again. Could that be it? She sought out the letters one by one, making sure they were there, making sure they fit. S–h–a–d–o–w...

'*Shadow.*'

She locked eyes with Olivia. '*Shadow of the Wind,*' they chimed.

'God, I love that book,' exclaimed Fran.

'Me too,' said Olivia. 'The whole series... and the Cemetery of Lost Books. I'd forgotten about that.'

Adam looked from one to the other. 'Carlos Ruiz Zafón,' he said, pleased. 'But was that a book Clarence liked?'

'It was him who introduced me to it,' replied Olivia. 'That has to be it.'

'And if it was one of Clarence's favourites,' said Fran, 'then he must have had a copy.'

Olivia's eyes lit up. 'Yes, it's on the bookcase. In the Inventing Room.'

Fran slammed the boot shut. 'Come on then – quickly – let's get over there.'

Adam climbed into the passenger seat and buckled up his seat belt. 'To Justice House, Fran, and don't spare the horses.'

Fran was about to turn up the drive to the house a few minutes later when a car suddenly flashed past them and out onto the road. Dark, low and sleek, it was unmistakably Marcus driving, and Fran just caught a glimpse of Cate's blonde hair as they sped by.

'I was about to say we need to hide the car this time,' she

said, 'because I'm not changing another bloody tyre, but there's probably little point now. We're obviously last here.'

Adam shook his head. 'There's Saul too, don't forget, and no sign of him yet. I still don't think we should take any chances.'

Olivia leaned forward and pointed to a track on the other side of the driveway. 'Turn up there,' she said. 'And follow it round to the left. It leads to the old graveyard at the side of the church. It's little used now, but there's no parking at the front of the church so anyone visiting a grave goes up there. You can pull in beside the shed the gardener uses and the car will be completely hidden.'

Fran did as she suggested. 'Which way do we go?' she asked. 'Front or back?'

'The windows in the Inventing Room overlook the side of the garden, so if we go around the back we should be able to sneak over to the window first and check in case Saul is there. If the coast's clear, I don't suppose it much matters after that.'

'Keep your eyes peeled,' said Adam.

'I've lost us at least half an hour,' said Fran. 'I should think he's been and gone too.'

Adam threw her a sympathetic look. 'We all could have thought about where we left the car back at the woods, Fran. It wasn't solely your responsibility.'

But Fran still wasn't comforted. This wasn't some light-hearted bit of a lark for a sunny weekend's entertainment. It was serious. The phrase *life or death* flashed through her head, but she pushed it away.

'Olivia, you lead the way,' she said. 'You'll know the best route.'

They made it all the way to the house without seeing anyone or being seen themselves. And, as they peered cautiously through the window, the Inventing Room was empty. No one wanted to voice the thought that it was obvious they were the last to arrive, but Fran felt it keenly.

Retracing their steps, Olivia let them in through the back door, and they soundlessly made their way through the house. A quick scout of the rooms confirmed what they already suspected: they had the place to themselves.

'*The Shadow of the Wind* is over here,' said Olivia, walking purposefully to the bookcase nearest the fireplace. 'It hasn't been moved,' she added. 'Or, if it has, it's been put back in the right place. See, the other books in the series are all here, and in order too.' She lifted it from the shelf and carried it over to Clarence's desk, laying her notebook beside it. 'So what are we looking for?'

'The most logical thing would be a cipher of some kind,' said Adam. 'But for that to work, we should have received another piece of information – a key word, or maybe some numbers.' He picked up the book and checked the front and back pages.

'Shake it,' said Fran. 'There could be something tucked inside.'

'No, nothing,' added Adam after a moment, when it was obvious that nothing was about to fly loose. 'Perhaps there's something written inside. Or on the jacket.'

He put down the book again and removed the dust cover, turning it over to examine it. He pulled a face. 'Nothing here,' he said. 'Inside it is then. This might take a while. Bear with...'

Fran watched as Adam began to turn the pages. He was right, *Shadow of the Wind* was quite a lengthy work and examining each page was going to take a while. That's if there was anything to be found. Adam obviously thought there would be a code of some sort, but surely that would be in a separate place, away from the book? Somehow Fran couldn't see Clarence defacing a much-loved volume, but where else might you leave another clue? Idly, she picked up the dust jacket, turning it over in her hands and running her fingers over the embossed title. She did it again, and then stopped, frowning.

As she'd run her fingers along the raised surface of the title, she had felt another series of bumps a little lower down, as if something else had marked the cover. Turning the jacket over so that the blank side was facing her, she began to study it more carefully, holding it up to the light.

'Guys...' she said. 'I think I might have found something.'

Olivia hurried to her side.

'See this?' Fran held the cover so Olivia could check it too. 'Does it look as if something might've been written here? You can see indentations on the paper.'

'May I?' Olivia took the cover. 'There's definitely something there,' she said, excitement raising her voice. 'I wonder if Clarence could have stuck something here, it would be a good hiding place, wouldn't it? With the dust jacket on the book you might not think to look underneath it.'

'A note most likely,' said Adam, coming across. 'That makes a lot of sense. Clarence loved books, it seems odd that he would have willingly defaced one.'

Fran smiled, pleased that Adam had also come to this conclusion. 'Well, if there was one, someone's made off with it.'

'So now what do we do? If the clue has been sabotaged, we've got no chance,' said Olivia, her face falling again.

'Not so fast,' said Fran, crossing back to the desk. 'I've watched far too many spy thrillers to let this defeat us.' She pulled open the top drawer. 'Would Clarence have had a very soft pencil?'

'Yes, he used them when he drew the maps for his books. I'll get one for you.'

Fran stood back as Olivia pulled out the drawer a little further and fished at the back of it. 'There you go. Hopefully, that should do the trick.' She passed across the stubby end of a pencil.

Fran took it, lay the dust jacket on the desk and began to rub the pencil tip very softly over the surface of the paper, as if she was doing a brass rubbing. 'God, my hands are shaking.' But almost immediately she could see the indentations beginning to appear against the dark background she was creating.

'Fran, you're a genius,' said Adam. 'And that looks a lot like a list of numbers. I think we might just have found our cipher.'

Fran beamed at him and, after a couple more moments, she straightened up, peering at the page. She pulled out her phone and snapped a quick shot. 'Just in case any of it gets smudged,' she said.

'So, how do the numbers work?' asked Olivia.

'There are various ways,' replied Adam. 'The first number could be a page number, followed by a line number, followed by the number of the word within that line, or paragraph. Or they could just be chapters, or individual letters even. We won't know until we see what makes sense.'

'If this clue follows the pattern of the others then we're looking for a location,' said Fran. 'That might help.'

Olivia sat down, looking at her notebook. 'From memory I don't think this book has enough chapters for some of the numbers here, so let's start with page number six then line seven and then...' She turned to the appropriate place and moved her finger down, counting as she went. ' Then the number nine is the letter we're looking for, or the word. In this case either a *B* or *broad.*'

She carried on in the same fashion for a few minutes, while Fran and Adam peered at what she was writing, trying to make sense of the mixture of letters and words.

'Next it's...' All eyes followed Olivia's fingers as she turned over the pages, scanning the bottom for the number. Her finger stilled. 'Oh...'

She flipped the page back and forth, but there was no mistaking what had happened. It had been done neatly, there were no jagged edges giving the game away, but the page they were looking for had been cut from the book.

'I guess that well and truly answers our question about whether we're the first ones here,' said Adam. He gave Olivia a pointed look. 'And whoever *was* here has clearly decided that cheating is the way ahead. They've tried to sabotage this clue in more ways than one.'

Fran stared at him, anger flushing her face. 'What do we do now?'

'It's obviously against the rules,' replied Olivia. 'You heard what Margaret said: anyone found cheating or sabotaging the others' chances in any way will forfeit the win.'

'*If* they're found out,' said Fran. 'And if my car tyre was deliberately let down then this is the second time they've acted. We need to stop them.'

'We need to work out who it is,' said Adam. 'And get word to Margaret.' He pointed at the book. 'Can you take a photo of that, Olivia, and send it to her? Alert her to what's going on?'

'I can. But without knowing who it is I can't see how that helps us. Margaret could just as easily say we'd done it and were covering our backs to make it look like someone else was guilty. The others could make the same argument.'

Adam sighed. 'Good point. I still think we should do it though.'

'Wait a minute,' said Fran, her mind racing ahead. 'Maybe, unwittingly, we've been given an extra clue.' She tapped the place where the missing page should be. 'Why only remove that page? Why not several?' She looked at Adam's blank face. 'The way we've been looking for the clue letters utilises numerous pages, in which case removing a page wouldn't really make any difference to our ability to solve it, we'd possibly still be able to work it out even with one letter missing. Removing only one page suggests that all, or most, of the pertinent information was on that page, or at the very least something crucial to the overall clue.'

'Also a good point,' said Adam, smiling at her. 'In which case we're completely scuppered.'

'Only if this is the sole copy of the book,' replied Fran, the corners of her mouth crinkling. 'So it's very lucky that this is also one of *my* favourite books. I have a copy at home.'

Olivia snapped a quick photo and, picking up her notebook, replaced *The Shadow of the Wind* on the bookcase. 'Plan B it is then,' she said. 'Come on.'

They'd made it as far as the kitchen when she suddenly stopped.

'What was that?' she asked, holding up a hand to communicate that they should stand still.

Fran strained her ears, listening for any sound within the silent house. Not even a clock was ticking. She was about to whisper that she couldn't hear anything when Olivia shushed them again. And that time Fran did hear something.

A low moaning sound of something in pain. Or someone...

12

'It's coming from the cupboard,' said Olivia. 'The pantry, over there.'

Fran darted a glance at Adam, who looked just as anxious as she felt. This was beginning to be not very much fun at all. One of them needed to open the cupboard door. She reminded herself that if someone was able to make a noise then at least they were still alive...

With a look at Olivia, she moved forward and, grasping the door handle, yanked it open, jumping backwards as she did so.

Saul tumbled head first into the room, and would have fallen had Adam not dashed forward to intercept him, gently lowering him to the ground, where the sounds of pain he was making intensified.

'It's okay,' said Adam as he tried to pull away. 'It's okay...'

Fran had already noticed the wound on the back of Saul's head, where dried blood had mixed with his fair hair, turning it dark. His hands were tied behind his back, his mouth a bright blue gash of tape. Frightened eyes met theirs as he tried to get to his knees.

'It's okay, Adam is a friend of mine, Saul,' said Olivia

quickly. 'A friend of Fran's. I went to school with her, if you remember.' She touched a hand to his face. 'Let's get this off. May I?'

He nodded, and she carefully removed the tape from his mouth, wincing as she did so.

He looked at Fran, as if still trying to focus on her face. 'You're the caterer?'

She nodded. 'Yes, that's right.'

With Adam's assistance, Saul was able to kneel, wobbling a little as he tried to find his balance. 'Christ, my arms hurt.'

'I'll get some scissors,' said Olivia. 'Hang on.' She rooted around in a drawer, returning with a pair in her hand. 'Jesus, Saul, what happened?' she asked, crouching beside him as she began to cut through the ties which bound his hands.

He shook his head. 'I don't know. Something hit me... hard. It bloody hurt and then...' He squeezed his eyes together. 'I don't think I passed out but I couldn't really make out what was going on, like I was... it's true, it's like seeing stars. Someone tied my hands. I couldn't even struggle.'

'How long ago was this?' asked Adam.

Saul paused until his hands were finally free, rubbing at his chafed wrists. 'I don't know. Not long. I shouted for a while but I couldn't hear anything and all that did was make my head hurt, so I stopped. I've just been lying there.'

It seemed an obvious question but Fran asked it anyway. 'Who did this to you, Saul?'

To their surprise he shook his head. 'I don't know. Stupid, but it all happened so fast. And from behind. I literally didn't hear a thing. I opened the kitchen door and bang. It felt like my head exploded.'

Fran took in his bright-red jacket, wondering if Adam had noticed it too. 'Was it Marcus?' she asked. Given that he and Cate were the only people not at the house, it had to have been one of them. Unless Saul had been very unlucky and was accosted by a would-be burglar.

'It's possible. It wouldn't be the first time he's thumped me, he was very handy with his fists even as a child.'

Fran could see the pain of memories in his eyes. What on earth had gone wrong in this family? Because something had, badly.

'I really didn't see who it was,' added Saul, stretching his neck and grimacing as he sought to loosen the taught muscles there. 'I thought I smelled something sweet, but maybe I was hallucinating.'

'We saw Cate and Marcus leaving as we arrived at the house,' said Olivia. 'Which means everyone beat us to this clue.' She studied Saul. 'Fran and Adam have been helping me,' she explained. 'And someone let down the tyre on Fran's car. At least it's beginning to look more and more like that's what happened. Whatever the reason, it delayed us getting here. Now we've discovered that the particular book page we need to solve the next clue is missing.' She gave him a pointed look.

Saul groaned. 'I didn't even get that far. Was it *Shadow of the Wind*?'

Olivia nodded. 'But we haven't figured out any of the message yet.' She looked first at Adam and then at Fran. 'What do we do now?' she asked.

Fran shrugged. It wasn't her place to make a decision when this affected Olivia's future. She knew what she would do, and she was pretty sure she knew what Olivia would do, but...

'Saul, we can't leave you like this,' said Olivia. 'And if it was either Marcus or Cate who did this, then I'm doubly determined that they shouldn't profit a penny from Clarence's death. What do you say to joining forces?'

'I can't ask you to do that,' he replied, running a hand over his face. 'I'm just going to slow you down. Look, I'll be fine. Give me

ten minutes to get myself together and I'll be right behind you.
So you'd best get going. You've already given me a helping hand
– two, actually, because you've told me there's a page missing in
the book. Which means I need to find another copy, as do you.
Go on, I'll be fine.' He pushed himself to his feet, wobbling
alarmingly as he did so. He forced a smile. 'Ten minutes...'

Fran could see the tussle on Olivia's face. She wanted to
win this – who wouldn't? – and given her circumstances you
could argue that she alone deserved to inherit Clarence's estate.
But it was clear she also didn't want Marcus and Cate to win. It
was just a question of which she wanted more.

'Bugger that,' Olivia said to Saul. 'We're not leaving you, it
isn't right. You need a rest, very probably someone to look at
your head, a drink, something to eat for the shock and—' She
glanced up at Fran to check she was following her line of
thought.

Fran smiled. There was a lot to lose but she was pleased by
the stance Olivia had taken. Money was at the root of this family's problems, and to follow it blindly with no regard for what
was important was allowing yourself to be ensnared by its lure.
Olivia was better than that. Besides, there might well be other
ways to resolve this situation, ones which would still lead to the
right outcome. For everyone.

'Absolutely,' replied Fran. 'Saul, my car isn't too far away. If
you can walk okay, I suggest we go back to my house. I have a
copy of the book there and we can make sure there's been no
lasting damage done to you at the same time.'

'Good idea,' said Adam. 'Fran always has cake. It cures all
ills.'

Saul smiled gratefully, although he was still alarmingly pale.
Whether through his injury or the realisation that his brother or
sister had no qualms about hitting him over the head, Fran
wasn't sure.

It was slow-going back to the car. Saul trod as if walking on eggshells and what had felt a short journey on the way out to the house now seemed to have trebled in distance. Every extra moment they took was another where Marcus and Cate were closer to the treasure. But Fran thrust the thought from her mind. If they were out of the running, then they would simply have to concentrate their efforts on proving the others were cheating. A flat tyre could have been used by them as an attempt to derail the hunt, making sabotage look like a possibility, but there was no way that Saul could have hit the back of his own head. Not unless he was a total psychopath... Fran shook her head as if to clear it. *Francesca Eve, stop it this instant, you and your overly active imagination...*

They were almost at the car when Fran realised something else.

'Saul, how did you get from the woodland back to the house? Where's *your* car?'

'It's still there,' he replied. 'When I realised where I was, I ran back, it's quicker.'

Fran stared at Olivia, who was looking equally as puzzled.

'And where exactly were you?' she asked.

'We used to play in the woodland as kids,' explained Saul, pointing behind them. 'There's a public footpath a little way along on the other side of the road from the house. It takes you past the grounds of another house, but eventually leads directly into the woods, only to the opposite end of where the clue was hidden. Like you, when I was trying to get to the what3words clue I looked for the nearest road, which is misleading, really. It's closest to where the clue was hidden but not as the crow flies. I only realised where I was when I saw our tree.'

'Your tree?'

Saul nodded. 'We carved our names into it years ago. Dad would have been furious if he'd found out. Which, come to think of it, was probably why Marcus suggested it.'

'So could Clarence have got there?' asked Fran. 'To place the clue, I mean.'

Saul shrugged. 'I guess so. It's about a mile, I reckon. Could he walk that far?'

Olivia nodded. 'If he took it steady.'

'Well, that explains that part of the puzzle at least,' said Fran.

Adam turned to Saul. 'Do you think Marcus and Cate would have worked out where they were?'

He nodded. 'I'm pretty sure they did. I drove past your car, but I didn't see either of the other two. And there were no cars at the house when I got here. So if they didn't leave theirs back at the woodland, they must have hidden it too.' He stopped a moment, looking overwhelmingly weary. 'We might as well give up, they're so far ahead of us now.'

Fran saw Olivia's jaw clench.

'They're not going to win,' Olivia said. 'Not if I have anything to do with it.' She frowned as another thought popped into her head. 'The car which passed us earlier was a dark-blue thing. Does that belong to Marcus? Only I'm wondering how Cate travelled here for the funeral. Does she have a car with her as well?'

Saul shook his head. 'Cate said it was in the garage being repaired. She was bitching about it when she first arrived. And about the cost of train tickets. Marcus gave her a lift, apparently.'

'But they live hours apart from one another,' said Olivia.

Saul shrugged. 'Well, that's what she said.'

By the time they arrived back at Fran's house, it was almost dark. She led the way straight into her kitchen, telling the others to take a seat while she made a beeline for the pantry. There were some biscuits there and a slab of chocolate which she had craftily hidden from Jack and Martha. She laid them on the table with an order for everyone to get stuck in and for Adam to put the kettle on while she went to fetch her copy of *The Shadow of the Wind*. It had been an age since she'd read it, but when all this was over she promised herself a return visit.

She handed the book to Olivia and sat down. 'I've been thinking,' she said. 'You might not like the sound of this but hear me out. I reckon we should split up.'

Adam's head jerked up. 'What? We've only just decided to stick together.'

Fran nodded. 'I know, and when I say split up, I mean into two teams, working together, but also apart, so we can tackle both sides of this challenge at the same time.'

'Go on,' said Olivia warily.

Fran took a biscuit. 'It seems to me that we have two very different paths ahead of us. We need to get to the final clue first, I think everyone will agree with that, but we also need to prove that if Marcus and Cate win, it will be because they've cheated and deliberately set out to sabotage everyone else's efforts.' She looked at Saul. 'You've been assaulted. That's a criminal offence apart from anything.'

'The police aren't going to be interested, if that's what you're suggesting,' he replied.

'No, I'm not, but it's proof of what Cate and Marcus have done. We also have photographic evidence that they cut a page from *The Shadow of the Wind*, but, as with my flat tyre, you could argue that we did it ourselves to make it look like everyone else was cheating and get them disqualified. Adam, you and I both know from past experience that supposition isn't enough, you have to have concrete, irrefutable evidence that an event happened the way you said it did. Saul's head injury is the only thing we have which falls into that category so if we're going to stay ahead of Cate and Marcus, not necessarily in the hunt, but in proving they've cheated, that's the piece of evidence we need. They're smart, they'll have an answer for anything we accuse them of.'

'That's actually a really good point,' said Adam.

'Thank you. So... we look at the book and work out the clue. Then, Adam, you and Olivia go on to the next location and carry on with the hunt.' She held up a hand. 'No, don't argue. Olivia, you have to go because you're the one playing, and Adam, you have to go with her because you're way better at the clue-solving stuff than the rest of us. Meanwhile, Saul and I can stay here and get in touch with Margaret, send her some photos and explain what's been happening. It will also give Saul a bit of time to recover and we can both join you as soon as we're done here. You should probably call your wife as well, Saul, let her know what's going on.'

But Saul's response was immediate. 'No, no way. She didn't want me to come for the funeral in the first place, and she wasn't at all happy to hear about the treasure hunt. If I tell her what's happened, she'll come and get me and that will be that. No, what she doesn't know, won't hurt her. I'm fine.'

Fran studied his face, but it was resolute and she could understand his point of view. She leaned forward and patted the cover of the book. 'Off you go then,' she said to Olivia. Getting to her feet to make some drinks, she smiled at the expression on Adam's face. He was doing a very good impression of a small furry animal facing oncoming traffic.

While the tea was brewing, she gave her hands a good wash, revelling in the feel of the warm water. She was only just beginning to thaw out and the thought of a hot shower hovered invitingly, but time was against them. Bringing a teapot and an assortment of mugs to the table, she sat down.

'Let's hope that wherever it is we need to go next, it's not too far away,' she said, nodding at the window outside. 'Or a place where it being dark won't matter. Otherwise we may have to think again.'

Adam caught her look and returned it with one equally as anxious.

'Almost there,' murmured Olivia, biting her lip. She had the index finger of her left hand on the list of numbers in her notebook and the one on her right tracing down the page of the book in front of her. She was clearly counting and there was nothing anyone else could do at this point. Three pairs of eyes silently watched her progress.

'Right, this is it... This is what the message says.' Olivia spun the notebook around to face Adam and Saul.

bothyberwickdropdead

Fran leaned across. 'Both... thy... no, that's not right.' She frowned.

And then she saw it. She picked up the pen from beside the pad, drawing three vertical lines to split the words so that it read: *bothy|berwick|drop|dead.*

'Charming, but I don't suppose that's what it actually means,' she said.

'Hopefully not,' replied Olivia. 'But what does it mean?'

'Well, the first bit's easy but I don't know about the second part, I—'

'You go with Olivia,' intoned Adam, imitating her voice. 'You're so much better at working out the clues than the rest of us.' He grinned. 'Come on then, clever clogs, why is it easy?'

Fran stuck out her tongue. 'Because I'm middle-aged and have a National Trust membership. Attingham Park is the country pad of the Berwick family, or was once upon a time, it's now owned and managed by the Trust. There's a rather fine Regency mansion, acres of land, a deer park, and, importantly, a walled garden where the gardener's hut is affectionately known as the Bothy. I've dragged Martha around it enough times hoping that one day she'll grow up to appreciate it.' Fran smiled, dipping her ahead. 'You're welcome...'

Adam got to his feet, seizing a couple of biscuits. 'I've no idea what the rest of it means, but we can work it out on the way.' He patted his coat pocket, rattling his car keys. 'You ready, Olivia?'

She jumped up, looking startled. 'Yes... No... I feel I should have, but I've never been there. I haven't a clue where anything is.'

Adam smirked. 'Don't worry, I know it. My mum used to drag me round it too.'

'Adam, it will be closed by now. You can't—'

'I don't think we have that choice,' he replied, his mouth a hard line.

And with that they were gone, Olivia with one last lingering look at the chocolate.

'I'll ring you!' she shouted from the hallway.

Saul, who had almost managed to stand up, sat back down again with a bump. 'Well, how is that going to work, if the place is closed?'

Fran pulled a face. 'How can I put this? Somehow, I don't think that's going to be much of a barrier to Adam. He can be really very creative when he puts his mind to it.'

Saul looked worried. 'Why, what's he going to do?'

'Hop over the fence, I would imagine. But you didn't hear me say that.' She reached forward. 'I'll have a look at your head in a minute, and we really should take some photos of it too, to send on to Margaret.' She smiled. 'But, first things first, Saul. How do you take your tea?'

13

_____

Adam had no idea how long it would take to get to Attingham House, but however long it was, he was determined to do it in half the time. Maybe they'd just got lucky because Fran knew the history of the place, but if the clue was that easy to work out, the chances were that Cate and Marcus were already there. Been and gone even – Adam knew the bothy and it was single-storey and only two-rooms big. Once Cate and Marcus had worked out the second part of the clue, it surely wouldn't take them long to find it.

Drop dead, drop dead... So far, Adam had no idea what that meant. He didn't think they were supposed to take it in its literal sense, to fall down deceased, so perhaps it simply referred to something inanimate. He concentrated on the road. They had to get there first.

Beside him, Olivia was quiet. Which he was beginning to find increasingly awkward. He didn't know anything about her, not really, other than she went to school with Fran, and that she was now a writer. If he were Fran, he'd be able to start a conversation, because Fran was like that whether she knew a person or not, she could talk to anyone. She'd make them a cup of tea and give them something to eat and whoever would soon be chatting away with her as if they'd known each other for years. Adam just didn't have it in him, and judging by the silence in the car, maybe Olivia didn't either.

'Sorry, Adam, I'm miles away,' she said. 'I'm not normally this quiet, as Fran would tell you.'

Adam smiled at her inadvertent reading of his mind. 'It's okay, you have a lot to think about,' he replied.

'I can't get my head around what's happening. The treasure hunt, that's Clarence all over, always larger than life. Why should that change just because he's dead but...' She sniffed. 'Sorry. I'm really going to miss him.'

Adam didn't know what to say. Half the time he didn't understand people at all, so empathy wasn't one of his strongest points. But then Fran always said that when people were emotional, mostly what they wanted to do was talk. Perhaps if he said nothing, Olivia would simply carry on.

'And, try as I might, I cannot understand why Cate and Marcus behave the way they do. Saul too, up to a point, although I might have to revise my opinion of him, given recent circumstances. Clarence really didn't like to talk about what happened, but I know how much their attitude towards him hurt and, from what little I did learn, I can't really relate their behaviour with events at all. There must be something I don't know about, something which caused the massive split in their family. I'm a historian for goodness' sake, cause and effect is my stock in trade, but sometimes I don't think I understand people at all.'

Adam risked a sideways glance, astonished that she could repeat exactly what he'd been thinking. 'Has Fran told you how we met?' he asked.

She shook her head. 'Not in any detail, just that you're the son of a friend of hers.'

'It wasn't my greatest triumph,' he said, smiling as he

recalled the memory. 'Although, to be fair, not hers either. It was during my mum's birthday party. Fran was providing the catering, but we were both hiding. Me, from the world in general, and she, dodging another friend who had Fran in her sights for something or other, something she didn't want to do anyway. So there I was, sitting in the understairs cupboard minding my own business when Fran snuck in. Nearly scared the life out of both of us, but as meetings go, it was pretty memorable.'

Olivia smiled. 'It sounds it. Was it the murder-mystery party she mentioned before? Where someone died and your mum looked like she was going to be in trouble?'

'Yeah, shortly after the party one of the guests died, poisoned, and all of a sudden my mum was in the frame for murder. Fran helped me clear her name. I couldn't think of who else to turn to.'

'That's Fran all over, always looking out for someone.'

'You were at school together, weren't you?'

'Mmm... Got up to all kinds of mischief. Mostly led by me, obviously. Fran was always the voice of reason.'

'I can imagine that.'

'She wasn't a goody two-shoes though, not by a long stretch, but she tempered my enthusiasms, mainly because she always had how other people were feeling at the forefront of her mind. I can see that hasn't changed.' She sighed. 'What are we going to do, Adam?'

'Well, I know where the bothy is, so get there as soon as possible. I'm hoping something clever will occur to me once we're there.'

Olivia cleared her throat. 'I didn't actually mean right now,' she said. 'Although, yes, I agree that's what we need to do. I meant what are we going to doing about all of this: the hunt, Clarence's family, the inheritance...?'

Adam frowned. 'I'm not sure I'm following, sorry.'

'I'm wondering if I should pull out, let them have it all, even though I know they'll fight and squabble over it. But they're family, Adam. Whatever's happened between them, I'm not sure I should be standing in their way.'

'So why are you doing it then?' He paused, wincing a little. 'Sorry, that didn't quite come out the way I intended. What I mean is, maybe you should ask yourself why you decided to take part in the hunt in the first place.'

'Well, because Clarence...,' She ground to a halt. 'Ah, I see what you did there,' she added, smiling. 'It just seemed that if Clarence had gone to the trouble of wording his will in a particular way so that I could join in, I would be turning my back on his wishes if I didn't. But I don't absolutely know that's what he had in mind.'

Adam thought for a minute. 'I like maths and physics best,' he said. 'They're subjects where there's usually a definitive answer. It's either right or wrong, black or white. But, even so, there are paradoxes and areas of research we don't yet fully understand that seem to defy our best thinking. So, when that happens, until someone works it out, all we can go with is our best guess. Sometimes that's all you have, until new information proves otherwise.'

'So you think I should carry on?'

'Yes, I do. And don't forget, someone hit Saul over the head and that's not right. Fran would argue whoever did that doesn't deserve a thing.'

'And she's probably right. She stood up to a bully on my behalf when we were at school, that's how we became friends. Even back then she always did the right thing, even when it hurt to do so.'

'There you go then,' replied Adam, indicating the sign ahead of them. 'Decision made and we're here so it's a good job. We'd better get our thinking caps on.'

· · ·

Adam had already worked out that entering Attingham Park via the front door was not the way forward, but beyond that, he wasn't entirely sure what to do. From memory there was a gatehouse at the entrance, from which a long winding driveway snaked its way through parkland and on into the car park. It was here that the ticket office stood. The estate ranged for miles, however, and Fort Knox it was not. There would be somewhere they could climb a fence or squeeze through a hedge, they just had to find it. Perhaps the back entrance would be a better bet.

Given the number of visitors Attingham attracted, the National Trust, in their wisdom, had devised a way of separating the cars leaving from those arriving. The village in which it stood was only small and at very busy times traffic liable to become a problem. For this reason, the exit from the park was on a completely different road from the entrance and it was here that Adam headed.

He scouted ahead for somewhere to stop, and, after a moment, he spotted the perfect place. A tradesman's van had pulled up under a large tree to one side of the road, perhaps to visit one of the neighbouring cottages, and he quickly swung in beside it. With any luck, anyone leaving the park would simply think he was associated with the tradesman and not look any harder.

The other benefit to parking near the exit was that it was very much closer to the walled garden where the bothy lay, and the clock was still ticking. With a grimace at Olivia, he climbed from the car and waited for her to join him.

'It's this way,' he said, setting a brisk pace. 'The garden is almost straight ahead of us, so we need to cut off to the left and come around to it that way. There used to be an orchard behind it that gave way to fields and with any luck, we can slip through somewhere.'

Olivia hurried behind him. 'Won't there be people still

here?' she said. 'We can't just waltz in and start looking for clues.'

He checked his watch. 'I'm not sure exactly what time it closes, but I'm pretty sure all the visitors will have gone by now. There may be one or two staff members left, but probably just the grounds staff, I would imagine. We'll have to be careful, that's all we can do.' He'd actually prefer to simply waltz right in – there was safety in numbers and they would more easily blend in if there were other visitors around. But that wasn't a luxury open to them.

By the time they had crossed the field, Adam's feet were soaking. And freezing cold. The grass was long, left unmown for the winter, and almost reached his knees in places. But there was no choice, it was this or nothing. Beyond were the trees he was looking out for, unmistakably apple trees, their branches gnarled and spindly against the darkening sky. And he was right, just a stock fence separated him and Olivia from the orchard. It took less than a minute to climb over.

Ahead of them was the rear of the garden, the walls of which rose in rich-red bricks to a height of twenty or so feet. Part way along, a tall gate led into an area which Adam seemed to remember was filled with vegetables at one end, and a formal flower garden at the other. As they slipped through, Adam put a gentle hand on Olivia's arm to stop her for a moment.

'We need to be on the lookout,' he said. 'As well as any staff, Cate and Marcus could still be here, and the last thing we need is a confrontation.' He pointed to another archway in the wall to his left: 'The bothy is through there.'

The day had rapidly lost its light and he hoped the dank chill had done little to encourage any remaining staff to linger. Sidling closer to the archway, Adam peered around, jerking his head back at the sight of a woman walking towards him. Only the fact that she was looking down at a clipboard saved him from being seen. He motioned for Olivia to flatten herself back against the wall and, pressing himself into the shadows, prayed that the woman would walk on past.

Moments later, he saw her shadow pass and he let out the breath he hadn't even realised he'd been holding. Risking another glance, he watched until the woman disappeared through another gate at the far end. Dressed in dark-green work trousers and jacket, with any luck she was the last of the gardeners making for home.

Leaning back, Adam drew in a deep breath, willing his breathing to slow. His heart was beating unaccountably hard. With a reassuring look at Olivia, he stepped through the archway, hugely relieved to find no one else waiting for them on the other side. He pointed to a single-storey building just beyond a long row of very old greenhouses.

'That's the bothy,' he whispered, frowning as he realised there was still a light showing inside. 'We need to be careful.'

They walked quickly along the path. Designed to allow visitors to take in all there was to see, it ran around the edge of the garden and Adam had to fight a strong urge to run across the lawn at its centre. He usually felt safer on the fringes, less exposed than in open space, but with every step he imagined that Cate or Marcus would burst out from the flower beds and the game would be up. He held his nerve and they reached the side wall of the bothy unchallenged. With a look at Olivia, and a slight nod, he edged his way along the front to the first of the two windows.

A quick glance through it showed the dim room beyond to be empty, but Adam wasn't taking any chances. Whispering to Olivia to stay where she was, he ducked underneath the window and, with an odd waddling crouch, made his way to the next. He gingerly raised his head until he was able to peep over the sill, sighing with relief when he saw the vacant room. He straightened, beckoning for Olivia to join him.

'Coast's clear,' he said. Gently, he lifted the latch and pushed against the door.

To his amazement, it opened, and he was immediately struck by the glorious warmth in the room, coming from the fireplace in the centre of one wall. It was also the source of the soft light. He automatically walked towards it, holding out his chilled hands to the dying embers. Olivia closed the door behind her and did likewise, head swivelling as she looked around her.

Adam couldn't even remember when he had last been here, but on that occasion he seemed to recall the building had been virtually bare, a place for storage and somewhere for the estate gardeners to take their breaks. Now, however, it had been put to more effective use and appeared to be part museum, part information centre. Importantly, they were the only two people there.

The space was divided into halves. The side they were standing in held several chairs, gathered around the fireplace, but beyond that, the only other items were a collection of battered gardening books which sat on a series of shelves lining an alcove beside the fire. The other half of the room, however, looked far more promising. Various gardening implements, both new and old, stood against the walls, and an old desk perched against one wall held what could only be described as a cabinet of curiosities.

An old watering can sat on the desk, amid several small terracotta pots, a pine cone, an old bird's nest, and the long russet tail feather of a pheasant... all treasures found and brought back to be displayed. A bunch of dried flowers were propped in an earthenware pot and an old hurricane lamp lurched on one side, having seen far better days. Adam peered closer as something caught his eye.

It was the skull of a small mammal, tucked onto a shelf in

the cabinet, the old bones gleaming softly in the dim light. *Drop dead...*

Adam lifted the remains from their resting place as carefully as he could, turning over the small label which told him what he was holding. The clue had been easy to solve this far, but surely not this easy. Eyes narrowing, he turned the object this way and that, holding it out so that Olivia could see. She too toyed with the label, but, beyond the handwritten description, there was nothing else to see.

'What are you thinking?' she asked, her voice almost a whisper.

Adam shook his head. 'I'm not sure, but... that part of the clue, drop dead, it must have relevance to something here, only this seems, I don't know, too easy?'

Olivia looked surprised. 'But we haven't found anything yet. We haven't even started looking... and everything's easy if you know the answer.'

'True...' He turned the skull over again in his hand before replacing it on the shelf. 'And this doesn't seem to be what we're looking for. But it has to be something like this, something connected with death, morbid though that is.'

Olivia's eyes were raking the shelves. 'Logically, if this location follows the pattern of the other clues, then it's where we should find another phone number.' She picked up the skull again. 'Perhaps there's something hidden on the label.' She frowned. 'I can hardly see a thing, it's too dark in here.'

Adam pulled out his phone. 'I didn't want to risk using the torch, but I don't think we've any choice.' He flicked it on, moving closer. 'What do you think we're looking for? Maybe one of those microdots you see in spy films?'

She raised her eyebrows. 'I was thinking more along the lines of markings, like we found on the inside of the book jacket earlier.'

Adam gave her a sheepish look. 'Don't mind me, I always go for the most wayward option.'

He shone the light at the label as Olivia twisted it this way and that. She shook her head.

'Nope, I can't see anything.' She peered closer. 'Maybe it is a microdot. Or invisible ink?' She smiled. 'You've got me at it now...'

'If it is, we'd need a reagent. Something which makes the ink reappear,' he clarified. 'And that doesn't seem like something Clarence would do, not here anyway, with nothing to hand.' He shook his head again. 'No, it can't be that. Think about the other times we've found the phone numbers. They were all written on slips of paper and hidden in empty film canisters. So that's what we're looking for, surely.'

Olivia glanced at her watch. 'So, ultimately we're looking for a place where you can hide a film canister, somewhere that relates to dropping dead.'

'Dropping dead...' repeated Adam, screwing up his face. 'All I can think of is what it literally means and somehow I get the feeling that's not what's intended at all.'

'Me neither. It sounds like something a petulant teenager would say to someone they didn't like.' She frowned. 'Still, as it's all we have to go on at the moment, let's get looking. I'll start on this side of the room.'

Adam nodded and moved opposite to where a large chalkboard was fixed to the wall. On it was a list of names, all gardeners who had worked at the estate over time, starting with the current day, and moving backwards. As well as their names, the list showed the positions the gardeners had held and the dates they served. It was a fascinating glimpse into the social history of the place but probably not relevant to what they were seeking. Taking a final good look all around the board, including behind it, Adam moved on.

Every artefact he came across, and every fixture and fitting of the room was closely examined, but the more things he dismissed, and the longer time went on, the more it felt like something wasn't right. He wandered back through the archway to where Olivia was systematically combing through the gardening books.

'Is there something about the way this last clue was written that seems odd to you? It reminds me of something but I can't think what.'

'It's pretty straightforward,' she replied, replacing the book she was holding on the shelf.

'I know,' replied Adam. 'That's what worries me.'

Olivia cocked her head to one side. 'What do you mean?'

'It's almost as if the clue is too easy. And I know it might only feel that way because we worked it out quickly, but it seems too simplistic for Clarence. I just get the feeling that we're missing something.'

'We must be,' replied Olivia, pursing her lips. 'Because I haven't found a thing that even seems to fit. I thought I'd cracked it when I came to look through the books. I fully expected one of them to have a secret compartment cut out from the pages, somewhere you could hide a canister, but you're right, that's far too easy. There isn't going to be anything here.'

'But there must be, otherwise why make the clue so obvious?'

Olivia sighed, moving back towards the fireplace, and idly trailed her fingers along the mantelpiece. A set of fire irons stood on the hearth and she lifted them up to check underneath. Nothing. None of this made any sense. She gave a wicker bin beside the fireplace a desultory kick and it toppled over, spilling some balled-up tissues. She pulled a face at Adam. 'Yuck.' Wearily, she bent down to pick them up with the very tip of her thumb and forefinger.

'Hey,' said Adam before she could drop the first of them back in. 'Is there something else in there?' He crouched down and pulled the bin towards him, lifting out a white lead of some sort. He frowned and dropped it back inside. 'Huh, just a charging cable. Broken, by the looks of it.' He stood back up and expelled a frustrated breath. 'Right, let's think about the clue again – *bothy berwick drop dead*. Why does that sound weird?'

Olivia shrugged. 'I don't know, does it?'

'Yes, it's just... it reminds me of something. When you say it out loud, it has a kind of rhythm to it, sing-songy if that's even a thing and ' He blinked as the answer came to him. Blimey, that was weird, even for him... *It couldn't be, could it?* 'I think I'm going mad...'

'Well, if you have any theory at all, let's hear it, because we're getting nowhere fast.'

'Have you ever watched *Mary Poppins*?' he asked, continuing when she nodded. 'There's the song, "Supercalifragilistic-expialidocious", which I think everyone knows. But at one point in the song, Mary Poppins says, "Of course you can say it backwards, which is docious-ali-expil-istic-fragi-cali-rupus."'

He smiled at Olivia's astonished expression. 'Even as a child it bugged me, because that's wrong. That's not saying it backwards at all. Instead, it's breaking up the word. Instead it's breaking up the word into its component parts and then repeating them backwards. Except even that doesn't work because the last part, *super*, gets changed to *rupus*, which neither fits nor is actually backwards, instead it's more like an anagram.'

'Adam, has anyone ever told you that your mind works in very mysterious ways?'

'Several people, actually... ah, rhetorical question.' He smiled. 'Anyway, that's what our clue reminded me of, don't ask me why. That same sing-songy phrasing. And what you get if you say *that* backwards is *dead drop berwick bothy*, which is an altogether different thing.'

'Is it?'

'Oh yes.'

Olivia stared at him. 'Sorry, I'm still not getting it. Drop dead or dead drop, what's the difference? Surely, they both mean the same thing. Although maybe a dead drop could be to fall off something, a cliff or a...' She trailed off, frowning at his gleeful grin.

He couldn't help himself, this was very exciting.

'A dead drop is the opposite of a live drop, both of which are terminology used by spies when leaving messages or information for someone else. With a live drop, the message is given in person, but with a dead drop, the information is hidden inside something, the point being that you don't have to be present to pass on the information. It's essentially what we've been doing all along. Each of the film canisters we've found are dead drops.'

Olivia stared at him. 'That's really clever, but fascinating though it is, it doesn't tell us anything we don't already know.'

'Not on the surface, but you have to think like Clarence. He's been leaving us clues in dead drops all along, so why suddenly make the dead drop a part of the clue...? *Unless* you wanted to somehow draw attention to the thing itself. He was fascinated with games and puzzles of all sorts, ciphers and codes too, you know how much he used them in his books. And what's important to understand here is that there are different types of dead drops. Some, like the ones we've already found, are simply containers hidden out of sight, but others can be camouflaged so they're hidden in *plain* sight, inside a brick or a moss-covered stone, for example. Some are simply thin cylinders with a spike on one end, which are pushed into the ground with the message concealed inside. They're incredibly hard to spot unless you know what you're looking for.'

'So which is it in this case?'

'I've no way of knowing for sure, but—' He suddenly broke off as another thought came to him. 'Hang on a minute, let's have a look at that lead again, the one in the bin.'

Olivia carefully fished it out and handed it to him.

'I thought this was just a charging cable, but it isn't, look... one end has a USB adapter.' He shone his torch on it, peering closer. 'And it hasn't been thrown away because it was damaged, the wire has been hacked at, almost cut through, deliberately.' He looked up, staring at Olivia. 'This changes things no end.'

'Does it?'

Adam nodded. 'Oh yes. As times change, so does technology, and some of the most modern dead drops are digital. Think about it, if you need to pass on a message, the size of it is limited by the size of the container you're hiding it in, but with digital technology, you can store large amounts of information on tiny objects.'

Olivia looked around her. 'Like a USB stick.'

'Exactly. I don't think we'll ever know where the cable was hidden originally, but my guess would be somewhere in this room, as a further clue, not to the hiding place, but to the type of dead drop being used. That's what's important here. It's also a necessary piece of equipment for what comes next, and one that's obviously been sabotaged, I'm afraid.'

'What do you mean?'

'If the next clue has been saved onto a USB stick, we'd need a way of accessing it – that's what the cable was for. With an adapter on the end, you can plug it into your phone to read the data from the stick.'

Olivia's face fell. 'But we no longer have a cable that works, so what do we do now?'

'Well, as luck would have it,' said Adam, smiling, 'I happen to have one in my car. I'll run back and get it and then we can start looking for the USB stick. I've had an idea about that too. Come on.'

He led the way back outside, closing the door behind them. Keeping a wary watch, they walked quickly back to the orchard, where Adam paused beside a corrugated roofed lean-to butted up against the rear garden wall.

'Wait here,' he said. 'I won't be long.'

'No...' Olivia's eyes were round. 'I'm coming with you.'

But Adam shook his head. 'It's safer if I go by myself. Look, this is a bin store and I don't suppose this place has patrolling security guards, or anything like it. The parkland here extends for miles, they can't police all of it. Just stay put, and I'll be back as soon as I can.'

'Adam, I'm really not sure this is a good idea. It's dark and bloody freezing.'

'Yes, but two of us moving will be much easier to spot than me on my own. My car isn't in the main car park, so with any luck the remaining staff have all gone, and they won't even realise anyone else is here. Plus, there's less chance of you being spotted out here than by the bothy. Duck down by the bins, I'll be ten minutes, tops, and then, providing we find what we're looking for, we can be back out of here in about half an hour.'

He could tell Olivia didn't like it, but she could see the sense in his words as she muttered, 'Ten minutes,' then ducked under the cover of the lean-to.

It took nearly all of that to reach the car, but thirty seconds later he was on his way back with the spare cable. He ran as quickly as he could towards the orchard, keeping close to the hedge line the whole way. Once there, he'd have to run across open ground, but if he was careful, he could use the trees' shadowy silhouettes to hide his passage. Besides, he didn't imagine National Trust visitors were known for their subversive behaviour. Who would be looking out for someone sneaking around? Everyone would be long gone by now, cooking dinner and sitting beside a nice warm fire. He almost groaned at the thought.

The lean-to was only a faint dark outline by the time he got there but, importantly, he hadn't seen sign of a single person.

'Olivia,' he whispered, as he neared the bin store.

He paused, expecting her to appear, taking another step forward when she didn't. 'It's me, Adam.'

Maybe she hadn't realised who it was. Cate and Marcus had obviously been and were long gone, but Adam didn't blame Olivia for being cautious. Just the dark alone was enough to make you feel jumpy.

He ducked his head under the low roof of the store, whispering Olivia's name again. However, it soon became obvious that the reason she hadn't answered was because she wasn't there.

Heart thumping, he ducked back out again. For goodness' sake, where had she gone now? Perhaps someone came by and she'd had to move or...

It was at that moment that light bloomed, although peculiarly, all of it was inside his head. He was about to muse on the wonder of the fantastical colours he could see when a spike of pain shot through his skull, at which point, mercifully, everything went black.

14

Fran studied Saul's face. With the others gone from the room, leaving just the two of them, she realised it was the first time she had properly done so. And she was struck again by what she'd noticed before, that Saul looked very different from his siblings. Not different in looks particularly, he had the same fair hair and dark eyes as his brother, but more so in his manner, in the way he carried himself. It was less obvious in the grandeur of Justice House, or perhaps it was simply that when there the setting and circumstance had caused Fran to lump the three siblings under the same rather uncomplimentary umbrella, one which had haughty arrogance emblazoned across its front. In her quiet kitchen, however, Saul looked very different.

His hair was similar in style to Marcus's, but whereas Marcus's was exact and held firmly in place by some product or other, Saul's was far more relaxed. It had a softer and slightly more ragged look to it. His facial features were less defined too, his jaw less chiselled, and cleanly shaven rather than sporting the trendier almost beard which Marcus wore. But it was his eyes which struck Fran the most. They were slightly lighter in colour than Marcus's, amber rather than brown, and perhaps being in pain had made a difference, but there was a vulnerability there which neither Marcus's nor Cate's showed. Instead their eyes were hard and flinty, entitlement shining from deep within.

She brought Saul's tea to the table and placed it in front of him.

'Shall I have a look at your head?' she asked. 'The bleeding looks to have stopped at least, but you might need to get it checked out.'

'It's fine, it's…' He raised his hand to gingerly locate the sorest spot. 'It's probably just a surface wound. Looks worse than it is.'

'Quite possibly, but let me have a look to be on the safe side. I can take a photo too, as evidence, and send it on to Margaret.'

'You could, but as evidence of what? I could have fallen, or simply hit my head on something. In the end, it falls into the same category as your flat tyre.'

Fran's hands were on her hips, her best 'don't argue' expression on her face and, after a moment, Saul sighed.

'Okay, you can have a look.'

'I know it's none of my business,' said Fran, taking Saul's head in her hands. 'Can you turn a bit, so you're facing the light?' She peered closer. 'But you have to admit this is a bizarre situation. Clarence may have been a little eccentric, but a treasure hunt to decide who inherits goes off the scale.'

Saul's breath hissed between his teeth as Fran probed his head wound.

'Sorry…' she murmured. 'Almost there.'

'Yeah well, that's Dad for you.'

Fran paused. 'He must have felt he had good reason though. And I can see why. Forgive me, but aside from what's just happened, you were on one team and Cate and Marcus another. That can't feel good. I haven't always seen eye to eye with my brother, but we've never come to blows.'

Saul took a sip of his tea. 'Fran, I appreciate what you're trying to do, but it's complicated and, with respect, it is none of your business. Let's just try to get through these blasted clues and have the whole thing over and done with. That way, we can all get back to our lives and carry on as we were before.'

'With nothing resolved...' Fran knew she was arguing but it seemed so senseless to take that attitude. 'Why would you want to go back to a situation where things are clearly not right? If nothing else, what your dad's done should make you examine the way things are. That's clearly why he did it in the first place – in the hope that you could move forward.'

Saul's shoulders may have hunched a little more but that was all the reaction he was going to give her. He certainly wasn't about to speak.

Fran released his head. 'You're right, I think it's just a flesh wound,' she said, exasperation clipping her words. She stood back, moving around the counter to face Saul. 'You know, if you're not going to tell me anything, I'm just going to jump to conclusions. Your head injury for one. Someone *has* been trying to slow us down, so how do I know that wasn't just a convenient ruse? That you just happened to be tied up right at the time when we would find you? How do I know that what we're being led to believe is anything like the truth?'

But the moment she said it, she realised how stupid she'd been. If she was right and there was some sinister motive behind all this, she'd just placed herself firmly in the middle of it. And, worse, now Saul wasn't saying a word, but instead looking at her with an unfathomable expression on his face.

He got to his feet. 'Then perhaps I'd better go,' he said stiffly. 'Thanks for the tea and first aid. I'm sure I can take it from here.'

'But you don't even have your car. How are you going to go anywhere?'

'I believe that's my problem, not yours.'

Fran tutted, cross with herself. She'd only wanted to help, but she could be so stupid sometimes.

'Saul, wait! I don't want you to go. Neither do I want to disbelieve you, but there's very clearly more to this whole affair than you're telling me. And if you want me to trust you, you need to start being honest about what's going on and unbutton your lips. I can't help you otherwise.'

'What, and you think I'm crazy enough to let Marcus hit me over the head to set up some elaborate bluff, do you?'

Put like that, Fran could see how wide of the mark her question had been.

'Because if not, how on earth did I manage to bash myself over the head? Tie my own hands behind my back?'

Fran dropped her head, raising it with a sigh of frustration tinged with embarrassed apology. 'Now you know why I leave the deducting to Adam. I'm a bit clueless sometimes... no pun intended.'

She saw the beginnings of a weak smile.

'Listen, Saul, why don't we start again? I'm not just trying to be nosy, I'm trying to understand everyone's motives here in case that helps.' She paused, wondering just how much she should say. But if she was asking Saul to be open about his own life, maybe he deserved the same from her.

'Sometimes knowing why people are doing the things they do can give you an idea of what they might do next. This isn't something that's easy to drop into conversation, but Adam and I have got involved in...' She still found it hard to say. 'A couple of police investigations. Cases where people have died. You could say we were in the wrong place at the wrong time, but what I *have* learned is that when people feel very strongly about something, particularly when large sums of money are involved, then the potential is there for some very nasty things to happen.'

Saul's eyes roved her face, an almost amused expression on his face. 'So you want to know why I'm doing this? Playing along with Dad's wishes even when, despite how he framed it, we all know how ridiculous they are, manipulative even. Well, the simple fact of the matter is that I loathe my brother and sister. They've ruined my life and I actually don't give a flying —' He stopped abruptly, clamping his mouth shut. 'I don't care about Dad's money. What I care about, more than you could possibly know, is that neither Cate nor Marcus should ever receive a penny of it.' He rubbed a hand around his eyes, looking incredibly weary. 'And maybe I could use a little help.'

Fran pushed his mug towards him. 'In that case, I think you'd better tell me why...'

He accepted his drink as a wry smile crossed his face. 'I think it's safe to say that we pretty much fit every stereotype for the dysfunctional family – absentee father who was always working – children spoilt irreparably by their mother to compensate – sibling rivalry that got out of hand. The weird thing is that, growing up, I always considered I had a happy childhood, but looking back, I think I just shied away from thinking about it too much. Path of least resistance, that was me. I regret that more than anything.'

Fran held up a hand, seeing the sadness in his eyes. 'Hold that thought... this sounds as if it might need a piece of cake to go with it. That's if Jack and Martha haven't finished it off.' She fetched another tub from the pantry and returned to the table with it, cranking off the lid. A sweet lemony scent filled the air. Cutting them both a slice, she handed one to Saul. 'Maybe start at the beginning,' she said.

'I won't bore you with all the details of our childhood,' he began, taking a bite of cake. 'I'm sure you can fill in the blanks. But things didn't really begin to go wrong until Marcus started working for Dad. His books were already very successful by then, but weirdly, where Dad made most of his money was from all the spin-offs – the board games, the puzzles, jigsaws, action figures, it was a pretty long list. He never anticipated that his books would spawn a whole generation of children who wanted to carry on playing his adventure games long after the last pages of the books had been turned. And Dad had been clever. He'd been approached by countless companies over the years all looking to buy a licence for these things, to take over their manufacture, but Dad would never agree. Why give some middle man a cut when he could do it all himself? So he set up his own company, and kept everything in-house.

'And that was fine in the early days, but Dad was never really a business man, ideas were what it was all about for him. But the demand for his products was going through the roof and that's where Marcus came in. He *does* have a business head and the short version of the story is that he took over the production side of running the company, and things really began to take off. Once he'd done that, he brought Cate and I into the fold. It seemed the most natural thing in the world.'

Saul stared at his cake, his head clearly full of the past and Fran wondered if he was actually going to continue. But then he took another bite, pulling himself out of his reverie.

'That's when the problems started,' he continued. 'And also when the differences between the three of us became more noticeable. I wanted to learn about the company – what we did – why Dad's games worked – what people loved about them. I saw myself becoming a creator, just like he was, but I knew in order to do that, I had to understand what made him so successful in the first place.'

'And Cate and Marcus were different?'

He nodded. 'They just wanted to make as much money as possible and so, gradually, Marcus began to involve himself in other areas of the company. He started to make suggestions to improve its running, or more specifically, its profit margin, tinkering with staff pay and conditions, changing job descriptions, little by little eroding the responsibility of other people in the company and transferring that power to himself. I didn't even notice what was going on to start with, until Marcus began restructuring the senior management team and I realised he might have some ulterior motive. Particularly when one of the first things he did was bring Cate into the team.'

'So they forced your dad out?' asked Fran. 'Is that what happened?'

'No, although that's what I thought too. But, it was much worse than that, they betrayed him. Went behind his back.' He touched a hand to the back of his head, wincing slightly. 'How much do you know about Dad's games?'

'As much as anyone else probably,' replied Fran. 'I grew up playing them, loved them. Still play them with my daughter sometimes, especially at Christmas, but beyond that, not much more.'

'Olivia could tell you, no doubt, but the thing you have to know about Dad is how passionate he was about learning. That's why he wrote the kind of books he did. He didn't want to settle for simply telling a good story, he wanted to write something which would not only be enjoyable but would challenge children's minds, make them think, and let them learn almost without realising they were doing so. And when those adventure books became adventure games, he couldn't have been happier. He always said it was the act of playing which drove him on, the bringing together of families or groups of friends to have fun. Trouble was that, as the years went by, the ways people played games changed. Video and computer games became hugely popular, and successful, but Dad was adamant those type of games weren't for him, and he refused point-blank to discuss them.'

'But why?' Fran asked. 'What's so wrong with them?'

'Nothing at all. Except that all Dad could see was that they stopped people playing games *together*... Instead, people played on their own, glued to a screen, or pitched their wits against computers instead of each other and he said it spelled the end of the game as he knew it.'

Fran chased a crumb around her plate with a finger. 'You won't know this, but Adam is a computer games designer, a very good one actually. Neither will you know that he loved your father's games. Clarence was a massive influence on him, still is. And since I've known him, I've begun to understand how much skill goes into creating these games, how carefully thought out and executed the plots are. I know they have their addictive qualities – I have a teenage daughter – and show me a parent who isn't concerned about the amount of screen time their children have, but now I know more about the games, I've come to admire them for what they are.'

Saul acknowledged her concern with a nod of his head. 'I tend to agree, but...' He trailed off, smiling awkwardly. 'I can also see it from Dad's point of view. And as far as his business was concerned, the games were his brain child and that earned him the right to run it any way he wanted. I just didn't have the guts to say so at the time.'

Fran gave him a sympathetic smile. 'But you said Cate and Marcus betrayed Clarence. What did they do? Is it connected?'

'Mmm... It was twenty-five or so years ago now, but when Dad's last book was released, Marcus and Cate set up a deal with another company, an exclusive deal for a computer game version with one particular addition – a new element that didn't, and couldn't, exist within the book. And because of the popularity of Dad's work, and the exclusivity this new edition promised, they were going to charge a really high price for it and everything was set for it to acquire something of a cult status.'

'And Clarence didn't know anything about it?'

'No. That might sound ridiculous, the fact that they could even get away with such a thing, but Dad was too busy being creative to worry about the running of the company. Besides, why would he? He trusted Cate and Marcus. But, he'd also let them have power, allowed them to have positions in the company which meant they could sign off on things. And they used it to their advantage.'

'Clarence obviously found out in the end though?'

Saul nodded. 'Eventually, it was inevitable really. But by then the deal had almost gone too far. The gaming company were convinced they had a massive smash on their hands and the publicity they were set to generate was immense. Up until that point, they had kept all the details secret from the public, everything except for the fact that *something* was coming. It was all part of their marketing strategy and they whipped up a fever pitch of anticipation.' Saul pulled a face. 'To cut a long story short, Dad pulled the contract, they sued him for breach, and eventually he settled with them out of court. But it cost him dearly. Financially, as well as emotionally. It was the last book he ever wrote, and no more games followed either. It all but destroyed him.'

Fran frowned, puzzled. 'But there *were* games that came after, I have some of them at home.'

'You have games made by the company,' Saul replied, 'but they weren't Dad's games, someone else designed them. The irony was that anything with his name on was still successful, so he carried on making a fortune even though he had nothing to do with anything new the company produced. And that's how it stayed. The company remained his, but he brought in new people, promoted people he trusted to run it for him and, from that day on, hardly ever set foot in the place again.'

'So what about the three of you?' asked Fran.

'We were sacked on the spot when Dad found out. Marcus and Cate might have been behind the whole thing, but I was just as guilty. I knew about it – not the detail, but I was aware it was going on, and I did nothing about it. What you sow you reap.'

'My mum always used to say that.'

'It's true. And it's taken me far too long to understand that I couldn't demand and expect Dad's love or respect simply because I was his son, when I'd done nothing to earn it.'

Fran thought for a moment. 'Well, it's obvious none of you ever mended your relationship with Clarence. So what happened after that?'

He shrugged. 'We went our separate ways. Marcus started work for a rival company, which was so typical of him, but it didn't last. He works as a production manager now, for a company which makes plastic bottles. Cate decided she'd try to use her brain and retrain as a medical professional of some sort – she was always good at sciences as a kid – and that seemed to be going well up until the point she married a con artist who stole her money and her house from under her. She's a pharmacist now and still paying back her debt. Oh, and embittered and cynical, obviously.' He paused, giving a wry smile. 'And that just leaves me... happily married with two point four children, a mortgage, two labradoodles and a steady but very boring job with a firm of accountants.'

'Yeah, I get that life goes on,' replied Fran, still certain there was more to come. 'But I'm sorry, Saul, what happened with your father was well over twenty years ago now. Did none of you ever try to rectify what had happened?'

Saul's posture stiffened. 'With respect, Fran, you don't know any of us, and Dad didn't exactly make it easy. He made it very clear he wanted nothing to do with us. Marcus and Cate were too busy harbouring grudges against him to care particularly, and I made a few attempts to patch things up, but Dad let me know in no uncertain terms how weak he thought I was. I've always been very good at playing second fiddle to the others, I didn't need him rubbing my nose in it as well.'

Fran studied his face. Saul's grudge may not have been the same one his siblings held, but he held one just the same. And although his words made sense on one level, she was still a little puzzled by something. 'But the three of you seemed close enough at the funeral dinner.'

'That's because...' He trailed off, running a hand across his face. 'This is the really pathetic bit. Whenever I'm around them, I can't stop myself from falling into the role I've played all my life, that of the younger, duller sibling with nothing to say, hanging on their tailcoats because I'm desperate to be a part of their gang, just like I did when I was a child. I did anything to be in their good books. They were always the ones having fun, the ones with all the friends, while I dragged along behind, slip-streaming off everything they seemed to achieve so effortlessly but which I struggled with. It's something which continued into adulthood for far too long.'

Fran could understand that, but she still didn't think she was seeing the full picture. 'So... coming back to present day for a moment,' she said, thinking yet again how complicated other people's lives were. 'I get that you don't want Cate or Marcus to inherit what they clearly don't deserve, but why do I get the feeling there's something else going on here too?'

'Because someone bashed me over the head, Fran. And let's just say, it's changed my perspective a little.'

Fran's eyes narrowed. 'And you're saying it was one of them?'

'I don't see who else it could be,' Saul replied. 'But that's not just sibling rivalry. Nor is it the machinations of our past playing out, it's something a whole lot worse.' He took a large gulp of tea. 'I could have been killed,' he added, voice rising. 'How desperate do you have to be to do that kind of thing? What kind of a person do you have to be?'

Fran stared at him, at the flush of colour which heated emotion had brought to his face. And suddenly she realised what their conversation had been leading up to.

'My God... You think they had something to do with your dad's death, don't you?'

Saul's mouth set in a thin, hard line. 'I wouldn't put it past them. Marcus still believes that what he and Cate did was right. He deserved his punishment but he'll never see it that way. Worse, he thinks Dad made a fool out of him when he broke the contract that Marcus had set up. He lost face and he's never forgiven Dad for that. And Cate... Cate's desperate. She's keen not to show it, there are appearances to be maintained, after all, but she was left so deeply in debt when her sham of a marriage broke up, she's never really recovered from it.'

Fran's mind was racing ahead, struggling to take in what he was saying. She looked with horror at the mugs and the half-eaten pieces of cake on the table. That they could be sitting there calmly chatting when...

She jumped to her feet, almost knocking over her stool in her haste. 'Saul, I really hope your head's okay because we need to go. Now!'

The urgency in her voice transmitted itself instantly and Saul's head jerked up. He stared at her, mouth hanging open.

She grabbed her car keys and bag from the side, and pulled off her coat from the hook on the back of the door. 'We have to go,' she repeated urgently. 'Olivia and Adam could be in terrible danger.'

15

It had been dark for some time when they arrived at Attingham, Fran speeding through the country lanes as fast as she could. She'd deliberately taken Jack's car, partly because it was far more powerful than hers, but also because she'd learned her lesson from before. Neither Cate nor Marcus would recognise Jack's car and that had to be a good thing.

Fran headed straight to the back gate, not even realising she had followed in Adam's footsteps until she spotted his car parked a little way along from the gatehouse cottage. Another vehicle that only she would recognise, thankfully. And at least it meant that Adam was still here... although not, she reminded herself, that he was safe and well. She checked her watch.

'They've been here ages already,' she said. 'That's what worries me. The bothy isn't very big, it shouldn't have taken them this long to find the clue. I should have got in touch with him.'

'Or perhaps realised he hadn't got in touch with *you*,' said Saul. 'Which might be more to the point. Something you would have done, had I not been so busy telling you my tale of woe.'

'Saul, none of this is your fault. I know we got talking, but in fairness, I asked you to. Besides, I think they were things you probably needed to say, if only to get them off your chest,' she said kindly. 'In any case, maybe they've already found the bothy clue. The fact that Adam's car is still here doesn't necessarily mean anything – the next clue could also be on the estate.'

'I hadn't thought of that,' replied Saul, eyes narrowing. 'Let's hope so.' He took hold of her arm lightly. 'Come on, we shouldn't waste any more time. If my memory serves me right, the gardens are behind the house, so to our left?'

Fran pulled out her phone, checking for signal. 'Agreed. Let's go.'

Once their eyes had acclimatised to the dark it was easy enough to navigate the fields. Fran quickened her pace. She couldn't be certain, but she wouldn't be at all surprised if this was the way Adam and Olivia had come. She'd already fired off another text message and neither of them had replied. It was becoming harder and harder to keep a lid on her anxiety with every minute that passed, and by the time they reached the orchard, her heart was thumping in her chest. It was now fear, rather than anxiety rippling through her.

She paused a moment, catching her breath.

'Where do we go now?' she whispered. 'Everywhere will be locked up.' She swung her head from side to side, straining to see. Her eyes caught movement a little distance away, but it was only a bird.

'Let's try the gardens anyway,' replied Saul. 'We have to start somewhere.'

They headed for the nearest gate, but the padlock hanging from it wasn't hard to spot.

Fran pointed to her left. 'This way,' she said. 'I think there's another door further down.'

Beside her, Saul spun around.

'What is it?' she said, scouring the ranks of trees behind them.

Saul moved closer. 'I thought I saw something,' he whispered. 'Over there.' He pointed to the far side of the orchard. 'Moving away from us, I think.'

'There always used to be a play park there,' she replied. 'But why would anyone be there now?'

Saul shrugged, peering into her face. 'I've no idea, unless that's where the next clue has taken them. But I think we should take a look. Stick close.'

Fran nodded and crept after him as they cut through the trees rather than taking the path which she knew lay to the far side of the orchard. She kept her eyes trained on the way ahead but nothing interrupted her field of vision.

'Are you sure you saw something?' she asked.

'Yes... there, look. I think it was a light.'

But she still couldn't see anything beyond shades of darkest grey. Maybe she just wasn't looking in the right direction. She stumbled slightly as they approached a small brick building at the edge of the play area and she wondered if they still used it for selling ice creams in the summer.

Saul pointed to the looming wall, motioning that they should approach from behind. Did he think there was someone in there? She moved closer, frowning. Because if memory served her right, the building had no windows, just a hatch at the front to serve from. Saul couldn't have seen a light inside.

If she'd been a split-second quicker in her thinking she might have realised what that meant, but Saul's vice-like grip circled her arm before she could take another breath.

'I'm sorry, Fran, but this is for your own good. I don't want you getting hurt.'

She tried to pull her arm away. 'What?' The word sounded incredulous even to her. She stared at the key which had materialised in Saul's hand. 'Really?' she demanded. 'You're going to lock me in there?' She aimed a vicious kick at his ankle. 'I don't bloody think so...'

He held her at arm's length, still pinned. 'Fran, please. *Please*, just listen. I don't want to hurt you, I swear, but you don't understand. Just go in there, do as I ask, and I'll come back for you, I promise. I just need to check something out.'

'But what about Adam and Olivia?'

'I'll look for them, I swear on it, but too many people are getting hurt, and I can't do what I need to with you in tow.'

She should fight. Saul might be bigger than her, and much, much stronger, but he'd never seen Fran when she was angry. She could be very determined when she put her mind to it, and... the expression on his face stopped her; bleak and weary to the bone. She stepped back as he pulled open the door. 'You better bloody come back for me,' she said, walking inside.

'Give me an hour,' he said. 'And if I'm not back by then, call the police.'

'Why? What are you—'

'Just do what I ask. One hour and not before.'

And with that, he pulled the door closed and everything went black around her. She heard the sound of the key being turned in the lock and, for a moment, she thought about yelling – screaming at the top of her lungs – but in truth what good would that do? Saul wasn't about to change his mind. Still... 'Bastard!' she yelled, for no other reason than it made her feel better.

She pulled her phone from her pocket, fumbling with cold fingers. She'd had enough. It was time other people got to hear about what was going on. She was ringing the police. Now. But then she froze.

There was something in there with her. She could feel it.

The hairs began to stand up on the back of her neck as she pressed herself against the wall. Whatever it was, was close by.

She swallowed. She was just being silly, imagining things because she was in the dark, and disorientated, but the thought was in her head now and it wouldn't shift. Like when she was a child and convinced there was a monster under the bed. Think about it for long enough and, any minute now, it will grab your ankle and drag you under... so you lie, as quiet as a mouse, not daring to move a muscle lest you give yourself away. But what if the monster can smell you anyway? Then there really is no hope, no way—

She jumped as something touched her foot. Almost screamed when a sighing breath that wasn't hers broke the silence. And whatever it was, was still there, resting on her boot. She should bend down, she should check what it was...

'Are you a really big rat wearing shoes... or am I in the deepest shit imaginable?'

The voice came out of nowhere, but the moment after shock fired through her, she realised not what had been said, but who had said it. She'd recognise that voice anywhere.

'Adam? God, is that you?' She dropped to her haunches, feeling with her hands, starting as she touched skin. 'It's me, Fran.'

She ran her fingers over clothing, a coat, jeans... until she found an arm, at the end of which was Adam's hand. He was slumped – half-sitting, half-lying, she realised. Fumbling with her phone, she flicked on the torch, lighting up Adam's features like a ghostly apparition. It was far too reminiscent of their first meeting, when they'd both sought a hiding place in the same cupboard and the only light had been the glow from Adam's laptop. She squeezed his hand.

'God, you scared me. Why didn't you say anything? You must have heard me yell?'

'I think that might have been what woke me up.'

'Woke you up? For God's sake, Adam, how could you possibly sleep—' She broke off at the expression on his face.

'I think "regained consciousness" might have been a better choice of words.' He pulled himself into a more upright position. 'Whoa...' He splayed out his hands. 'Is everything supposed to spin like that?'

'What on earth happened to you?'

'Actually, that should be *who* on earth happened to you...'

'Someone hit you?' She swore under her breath, shining the torch at him. He blinked furiously. 'Sorry... where does it hurt?'

'Same modus operandi as Saul, I'm afraid. Back of the head.' He explored a little with his fingers, wincing as he did so.

'You think Marcus did this?'

'A best guess,' Adam replied, submitting to Fran's gentle touch. 'Or Cate, perhaps. I was too busy wondering what the incredible lights were inside my head, followed a split second later by white-hot pain. I forgot to think about who might have hit me.'

Fran held the torch closer to Adam's head, parting his hair gently as her fingers sought out any damage. 'Where am I looking?' she murmured.

A sudden sucking in of breath told her exactly where, and her fingers stilled before moving very slowly around the whole area.

'Amazingly, I don't think the skin's broken. But you're going to have a mighty lump, I can already feel it.'

Adam reached up again to gingerly confirm what Fran was saying.

'We should get you to a doctor,' she added. 'In case you've got concussion.'

He stared at her, eyebrows raised.

'Yes, I know, we're in a locked room with a maniac on the loose and don't happen to have a doctor handy. Even so, that's what they recommend if anyone loses consciousness.'

'I'll be fine,' replied Adam, trying not to let her see the expression of pain on his face as he moved.

A sudden thought came to her. 'Where's Olivia?'

Adam groaned, though not through pain this time. 'She's

not with you? No, of course she isn't. Then I've no idea. Stupidly, I left her hiding by the back wall of the gardens while I ran to my car to fetch a cable. On my return, she'd gone and that's when whoever jumped me.'

Fran stared at him. 'And you didn't see anyone?'

'Not a thing.'

Fran didn't want to think it, but... 'So, whoever hit you, could equally have done something to Olivia and—' She swung the torch wildly around the space, heart thudding again, but there was no one else there. 'We need to find her, she could be badly hurt.'

'Anything could have happened, and that's what worries me. Fran, this has gone way beyond a treasure hunt. Saul getting thumped was bad enough, but this is really beginning to freak me out.' A thought creased his brow. 'Speaking of which, where *is* Saul? And how come you're in here? You're not hurt, are you?'

'No, I'm fine.' She blew out a breath from between her teeth as she sat back against the wall. 'This was his doing though, I'm afraid. Apparently for my own good.'

Adam frowned. 'What do you mean?'

'I have a horrible feeling he's taken off after Marcus and Cate.' She quickly explained the bones of the conversation she'd had with Saul earlier. 'So, not only does he actually believe Clarence might have been murdered but, having suffered at the hands of his siblings once too often in his life, he's now out to stop Marcus and Cate too. I have no idea what he's planning to do, but I'm really worried. Poor Clarence, to have been betrayed by his children like that.'

'Do you think Olivia knew what had happened?'

Fran shook her head. 'I don't think so. She'd have said otherwise. But it's no surprise it completely destroyed the family. And now Saul sees it as his mission to put things right, to atone for his lack of action in the past. When we realised how much danger you and Olivia could be in, we rushed over here. There wasn't a plan, as such, but I didn't imagine Saul would turn all vigilante on me.'

Adam sighed, easing his body into a more comfortable position. 'I haven't seen any sign of Cate or Marcus since we got here, but they obviously are. And I still need to get to the bothy clue. I worked out what it meant – that's why I went to get the cable from my car – but I never even got to finish looking for it before... lights out.'

'So what *is* the clue then?' Fran asked.

'It's a dead drop,' he explained. 'Not drop dead at the bothy, but rather a dead drop at the bothy.'

'Which is...?'

'Basically, a way of passing on a message or information to someone without you having to be present. And yes, that's essentially what Clarence has been using the whole time. Those little films canisters, they're dead drops too. But this time, the fact that the words dead drop were part of the clue itself was significant, and I'm pretty sure we're looking for a USB stick – a rather more high-tech version of the black plastic container. We found a USB adapter cable in the bin at the bothy and, although it's quite possible it could have been discarded by a member of staff, the damage to it looked deliberate. I think it's what we were meant to find.'

'Ah...' said Fran, light dawning. 'Which is why you went to get a cable from your car.'

A look of horror crossed Adam's face as he hurriedly began to pat his pockets. 'Oh, thank God.' He drew out both his phone and a lead. 'I thought for one minute someone had taken them.' He looked at Fran. 'Actually, that's not very smart. Whoever shoved me in here isn't thinking straight.' He peered at his phone to check it was okay.

'And do you know where the USB stick is?'

Adam shook his head. 'No, I went to get my spare lead first.

But it will be hidden, in much the same way the film canisters were. Usually, these type of dead drops are embedded in something so that only the end of the USB stick shows. It makes them much harder to spot. That's why I'm pretty sure it will be outside.'

'None of which is any help to us at all if we're locked in here,' said Fran. She flashed her light around the room. 'So obviously we need to get out, as soon as possible.' She opened her mouth and then snapped it shut, placing a hand across it for good measure. She'd been about to yell for help, when that was possibly the worst thing she should do. She shook her head as if to clear it. 'Hang on a minute, Adam. We need to think about this first. We need to work out what's going on, and what we're up against.'

Adam peered at her, blinking as if struggling to see. 'Run that by me again,' he said.

'We need to get out of here, that's obvious, but then what do we do? We don't know if anyone else has found the bothy clue yet, but it's probably safe to assume they have. So are Marcus and Cate still here? In which case, do we really want to risk running into them? We have no idea where Olivia is, and if you've been bashed over the head and locked up, she may have been too. Of course, all this is further complicated by the fact that Saul is now running around on his own, after telling me he doesn't care about the money, and only wants to stop Marcus and Cate from getting their hands on it. We need to work out what our priority is. Do we look for Olivia first? Or do we try to find the bothy clue and carry on with the hunt, hoping that somehow we might beat the others to it?' She frowned. 'No, that won't work because Olivia is the one who needs to find the clue – we're supposed to be helping her, so surely we need to get to her first and—'

'What?'

Fran stared at him. 'I've just had a horrible thought... What if Olivia has gone looking for the next clue herself?' She bit her lip. 'She doesn't know you're in here because she'd disappeared before you got back from the car so she has either been locked up herself or didn't wait for you... God, listen to me, I'm a horrible friend, she wouldn't ditch you.' She waved her hand. 'Ignore me. So, what we need to consider is whether we should be chasing down the next clue, or putting all our efforts into stopping Cate and Marcus because, apart from hitting Saul over the head, one of them may well have murdered their father.'

Adam groaned. 'Okay; I think I have all that. You couldn't slow down a little though, could you?'

Fran touched his arm. 'Sorry,' she said. 'I'm gabbling, I know. But events have suddenly got very confusing and if I don't say things out loud, I can't even begin to make head nor tail of them. Are you sure you're okay?'

Adam was staring straight ahead, as if he hadn't heard a word she'd said.

She waved a hand in front of his face. 'I said, are you okay?'

He was frowning now. 'You said Saul threw you in here?'

'Yes. Although he didn't really throw me in. He grabbed my arm, but then sort of invited me inside and said it was for my own good. Then he locked the door behind me, but... Oh...' She turned to look at Adam.

'Exactly,' he said. 'Where did he get the key from?'

'Shit,' she muttered. 'That makes it even more confusing. How on earth did Saul get the key? *Where* did he get it *from*?'

'And *how*,' added Adam, 'did he know he was going to need it?'

Fran stared at him. 'What on earth is going on?'

16

Fran scrambled to her feet. 'Okay, first things first. We need to get out of here, without letting anyone know we're out, because whatever's going on, as far as Saul is concerned, you and I are both out of the equation. If he's decided to carry on with the hunt himself, maybe even go after Cate and Marcus, then our only advantage is if he thinks we're safely out of the way.'

'Don't forget he said he put you in here for your own good so whatever he's planning, he doesn't want you to interfere with it, and that doesn't bode well.' Adam stuck out his hand, motioning that Fran should help pull him up. 'Plus, if Saul has a key to this place, it also begs the question who put me in here.'

'Well, it can't have been Saul. From the minute you left my house with Olivia, he was with me the whole time. And we travelled here together.'

'Then someone else has a key,' Adam replied, wincing as he stood up. 'Which makes it worse. Do you think Saul even knew I was in here?'

Fran thought for a moment, running through the sequence of events in her head. 'I can't say for certain, but I didn't get that feeling.'

Adam nodded. 'Okay, so as you said, first things first.' He fished inside an inner coat pocket. 'Let's get this door open.'

Fran tutted. 'I might have known,' she said, eyeing his lock-picking set.

Adam managed a smile. 'What? Don't look at me like that.'

'Funnily enough, on this occasion I'm all for your lock-picking prowess. Do you think you'll be able to open it?'

'Only one way to find out. Shine a bit of light, Fran.'

She followed him to the door, noticing how gingerly he was moving. She wasn't at all happy about the blow to his head, but what choice did they have other than to keep going? If they didn't act now, an even more serious crime could be committed. That's if it hadn't already been.

'Where even are we?' asked Adam, taking out the first of the slender cylindrical tools he needed. He inserted it into the lock, tongue between his teeth in concentration. 'That's it, shine it right there.'

Fran did as she was asked. 'We're in one of the buildings behind the gardens,' she replied. 'In the kids' play field.'

'So not far from where I got thumped then,' said Adam through gritted teeth. 'I left Olivia at the bin store just behind the walled garden. I don't remember much else, but whoever hit me must have had help to carry me here – it's close, but not that close.' He took out another tool and, holding the first still, proceeded to jiggle the other in the lock. Less than thirty seconds later, he straightened, a triumphant expression on his face. 'Open sesame,' he said, turning the handle. The door swung open.

Fran shivered as she stepped outside, a chill wind cutting through her. She shut off the light from her torch. 'So, where to first?' she whispered.

'I still think we need to solve the bothy clue,' replied Adam. 'Because otherwise we'll have no way of knowing where anyone else has gone. This is a big place, the woodlands stretch for miles. You could search all night and not find anyone. That's if they're even still here.'

They reached the walled garden without incident, but careful checking revealed that all the doors leading inside were still padlocked. Adam set to work, while Fran turned around to watch for any signs of movement.

'So tell me again what we'll be looking for,' she asked while she waited.

'I can't be certain,' replied Adam. 'But I'm convinced it's a USB stick – the damaged adapter cable is the best clue we have. Nothing we saw inside the bothy pointed to it being anything else. I'm also pretty sure it will be hidden somewhere outside the bothy. It makes sense if you think about it. If Clarence hid the stick inside, there was a possibility, however slight, that a staff member could find it, even a member of the public. Plus, depending on what time any of us got here, the place could also have been busy with visitors, making discovery very difficult. It's therefore much more likely that Clarence placed it outside where it could be found whatever the time of day.'

Fran groaned. 'That's not going to be easy to find in the dark.'

Adam undid the padlock. 'We just have to hope we get lucky then.'

A couple of minutes later they reached the bothy and Adam switched on his torch. 'You start that end,' he said, pointing to his left. 'I've seen these type of dead drops cemented into walls, so let's start looking there. And remember you're looking for the metal end of the USB, it should be sticking out somewhere.'

'Okay...' But Fran wasn't convinced. It was pitch-black, how on earth were they going to find something so tiny? She moved to the end wall and stared up at the eaves. At least the building was single-storey. She found the top left-hand corner and began to sweep her torch systematically along each line of bricks, paying particular attention to where the wall joined the roof.

She was halfway down the section when a noise sounded immediately behind her. She froze, ears straining for any sound. It came again, the unmistakable crunch of a foot stepping on loose material. Someone was on the path. Fear shivered down her back and, although all her instincts told her to hide, she also wanted to know what she was dealing with. Whoever was creeping up on her would have seen her torch, would have recognised her, and she was getting fed up with all this skulking around. It was time to find out what the bloody hell was going on.

She was about to swing her torch upwards when a whispered voice came at her through the dark.

'Fran, it's me...'

'Olivia?' This time she did swing the torch up, it's beam flashing across Olivia's startled face.

'Oh, thank God!' Olivia rushed at her. 'I couldn't find Adam, I didn't know where anyone was.' She threw her arms around Fran, who did likewise. 'Christ, I was scared,' she added as she pulled away. 'And I'm bloody freezing.'

Fran rubbed up and down Olivia's arms to try to generate some heat as Adam came crashing towards them.

'Are you okay?'

Olivia nodded. 'I'm fine. Fine... I just got scared. Where were you? I couldn't find you.'

'Me?' Adam flashed a look at Fran. 'I came back to meet you but you weren't there. I thought something had happened to you.'

Olivia shook her head. 'It nearly did. Marcus and Cate were here, I could hear them walking round, I was terrified they were going to find me. At first I ducked down behind the bins, but when they walked straight past where I was hiding, I realised they were going into the garden so I followed them. I managed to sneak in after them and hid behind the greenhouse.' Her face took on an urgent expression. 'Adam, I know where the dead drop is, they found it. But I was terrified I was going to get locked in here so I had to sneak back out again before they did. They followed just after me, but I don't know where they are now. Cate was not happy, though, I know that much. They were arguing furiously by the time they left.'

'What about?'

'Marcus being too slow. Marcus being gutless. Marcus basically being someone other than Cate. She clearly has a very high opinion of herself.'

'Which way did they go?' asked Adam.

Olivia pointed to her left. 'Back out towards the main path. When I saw them leave I went back to the bins to look for you, and I waited but you never came. I didn't know what to do. I've just been hiding under the lean-to.' She paused, looking at Fran. 'Where's Saul, isn't he with you?'

'Long story,' Fran replied. 'Adam got—'

'Never mind,' interrupted Adam. 'It doesn't matter now and we need to find the dead drop quickly. Olivia, can you show us where it was?'

She nodded. 'Yes. I couldn't see exactly, but they were standing right by the window there. The one immediately to the left of the door.'

Fran shone the torch to where she was pointing. It was an old window with a narrow wooden frame and a small sill. Underneath was a bench, slightly to one side, and a flower bed. Several plants partially screened the wall.

'Then let's hope whatever it is, is still here,' said Adam, moving closer. He dropped to his knees on the stone path by the bench. 'Fran, have a look among the plants, the stick could be pushed into the soil or—' He broke off, the beam of his torch flashing against something. He leaned closer. 'Now what do we have here?'

Fran angled her light to join Adam's, shining against a section of brick just below the windowsill. It was hard to tell what she was looking at but she could just make out the end of something metal.

'Can you bring the light over to me a minute?' asked Adam, dropping the beam of his phone away from the wall. He slid his free hand into his pocket and pulled out the cable, gleaming white against the darkness. 'That's it, shine it on my phone. I just need to connect this and...'

Fran watched as Adam fiddled with one end of the lead, swinging the light back against the wall when he was ready. She shuffled closer, realising how well the USB stick had been hidden.

It was sticking out from between two courses of bricks, with the body of the stick sunk into the mortar itself so that only the end protruded. It sat just beneath the level of the windowsill, and from a standing position would be impossible to see – the angle of the sill not only obscured it from view but protected it from the elements too. If any more concealment was needed then the plants growing up the wall were also doing a good job, even in wintertime.

Adam quickly attached the other end of the lead to the USB and directed his attention back to his phone. After tapping the screen several times, he turned to look at them. 'It's a Word document,' he said. 'Look.'

They both peered closer as Adam clicked to open it.

Fran's lips moved as she read what was written there: *Oh when to free hate, nigh know to sever no one.*

'Well, what the dickens does that mean?'

'It's just gibberish,' said Olivia. 'That doesn't make any sense at all.'

'Then why go to all the bother of typing it into a Word document, transferring it to a USB stick and then hiding that stick where it's almost impossible to see?' said Adam. 'It has to mean something, we just don't know what yet.'

Fran inhaled deeply and then expelled her breath slowly, puffing out her cheeks. 'Nope...' she said. 'Still nothing.'

'Another anagram?' suggested Olivia.

Adam screwed up his face. 'It could be, but somehow I can't see Clarence using the same kind of clue twice. It's a different type of puzzle, but which...' He shook his head. 'Nothing obvious is coming to mind.'

Fran stared at the bizarre list of words. Except that they weren't a list because they were separated with a comma, which meant that it was a sentence of some kind, and there was an order to the words. 'It must be a coded message then,' she said. 'Otherwise why put a comma in the middle of the words?'

'Hmm... that's what I was thinking too,' replied Adam. 'Yet if it's a coded message, there must be a key to *decode* it with. And there's nothing else on the document, just those words. There's nothing else on the USB either, only that single file.'

'Maybe we already have the key,' said Olivia. 'Although for the life of me I can't think what.' She frowned. 'What was the clue that brought us here again? *Bothy Berwick drop dead*. Is there anything in that which could be a key?'

'Well, there are two words that begin with the letter "B" and two beginning with "D", but I can't see how that's significant,' said Fran.

'You can have skip codes,' said Adam, 'where each letter in any given word skips forward by a certain amount. So if the key was two, for example, then the word "dead" would become "fgcf" – all you have to do is work backwards to solve the code. But I still can't see how that helps us. There are substitution ciphers too, loads of them, but they all need a code word to decipher them.'

'Then there must be something,' said Fran. 'Although I admit I was expecting to find a phone number, so perhaps Clarence had decided to mix things up a bit. Maybe there's another USB stick? And that one has the code word on it.'

'That's a really good idea,' said Olivia, turning back to the wall. 'Shine your torch back over here, Fran.'

'Hang on a minute,' said Adam slowly. 'What did you say about the phone number?'

'Only that it's what we should have found, really. Each time we've found one of the black canisters it's contained a number, and you said the USB was just another type of...' Fran trailed off at the expression of Adam's face. 'What?' she asked.

He stared back down at his phone, lips moving imperceptibly. 'Oh, that's genius,' he said. 'Listen... Let me read out the clue to you. *Oh when to free hate, nigh know to sever no one.* And you were right, Fran, the positioning of the comma is significant. But they're not words at all.'

Fran stared at him quizzically.

'They're numbers. Listen again. *Oh when to free hate* – 01238 – *nigh know to sever no one* – 902701. It's an area code, followed by the number, so the comma is there to make that clear. Well done, Fran.'

'You solved it, not me.'

He smiled generously. 'Team effort,' he said.

'Oh my God, that's brilliant!' cried Olivia. 'Quick, let me ring it.' She pulled out her phone and, looking at Adam's screen again, began to dial the number. 'Hello?' she said, as soon as the call connected. 'This is Olivia Turner.'

'Olivia! It's so good to talk to you. This is Stephen Forrester, congratulations on finding the clue. Now, I have the next part for you. A little different this time because it's a photo, and I'm going to text it to you now, so stay on the line a moment.' There was a pause and seconds later, Olivia's phone buzzed.

'Yes, I have it,' she replied. 'Thank you.'

'Excellent. The photo will lead you to the location of the next clue. Good luck, Olivia.'

The line went dead.

Immediately, Olivia clicked on her messages and double

tapped to enlarge the picture. It was hard to make out exactly what they were looking at. Whether that was because the light from the torch was making it hard to see, or because the picture was as grey as they thought, it was hard to tell.

'It looks almost like stone,' said Fran, pointing to an area in the lower half of the screen. 'See there, it looks like it's weathered.'

Olivia held her phone at arm's length, perhaps so that she could get a better sense of perspective, but the image still appeared to be flat, a close-up of something. Dull colour filled the screen, mottled in places, and the only part which was different was the top right corner, where a series of markings appeared raised, suggesting a relief of some sort.

'A building?' Adam suggested. 'It could be the mansion house.'

'Or a gravestone,' said Fran. 'A path maybe.'

'I don't think it's a path,' said Olivia. 'Otherwise, what are those markings there?'

'They could be flagstones?' said Adam. 'There are several courtyards here. Still doesn't explain the relief though.'

'Where even is it?' said Fran. 'It might not be on the estate at all.'

Adam sat back on his haunches. 'It might not, but there's just this one photo, no other clues at all.'

'Which must mean it's something or somewhere we know,' said Olivia. 'Or can easily find out.'

'Something here then?' said Fran. 'That *would* make sense. Particularly as you said you'd seen Cate and Marcus walking back to the main path. They must be looking for it too.'

'You're right,' said Adam. 'But what?'

'I don't know anything about this place,' said Olivia. 'What's the house like?'

'Big,' replied Fran, screwing up her face. 'As in enormous. With a massive courtyard behind it and a bell tower. There's a whole stable block too, with another flagged courtyard. Visitors have to walk through it to get to the parkland and around to the mansion house itself. Everything is built from the same stone.'

'It'll be like looking for the proverbial needle in a haystack.'

Adam huffed. 'Okay, let's think about this logically. The clue is the photo itself, so Clarence has shown us everything we need to work it out. Therefore, everything in it is relevant. *Therefore...* those relief lines in the top right corner must be significant.'

'It must be something on the main house,' said Fran. 'It's the reason most people come here, and there would be plenty of opportunities for carved details or...' She gave a frustrated groan. 'God, all the times I've dragged Martha around here. I should have paid far more attention to what I was seeing. We've even had a guided tour of the house, I should know this.'

'We'll find it, Fran, don't worry,' said Adam. 'But we'd better get moving. Which way do we go?'

Fran pointed to her right. 'The house is pretty much straight that way. We need to do what Cate and Marcus did and get back on the main path.'

Adam removed the adapter from the USB stick and replaced it in his pocket. 'You lead the way then, Fran.'

She nodded, but as they left the garden she felt her unease grow again. There was something very wrong here and, as time went on, the feeling was becoming harder and harder to ignore.

It didn't take long to reach the main path, but out away from the trees and the walled enclosure of the gardens, she felt horribly exposed. The main pathways around the estate had been designed to carry visitors, sometimes in great number, and they were wide and open. People could arrive at the house from multiple directions, and the building itself stood in the middle of a vast expanse of lawn, with a gravelled forecourt to the front. She put out a hand to draw the others to a halt.

'I think we should head off the path,' she said. 'It's too

exposed out here, and with the three of us together, we're far too easy to spot. It will take us longer to get to the house, but I think it's a risk we have to take.'

Adam nodded. 'Agreed.'

'If we walk through this stand of trees, I think there's a field on the other side,' said Fran. 'But we should be able to skirt its edge and come out behind the house.' She peered into the almost total darkness. 'It's so hard to get your bearings at night.' She turned to check with Olivia, who was peering at her phone.

'Sorry, guys, I was just thinking about what you said, Adam. How the markings on the stone in the photo are significant. I wondered if they could be part of a plaque, or a family crest. Is there anything like that here?'

'Almost certainly,' replied Fran. 'That's a great idea. And we know from the last clue that the house was built for the Berwick family. I'm pretty certain they would have had a crest or coat of arms. You're the historian, Liv, where is that most likely to be situated?'

'Google it,' said Adam. 'This place is owned by the National Trust, isn't it? There must be loads of information online, a guide for visitors, a map even. That's what we need, we—' He broke off at the sound of an engine, looking around him in horror. 'Through there,' he said, pointing at the trees. 'Hide!'

The three of them crashed through the undergrowth, their ungainly, noisy passage making Fran almost as anxious as the approaching vehicle. They would need to take a lot more care than they had been. If whoever was coming had heard them, or seen the light coming from Olivia's phone...

Fran had ended up behind a large expanse of sprawling yew, Adam beside her and Olivia a little distance away. She could see hardly a thing, but the noise of the engine was still increasing so whatever it was, was coming nearer. Adam inched sideways a little, peering around the outermost branches, before ducking back in.

'It's a buggy of some kind. Looks like one of the staff.'

'A warden maybe,' Fran whispered back. 'Which way are they going?'

Adam pointed in the direction they had been travelling. 'They're hopefully just doing the rounds, giving the place one last check over before they leave.'

'This is crazy,' she whispered. 'We're going to get caught.'

Adam shook his head as the sound of the engine receded. 'We just need to be careful.' He beckoned to Olivia, who cautiously moved across to them.

'Let's try to find what we're looking for before we move on, just in case we run into anyone else. It might save us a lot of time and aggravation. Fran, you look at the main site for this place. Olivia and I can search the internet for images.'

Fran and Olivia both nodded.

'I can hardly feel my fingers though,' said Fran, peeling off a glove again. 'It's getting really chilly.'

Olivia grimaced, and Fran could see she was feeling it too. Her face looked pinched with cold. 'Is anybody else thinking this is just not worth it?' she asked.

'About every ten seconds,' Fran replied. 'But I don't really mean it. You don't mean it either.'

Olivia shook her head. 'No, I do. Whoever wins, I should let them get on with it and carry on with my own life. What difference does it make to me?'

'Liv, we can't give up, because if we do then everything that Clarence wanted will come to naught. You clearly made a difference to his life, that's why it's important. This is his opportunity to give something back to you.'

'Then why stage this whole rigmarole in the first place?' she asked. 'Why not just leave his estate to me?'

'You know, that's a very good question,' said Adam. 'If Clarence didn't want his children to inherit, then why not just cut them out of the will, leave his estate to Olivia, or to charity like he threatened?'

'Because he liked a game?' offered Fran. 'Because he wanted to give them one last chance to come together as a family.'

Adam shook his head. 'No, that's not a strong enough reason. Olivia's right. There has to be a point to all of this.'

Fran thought for a moment. 'Maybe it's as much to do with redemption as anything. I'm just thinking about what Saul told me back at my house. Liv, did you know about the way Cate and Marcus betrayed their dad?'

'The bare bones. But it wasn't something he liked to talk about, as you can imagine.'

'I probably don't know much more than you then, but Saul told me how he regrets not speaking up when he had the chance. How he knew about Cate and Marcus's scheme, but he never did anything about it. He was scared to, essentially, because he'd spent his whole life trying to curry favour with his elder siblings, just like the stereotypical youngest child who only ever wanted to fit in. But, if that's true, and Saul deeply regrets his actions, and the missed opportunities he had to put things right, maybe this *is* simply just the last act of a man still trying to be a parent. Perhaps Clarence didn't just want to send his children on a physical journey, but on a spiritual and emotional one as well.'

Adam stared at her. 'Come again?'

Fran winced. 'Too deep?' she asked.

'That's definitely a rhetorical question,' said Adam. 'Even I know that. Sorry, Fran, but I'm not sure any of this is as well-meaning as you describe. Despite what Clarence's will stated, I can't help thinking the motive here is much darker.'

'I get what you mean,' said Olivia. 'And even though I found Clarence to be a very warm and generous person, it doesn't mean he was that way with his children. But if Saul does regret his actions then that's something at least. Maybe some good can come out of all this, the best man wins and all that.'

'But Clarence had no way of knowing who would win,' said Fran.

'No, he didn't...' Adam narrowed his eyes. 'Unless, of course, he did...'

Fran stared at him. 'Now what's that supposed to mean?'

'I need to think about it some more,' he replied, wrinkling his nose. 'And right now, we don't have the time.' He pointed at his phone. 'Come on, we need to get to this next clue.'

All three heads bent as they collectively began their searches.

Fran was the first to speak. 'Okay. So I'm on the Attingham website and there's a very helpful pictorial map of the grounds, with all the main features marked. And I can see where we are in relation to the house. I'll check the history pages and see if I can turn up anything about family crests.'

'Loads of pictures of the house,' added Olivia. 'But nothing close enough to be able to see any detail. I need to make the search more specific.' She bent back to her task.

'Here's something,' said Adam. 'This shows us the crest, but just a coloured image of it, not where we might find it. We might be able to cross-reference it with the photo though. See if any of the shapes we can see on it correlate with the crest.'

Fran nodded, although she wasn't really listening. Something had caught her eye. She used her fingers to enlarge the section of the map she'd been looking at. 'Dammit,' she muttered. 'Of course. Adam, can you search for a photo of the Berwick memorial? There's one in the grounds. And I could be wrong, but where else would you have your family crest other than where you were buried? Olivia, let's look at your clue photo again.'

She waited while Adam called up the page of search results,

scrolling through them to find one which might be suitable. He flicked past, stopped, then backed up.

'Here, this one, look.' He enlarged the image and held out his phone.

Olivia did likewise, placing it side by side with Adam's. Fran cocked her head, peering at both sets of images.

They all saw it at once.

'There!'

With both photos to compare, it was easy to see that the lines and patches of dark and shade on the clue photo were the same as those on the top-most part of the family crest from the stone memorial. It sat above the inscription, marking the burial place of Thomas Henry's ashes, the eighth Lord Berwick.

Fran turned back to the image of the map she held. 'So we're here... and the memorial is right at the far end of the park, just off this path which winds through the woodland.'

'That doesn't look far,' said Olivia.

'It's well over a mile,' said Fran, 'don't be fooled.' She tapped the screen again. 'That's a river. We have to cross it and there are only two bridges. One just along from the main house and the other, a suspension bridge, here, in the middle of the woodland walk.'

'Which is the quickest way?' asked Adam.

Fran pointed to the house. 'This one, but we'll be walking out across an open field. We have to go via the woodland if we want to give ourselves a better chance of not being seen.'

'Then come on. But stick to the edges of the path, under the canopy of trees.'

The going was easy enough while they were following the path. Paler than its surroundings, it threaded its way through the woods and was relatively smooth. Once they had crossed over the bridge, however, and passed through a gate shortly after, they were walking among trees and Fran stumbled more than once over the uneven ground, which was thick with brambles. Knowing they were nearing the memorial, no one dared use the torches on their phones and the darkness was absolute.

Fran crept forward, cursing as more brambles caught at her clothing. Trying to unsnag her coat, she almost jumped out of her skin when a hand touched her arm, pulling her back.

'Wait,' hissed Adam quietly. He spun around to attract Olivia's attention too. 'Shh, I heard something. Listen.'

Fran's heart was beating so hard that for a moment its heavy thud in her ears was all she could hear, but then she heard voices too. A loud shout, ahead of her. Then nothing. A flash of light swung around wildly and she ducked instinctively. 'Who is it?' she whispered. 'Could you tell?'

Adam shook his head. 'No, it sounded male. So Marcus, or Saul?'

All three of them crouched to the ground, waiting, as the seconds ticked past.

When a couple of minutes had passed without incident, Adam got cautiously to his feet. 'Come on,' he said. 'Carefully now. And slowly.'

For the second time, Fran felt a hand on her arm. She whirled around to see Olivia's anxious face peering at her.

She immediately looked apologetic. 'Fran, sorry, but can we hang on for a minute or two more? I'm desperate for a wee.'

'But...'

'Yeah, I know.' She rolled her eyes. 'But what are my options? Wait here a sec, I won't be long.'

Fran whispered for Adam to stop before calling softly to Olivia: 'Don't go too far.' She could just make out Olivia picking her way between the undergrowth then disappearing behind a tree. She caught Adam's arm, turning them both around to give Olivia some privacy. 'Answering a call of nature,' she murmured to Adam's enquiring face.

He nodded. 'Okay. I could do with a breather myself. Is your heart going like the clappers too?'

'Like it's coming out my chest. Tiptoeing around in the dark really isn't helping. I feel like I'm in a horror movie and it's only a matter of time before...' She broke off. 'Perhaps I'd better not say it.'

Adam gave a faint smile. 'I know I have an overactive imagination, but mine is coming up with some truly spectacular stuff. I keep telling myself it will come in handy for a game some time in the future.'

Fran wriggled her shoulders, wrapping her arms around herself and shuffling her feet. The air was dank and bone-cold. 'Come on, Olivia,' she murmured.

She took out her phone again to look at the map of the park, shielding the screen as she did so. 'It's not far now,' she said, showing it to Adam. 'I think we're about here... and that's where we're headed. Once we get out of this wooded area, the memorial should be just a little way along. Out in the deer park.'

'The deer park? You mean we've got to look out for four-legged foes as well now? I'd forgotten they have deer here.'

'Adam, the deer aren't going to be remotely interested in you. They'll be more frightened of you than you are of them.'

'Don't bank on it,' replied Adam, scuffing at the undergrowth. 'I'm not good with animals, I make them nervous.'

'Isn't that just horses?' asked Fran, turning around slightly. There was still no sign of Olivia. She took a couple of steps forward.

'Olivia?' she hissed into the night. 'Are you nearly done?' She looked at the line of trees in front of her, merely darker shapes. And the more she looked, the more she couldn't be certain which one Olivia had gone behind. She moved a little further forward, thinking she had it right, and then stopped again. 'Olivia?'

She felt Adam move beside her. 'Where's she gone?' he asked.

'Just over there,' whispered Fran. 'Behind one of these trees, but I'm not sure which...'

A muffled cry sounded away to their left and Fran's head whipped around to follow the source of the noise. 'What was that?'

'Shit,' said Adam, swinging his head from side to side. 'What the hell is going on?'

'It could have just been an animal,' Fran replied. 'There must be all sorts of things here, foxes... rabbits...' But she didn't really believe that. Her heart was pounding, blood rushing in her ears. 'Olivia?' Her call was more urgent now. 'Olivia? For God's sake, where are you?'

She stumbled forward, fear turning her feet to lead. Something pulled at her coat and she jerked away, only to catch her foot on a tangle of brambles. She plunged headlong to the ground, landing hard as a sharp pain tore at her cheek.

Adam's voice came from behind her as she fought to lift her head, her hair snagged by the thorny branches. Her fingers pulled at them as she twisted herself free, pushing herself upright. A strangled sound split the silence.

In front of her, with his head turned slightly, lay Marcus, sightless eyes staring upwards, dark pools against the even darker night.

17

Fran shot backwards, scrambling for a foothold as bile rose in her throat. Her only thought was to put distance between her and Marcus's lifeless body, but as Adam's arms gripped her tightly, she sank back against them. The weird noises she could hear seemed to be coming from her.

'It's all right, Fran,' murmured Adam, pulling her up.

She twisted away, pushing at his chest. 'Of course it's not bloody all right!' she shouted, staring at him, eyes wide. 'It's not all right!'

But as she stood there, chest heaving, all she could think about was that this was the second dead body she had discovered in her lifetime thus far, and it was two too many. The whole thing was getting beyond a joke. She looked at Adam, standing helplessly, arms by his side, and trembling too if she wasn't much mistaken.

'Sorry,' she said, moving closer. 'I didn't handle that very well.'

'I'm not sure there's a right way *to* handle it,' he replied. 'Jesus, Fran, what's going on?'

She swallowed, her breath still coming in great heaving

gulps. 'Olivia's gone,' she said, although she knew Adam had already worked that out for himself. 'It's like someone is picking us off, one by one.'

He shuddered. 'Don't.'

She stared at him. 'What do we do? Do we try to find Olivia? Or...' And the minute she said it, another thought occurred to her. 'I can't call Nell and tell her I've found another body, Adam. I just can't.'

'We may have to,' he replied. 'And, to be fair, she's a detective chief inspector, it is her job.'

'Exactly,' said Fran. 'It's *her* job, not ours. Why do we keep getting involved in all this mayhem? All I want is a quiet life making cakes and cooking nice food for nice people.'

'That's kind of what you were doing. Only the nice people didn't turn out to be so nice. Aside from Clarence, perhaps... and some of the other guests.'

'And Olivia,' added Fran. 'What do we do?' she repeated. 'She could be in real danger, Adam, and we should—' She stopped at the look on his face. 'What?'

Adam blinked. 'Sorry, I was just... it doesn't matter. But yes, you're right. Except that... what do we do about Marcus?'

Fran still couldn't bring herself to look at him. 'He might have tripped,' she said. 'His death might have been an accident. He might not actually be dead.'

But they both knew that wasn't the case.

'Then we have to call the police,' she added. 'Whatever the cause of death, that's what we should do.'

He nodded. 'Except all that's going to do is slow us down.'

Fran was well aware that Adam and Nell didn't exactly see eye to eye on certain matters. They'd got to know the chief inspector rather better than they would have liked over the course of the last eighteen months. Firstly, when Adam's mum was almost accused of murder and, secondly, when Fran and Adam solved a murder just six short months ago after the host of a party Fran was catering for turned up dead. Nell didn't approve of their 'meddling' and had a particular issue with some of Adam's 'gadgetry', as she called it. She'd have a field day over the latest turn of events.

'We can't leave Marcus here,' Fran replied. 'Apart from anything else, this place will be open to the public tomorrow.'

'Fran, I don't want to do that any more than you do but, thinking about this logically, we can't help Marcus now. What we *can* do, however, is help whoever's next, because we're running out of time. I'm convinced this isn't the end of it.'

Cautiously, Fran turned back around. Letting her eyes become accustomed to what she was seeing, little by little. 'We'd better have a look at him, hadn't we?'

Adam nodded. 'Do you want me...?'

But Fran shook her head. Given their age difference, Fran still felt there were certain things she had to protect Adam from, not that he needed it, just... She swallowed again. 'No... I'll look.'

She crept closer. With any luck there wouldn't be any... but she couldn't finish the thought.

Marcus was lying almost face down and she had a sudden image of him falling to his knees before sagging forward, twisting as he fell so that he was partially on his side. She pulled out her phone and flicked on the torch, covering the light with one hand so that it only just spilled from her fingers. She aimed it at his feet, slowly playing the light along the length of his body, until she reached his neck. Nothing untoward so far. But she didn't need to look very much higher to see how Marcus had died.

'Whoever is doing this has a particular penchant for bashing people over the head,' she said. 'At times rather harder than others.'

Adam's face was pale in the dim light. 'That could have been me,' he said quietly.

'Maybe they didn't mean to kill him,' she replied. But as soon as she said it, she realised that wasn't what she thought at all. 'Actually, I think whoever is doing this knows exactly what they're about. Whoever hit you meant to slow you down, not kill you. Saul too, I reckon. I think if the intention had been to kill, you'd both be dead by now.'

'I think you're right. But doesn't this change what we've been thinking? I don't know about you, but I certainly had Marcus pegged as the one who'd been doing the head bashing. But now we know that can't be true.'

Fran frowned. 'Then who? Saul?'

'It's possible, but that would also mean that Saul managed to somehow hit himself over the head and tie up his own hands. He's either some kind of contortionist or there's someone else at work here.'

'But the only person left is Cate. Would she have the physical strength to hit someone that hard?' She thought for a moment. 'Maybe she and Saul have teamed up together.'

'I can't see it,' replied Adam. 'The way Saul was talking to you earlier, he hates both his siblings equally. And something has very clearly tipped him over the edge. I think he's out to take them down.'

'Then Cate's in danger too... And Olivia. Adam, if she gets in Saul's way then who knows what could happen.'

Adam's look held hers. 'There is another possibility,' he said quietly. 'And the more I think about it, the more I realise I already knew something was wrong when I was ambushed.'

'What do you mean?' asked Fran, alerted by something in the tone of his voice.

'If we look at the sequence of events, nothing makes sense.'

'Go on...' she said, beginning to feel very nervous.

'When I ran back to the car to fetch the USB adapter, I returned to find that Olivia was gone. According to what she told us, this would have been when she followed Cate and

Marcus into the gardens and watched them find the bothy clue. Then, once they had, she said she slipped back out so she wouldn't get locked in, saw them leave, and watched them walk away in the opposite direction, towards the main path. She then waited for me. Except that by then, of course, I'd already been thumped and carted off.'

'So it couldn't have been either Cate or Marcus who hit you because they would have still been at the bothy.'

'Exactly. Besides, Olivia was watching them.'

'And it can't have been Saul... because he and I hadn't arrived by then.'

'So do you see my point?' asked Adam.

Fran had a horrible feeling she did.

'If what Olivia said was true, then there would have been no one around to clonk me over the head. So either Olivia was mistaken, and she only saw one of the siblings in the garden...'

Fran stared at Adam, a wave of heat rolling up her neck. 'Or Olivia's lying...'

'I'm sorry, Fran. But she must be. There's also the fact that by the time Olivia and I found the lead in the bothy, it had already been sabotaged. So who did that, if not Cate and Marcus? I think they found the bothy clue much earlier than Olivia said they did.'

And now it was all beginning to make sense.

'That's why you cut me off earlier, when I began to tell Olivia what had happened to you. You didn't want me to talk about it, because if she acknowledged what had happened, and when, we would have seen straight away that what she'd told us didn't made sense.'

'And the more I think about it, the more I realise that there could be an explanation for some of the other things which have happened too. Think back to the what3words clue and the pipe in the woodland. You and Olivia went to fetch water from the ditch and on your way back, thought you saw something, or someone.'

'We did. A flash of red. I saw it too.'

'Yes, but what we didn't realise was quite how close we were to Justice House, because we'd approached the location from a completely different direction. We only found out how close it was when Saul told us he had run back to the house because it was quicker.'

Understanding flashed through Fran. 'And when we were trying to float the film canister out of the pipe, we heard something and Olivia ran off to give chase...'

Adam nodded sadly. 'I don't know for certain without checking the timings, but what if Olivia had time to follow Saul to Justice House, hit him over the head and tie him up, and then run back to meet us? We waited for her in the woodland for a while before deciding to walk back to the car. A car which had a conveniently flat tyre.'

'And Olivia was out of puff when she met us...' Fran bowed her head. 'Oh God... I can't believe it.' She put both hands on her cheeks. 'Adam, this is all my fault. I hadn't seen Olivia for years and I just assumed she was the same person I'd known way back when. I don't really know her at all.'

Adam gave her a soft smile. 'And this is where it gets really complicated. Because we need to look at two different things. The first is the treasure hunt and Clarence's inheritance. And the second is the notion that Clarence may have been murdered.'

Fran closed her eyes. This was getting worse by the second. That Olivia could be guilty of all that. That she could have killed the old man and then... But something else was puzzling her. 'So you're saying the person who will seemingly stop at nothing to inherit doesn't necessarily have to be the same person who might have killed Clarence. Logically, there could be more than one culprit.'

'Exactly. Saul said to you he wasn't interested in the inheritance so much as making sure that neither Cate nor Marcus saw a penny of it. But then he also went on to surmise that either one of them might have killed Clarence in the first place. Now, what he told you about his regrets might all be a pack of lies, but his endeavouring to finally make amends for his past behaviour makes far more sense to me than him being Clarence's killer.'

'Though you can hardly make amends for your behaviour by killing your brother and sister, even if it is to stop them getting their hands on Clarence's inheritance. Wouldn't a much better way be to expose them and what they've been doing?'

'That, is very true. So we still don't know what's going on. But is Saul innocent, do we think?'

Fran frowned. 'I can't stop thinking about your earlier question – what this whole thing has been about. Because, like you said, if Clarence didn't want his children to inherit, then why not simply strike them out of the will? And it's not just for the love of a puzzle, or any desire to see his family reconciled. I think Clarence knew his children very well, I think he knew exactly what they could be capable of. And maybe *he's* also a whole lot cleverer than we've been giving him credit for.'

'Okay... I like the way you're thinking. Go on...'

'Before the family dinner had even taken place, Olivia told me that Clarence mentioned to Margaret that if he died of a heart attack it would be because of foul play. Margaret herself corroborated this later. He was in his eighties, so citing a heart attack as the cause of death wouldn't be at all surprising. But yet, something convinced him that it would be. It's a little specific, don't you think? Maybe the dinner, the treasure hunt, all of it, is part of a very elaborate ruse to catch the killer. *His* killer.'

'The game's the thing wherein I'll catch the conscience of the king,' mused Adam. 'So Clarence hoped that someone might trip themselves up, reveal themselves...?'

'That's it.'

'Except that someone has just upped the stakes. It still doesn't mean that whoever killed Clarence killed Marcus too.'

'No, it doesn't. My gut is telling me that Saul isn't behind all this, but he could have equally spun me a story, a very good story, and I fell for it. In fact, it's very likely that I'm not so good a judge of character as I thought I was... I want to believe it's either Saul or Cate who are guilty, but now I know we have to add Olivia to that list. You know, she must have realised that Margaret might tell me Clarence had suspicions about the way he would die. In which case, that suspicion could fall on Olivia just as equally as any of Clarence's family. So she got to me first – revealing what Clarence had told Margaret and pooh-poohing the whole idea as ridiculous. She was banking on the fact that we're old friends and I would naturally take her word that it was an absurd notion. She managed to completely change my perspective on it, without me even realising. God, that's clever.'

Adam looked at Fran, compassion in his eyes. 'You know, on our way over here in the car, Olivia and I talked about how you met at school. She said you'd stood up to a bully on her behalf and that, even when you knew the consequences wouldn't be good, you always did the right thing. I'm sorry, Fran.'

Fran lifted her chin a little, biting back a sudden rush of tears. 'Then we'd best get going,' she said. 'Because we have a killer to catch.'

She turned around for a moment, facing Marcus's body. 'I promise we'll get whoever did this to you,' she said and, bending down, she touched a hand lightly on his arm. 'I feel awful leaving him like this,' she added, wiping her nose. Her cheek was beginning to sting like crazy from the wound.

'I know, but there's nothing we can do for him except catch whoever did it. And we'll notify someone as soon as we get the chance.'

Fran nodded. She knew Adam was right. She straightened

up, swapping her phone into the other hand so she could flick off the torch. 'Hang on... what's this?' Her light had picked up the glint of something shiny lying a little distance away. She bent down again, realising as she neared that it was another phone, its crazed and cracked screen reflecting her light.

'Careful,' cautioned Adam. 'Here, let me...' He was still wearing his gloves. He gently lifted the phone from where it had fallen, or more likely been thrown.

'Do you think it belonged to Marcus?' asked Fran.

'Mmm...' Adam was tilting the screen this way and that. 'It's cracked to such an extent I'm pretty sure it's been damaged deliberately.'

'But why? What would be the point in that? He's hardly likely to ring for help, is he?'

'Which is why it's curious,' said Adam. 'Because if the phone was smashed before he was killed, then it could have been to prevent him from alerting anyone to what was going on. But I don't buy that for a minute. It's too near to the body. If someone intent on doing you harm was that close to you, you wouldn't be stopping to phone for help, you'd be running, or trying to defend yourself. I think it's much more likely that his phone was deliberately smashed, after he was dead. In which case, what's on it that someone doesn't want us to see?'

'Would we be able to tell?' asked Fran. 'Can you fix it?'

Adam shrugged. 'I don't know, but it's coming with us just in case.' He slipped the phone in his pocket, looking up at Fran. 'Right, which way do we need to go?'

Fran looked at the map afresh. 'Keep heading in this direction,' she said. 'Once we're out of the trees, the memorial isn't too far ahead.'

Neither of them needed to tell the other to be careful.

.   .   .

They reached the stone reliquary without incident, although Fran's heart was thumping painfully in her chest the entire way. She was convinced that at any moment someone would loom up at them out of the dark, brandishing a sword for some reason, although a whopping great tree branch would obviously be far more likely. But the effect was the same, she felt jittery, almost sick with apprehension.

Bizarrely though, as soon as they came out from under the line of trees and stood staring up at the stone monument in front of them, the feeling began to change. Perhaps it was simply the claustrophobic atmosphere of the woods at work; that, and an overactive imagination.

'So now what?' she asked.

Adam held her look, clearly thinking, and then began a slow circuit of the memorial, a puzzled expression on his face. He stopped as he drew level with her once more. 'I have absolutely no idea,' he said. 'None...' He tapped his fingers against his head. 'It's like, poof... nothing there at all.'

'I'm not sure what I expected,' said Fran. 'I know it's hardly likely there'll be a flashing neon sign which reads "next clue here", but I don't even know where to start. It's a stone plinth, with a solid finial on top. It doesn't look as if there are any hiding places.'

Adam directed his light onto the side of the memorial facing them, where Fran could just make out lines of engraved lettering. They looked to be gothic in style but were so weathered and faint she could only just about read what they said.

'Maybe there's something in the words themselves,' mused Adam. 'Although what, I don't know. The inscription is as you'd imagine, *to the memory of*, and so on.'

He angled the light upwards, illuminating what was obviously the Berwick family crest – a crown atop some kind of creature – but Fran couldn't make out what. It was clear, however, that the photo Olivia had been sent was simply a small section of it, magnified. Fran peered closer.

'So why take a photo of that specific part of the memorial? Was it simply to tell us what we were looking for? Or for another reason?'

'Exactly,' said Adam. 'But I can't think what. All we can do is search every inch of this thing and see what we come up with. Something hidden on it somehow, or...' He shrugged.

Fran nodded, but she wasn't convinced, and nearly twenty minutes later they mutually came to a halt.

'Have we missed something?' asked Fran. 'Or has it been taken away, do you think?'

Adam wrinkled his nose, pulling his beanie down further over his ears. 'Either of those things could be true. I think we *have* missed something, but not in the sense you mean. There's something we're not seeing here, something to do with the bigger picture.'

Fran stood back. She was acutely aware of time trickling through her fingers and of just how bizarre this whole situation had become. But Adam was right, she felt it too. As if something was ever so slightly out of reach, or out of their line of vision, and all it would take was a slight shift to see it. And the more she thought about it, the more she could feel whatever it was inching its way towards her.

'What?' asked Adam. 'You've got a weird look on your face.'

'I don't know... Just an odd sense of something which feels a bit like déjà vu, even though I've been here before.'

'I've been here too, I remember coming with Mum.'

Fran nodded. 'Hmm, Martha and I ate our picnic on a bench over there, but that's not it. I'm not remembering it from a time I've been here before, more that it's reminding me of something else.'

'Your photographic memory strikes again?'

Fran stared at him. 'Maybe...' she said. Yet where could she have seen something similar? 'There's something else as well, though... I'm very glad that we *haven't* bumped into the others, but we've been here about half an hour now. Where is everyone?'

'Been and gone,' replied Adam. 'They must be so far ahead of us.'

'Cate and Marcus possibly, but not everyone. I'm thinking about the sequence of events, and trying to make them add up. Because, if you believe what Olivia said, then they can't be that far ahead of us.'

'*If* you believe what Olivia said,' replied Adam. 'Although, whatever she said about them, I think we can still safely assume that Cate and Marcus found the bothy clue *and* worked out that they needed to come here, the proximity of Marcus's body tells us that. They must have found the next clue and left. Maybe Marcus was killed on the way back from here, rather than on his way to it.'

'That's one possibility,' replied Fran, nodding. 'But what about Saul and Olivia? Humour me,' she added at his perplexed expression.

'Okay,' said Adam.

'So let's start with Olivia. She could simply have followed Cate and Marcus here from the bothy, but if that were the case, would she have had time to find the next clue, hit Marcus over the head and then double back in order to meet us when she did?'

Adam stared at her. 'That's a very good point.'

'See, it doesn't make sense, the timing is all wrong.' Fran shook her head. 'I don't know. Maybe it's just because I don't want to believe that Olivia knocked you out, or killed Marcus, but if we assume she didn't follow anyone, then the sequence of events looks very different. What if she simply *did* hang around waiting for you to appear, or me? We're supposed to be helping her find the clues so that would be logical. So, she waits and remains with us right up to the point before we find Marcus's body, and then she disappears. She couldn't have been that far ahead of us, so where is she now?'

Adam swung his head around uneasily.

'Then there's Saul. He and I arrived after you and Olivia, quite a bit later, and don't forget, all he would have known was that the clue was at the bothy. He didn't know about the dead drop, unless of course he'd worked it out for himself. But he would have had to do so pretty darn quickly. I wasn't locked in with you for long and we were right behind him. Could he really be that far ahead of us?'

'That's a very good question... Hi, guys.'

18

Adam swung his torch upwards just as Fran spun around at the sound of Saul's voice. He was standing a few yards away from them and flung up an arm to shield himself from the sudden light.

'For God's sake, put that thing down!' he hissed. 'I can't bloody see!'

Adam lowered it, fractionally.

'And the answer to your question, of course, is that I wasn't very far ahead of you, not very far at all. I'm sorry you had to discover poor Marcus, though. I might not have had much time for him but even I draw the line at murder.'

Fran swallowed. 'How do we know it wasn't you?' she asked, suddenly finding her voice.

'You don't, so you'll just have to take my word for it that my darling sister is to blame. Interesting what you had to say about Olivia, though. I shall have to have a good think about that, and watch my step, just in case.'

He moved closer. 'You're a pain in the backside though, Fran, you really are. I thought I'd locked you in a storeroom.'

'Yes, well, we got out.'

Saul stared at her for a moment, puzzled. 'We?'

She flashed Adam a look. 'You obviously didn't realise that Adam was already in there.'

'Hmm, well, that's interesting too. And, no, I didn't. Although having both of you out of the way would have been even better, then neither of you could have tried to stop me from going after Cate and Marcus. Course I didn't know at the time quite what I was letting myself in for. I did, however, say I'd come back and let you out within an hour, and if I didn't, to call the police. So it's a good job I already have. They might be a bit surprised to find the storeroom empty, but I suspect Marcus might occupy their minds a little more.'

'So where are Cate and Olivia then?' asked Adam.

Saul shook his head. 'Cate's already gone, and I really need to get after her if I'm going to stop her. As for your friend, I have no idea. Isn't she supposed to be with you?'

'Yes, but she made out like she was desperate for the loo and then snuck off.'

'Then she'll have to look after herself, there's nothing I can do about that now.'

'So what are you going to do?'

Saul sucked in a deep breath. 'Sorry, Fran, you had to ask. You see, the thing is, I need to go now, and I can't risk you two ruining anything for me, so I'm going to insist you both stay here, I'm afraid.'

'Not bloody likely. We're coming with you.'

'No, I'm sorry, but you're not.' Saul slipped his hand in his pocket. 'But like I said, I've rung the police. I left an anonymous message so you won't be stuck here for too long. Someone will find you.'

Fran's eyes widened as she realised that Saul was holding a ball of twine in his hand.

'It's amazing what you can find lying around this place. So it would be great if I could have you both kneeling down, please, back to back, holding each other's hands. I don't want either of you thinking you can jump me while I'm trussing you up.'

'I'll give you trussing me up,' muttered Fran, wondering where she could kick him. 'You can't leave us here,' she added. 'It's bloody freezing. What if no one finds us? We might not make it to morning.'

'Then you should have stayed in the storeroom, shouldn't you? Kneel down, please.'

Fran did as she was told. What could either of them do? She didn't fancy her chances against Saul, nor those if she could somehow get away and run off. At least if she and Adam were together, they might be able to come up with something.

'And I'll take both your phones as well,' added Saul, removing Adam's from his hand first so that it went suddenly much darker. 'I'll leave the torch on for you and pop them both on the ground a little way over here. Then you'll have a bit of light.'

Fran squeezed Adam's hand as it met hers, gritting her teeth while Saul tied string around both their wrists in what felt suspiciously like a figure of eight.

Saul straightened once he'd finished. 'Look, lovely though it is standing here chatting, I don't have time for this. Cate's already gone and I need to get after her if I'm going to have a chance of stopping her. This is family business, and I intend to finish it. My way, without the two of you interfering. There's no way Cate's getting her hands on my inheritance. And I intend to make sure she pays for what she did.'

'So where's she gone?' asked Adam. 'You sound as if you know. Does that mean she's worked out where the next clue is?'

'Well, of course she has, and I need to be right behind her.' Saul began to walk away.

'No, wait!' shouted Adam. 'Where is it? For God's sake, if you're going to tie us up and leave us here, then at least tell us what this bloody memorial has to do with anything. We've searched it from top to bottom and there's nothing here.'

Saul's laughter split the air. 'I know, it's brilliant. At times I could have killed Dad myself but I have to hand it to him, he does make a damned good game, and this has been one of the best. It's all just become really very clear.'

'What has?' cried Adam. 'Tell me about the clue!'

'But that's what's so funny. The clue *is* the clue.'

'What the hell does that mean?' muttered Adam. 'Saul...? Saul?'

But it was evident from the silence that he'd already gone. Adam groaned, a long drawn-out, utterly fed-up groan. Fran knew how he felt.

'Great,' she said. 'Just when you thought things couldn't get any worse.'

'Don't,' said Adam. 'Because it could *actually* be worse.'

'I don't see how.'

'We could be dead.'

'Brilliant.' She tutted. 'And well done for kicking and struggling to get us free.'

'I didn't see there was much point,' replied Adam. 'Given that he had a weight and height advantage. I'm a wuss, I thought you'd realised that by now. Besides, I was thinking.'

'Oh great, thinking. Big help.' She sighed. 'Okay then, tell me, what were you thinking?'

'About this place, trying to fathom what the significance of it is. But of course now we have another clue. A clue which *is* the clue.'

'Which means?'

'I haven't the foggiest. But I'm sure it will come to me in the nick of time.'

Fran had never heard Adam's voice so flat before and she wriggled furiously. 'Sorry,' she said at his intake of breath. Her wrists were hurting too. 'Now what do we do?'

'I know what we *don't* do,' replied Adam. 'And that's scream and yell and basically draw as much attention to ourselves as we can so that the police practically fall over us.'

'Yes, but what—'

'Oh, hi, Nell,' pretended Adam, warming to his theme. 'Yes, we know there's a dead body in the woods, but really we had absolutely nothing to do with it. I know, it sounds crazy, doesn't it? Yes, we do seem to have a penchant for getting involved in murder, and no I don't know why that is either...' He trailed off, running out of steam. 'Sorry,' he added unnecessarily.

'It's okay,' said Fran in her best soothing voice. 'You haven't seen me when I'm really angry,' she added. 'But you might be about to.'

'Do you turn green and swell to four times your size with huge muscles, thereby breaking our bonds?'

Fran actually smiled. 'I wish... But, no, I get bloody-minded, and when I get bloody-minded, I sometimes have really, really good ideas.'

'And have you had one now?'

'No... But I'm working on it.'

'Did you by chance do that thing they tell you to do if you're ever tied up?' asked Adam. 'You clench your fists and then when you're able to escape, you relax them again, making your hands slimmer, allowing you to slip off the ties.'

'No, did you?'

'I forgot, sorry. I've only just remembered.'

'Hmm, that kind of clear thinking in a crisis is easy to write about, not so easy in practice,' said Fran, adjusting the position of her knees. 'Maybe if we stand up we can find something that might help us cut through the twine.'

'What, like a handily placed rock with a razor-sharp edge?'

'You know, most of the time I really like your dry humour, Adam, but... Shhh, what was that?'

They both froze, straining to hear. Something or someone

was coming their way, and whatever it was clearly didn't mind the noise it was making. Fran closed her eyes and prayed for it to be a deer. As far as she was aware they didn't eat people.

'Oh, thank God you're okay!'

Fran whipped her head round at the sound of a voice. One she really hadn't expected to hear.

Cate was standing only a few feet away from them, harsh breaths clouding the air. Her chest heaved with exertion as if she'd been running. Leaves tangled her hair and something dark was smeared across one cheek.

She ran forward. 'Christ, who did this to you? Was it her?'

Fran was so confused her words dried in her throat, but she could feel Cate's icy fingers touching hers, fumbling with the twine that bound them. 'Shit...' she murmured. 'Hang on...' She left them to pick up both phones, still lying where Saul had placed them. 'I can't see a thing. Fran, can you hold this?'

She thrust one of the phones into Fran's grip, bending her fingers a little to grasp it better. 'That's it, like that so the light's on the knots. I don't suppose either of you have a pair of scissors in your pocket, do you?' She tutted, muttering under her breath. 'No, of course not.'

Neither one of them had said a word. Fran was still desperately trying to process what was happening.

Cate continued muttering, uttering exhortations to herself to hurry up, and then a triumphant 'Hah' burst from her lips. 'Got it. Hang on...'

Fran felt the bonds tying her hands loosen and she hurried to pull them free.

'Are you okay?' asked Cate. 'Can you stand? Here...' She offered Fran her arm, half pulling her to her feet.

Even in the small amount of time they'd been tied up, a ferocious ache had settled across Fran's shoulders. She stamped her feet to try to get the circulation going again as Cate switched to helping Adam. He rubbed his wrists, rolling his shoulders back to ease out the stiffness.

Cate stood in front of them, watching them carefully. 'Are you okay?' she asked again.

Fran took back her phone and slipped it in her pocket. 'We found Marcus.' It sounded blunter than Fran had intended, but she still didn't know what else to say. Sorry didn't seem quite right given that Fran had more or less got used to the idea that Cate had killed him.

Cate's face contorted as she stifled a sob, clamping one hand against her mouth. 'I know,' she said. 'I didn't know what to do. I had no idea she'd go that far. I managed to give her the slip, but you've got to help me.'

Adam took a step forward. 'Hang on a minute, Cate. Are you saying that Olivia killed Marcus?'

She nodded, hand still clamped across her mouth.

'And you know that for a fact, do you?'

'Yes! I was there...' A puzzled expression creased her face. 'Wait a minute, you were supposed to be on her team. Why weren't you with her?'

Fran flicked a glance at Adam. How did she say that they'd got split up? That Olivia had sneaked off, first on Adam and then on them both.

Slowly, Cate's furrowed brow smoothed as she misunderstood Fran's silence.

'You think it was me?' she asked, staring at them in horror. 'You do, don't you? Jesus...' She trailed off, looking at the ground.

Fran swallowed, feeling torn. Her natural compassion meant she was instinctively drawn to Cate's plight, but could she really believe anything she was saying?

Cate's head came up slowly. 'He was my brother. We were working as a team... why on earth would I want to kill him?'

'Oh, I don't know,' said Adam. 'Maybe to get your hands on the inheritance without having to share it.'

Cate made a derogatory sound in her throat. 'The inheritance... Dad's final game for us all. Only he didn't count on one of the players being a psychopath, did he?' She looked first at Fran and then back at Adam. 'Olivia obviously had the wool pulled so firmly over his eyes he couldn't see what was happening. I know things went wrong between us and Dad, but Marcus and I, we tried... And you weren't there, you don't know how it was. You only know what you've been told... by Olivia, no doubt. I can see it in your eyes.'

'Actually, it was Saul who told me how you and Marcus betrayed your father. How you conspired to sell one of his games out from under him.'

'*We* didn't betray him at all. Everything we did, we did with Dad's full knowledge. It was Saul who betrayed us. Saul who was entrusted to put together the contract with the gaming company. Only what we didn't know was that he'd set up a deal with them on his own, a little extra kick-back just for him. He changed the wording on the contract at the last minute, meaning that when the deal was signed, rather than simply granting the company the rights to license a digital version, it gave them the rights in their entirety. Dad would have lost his most lucrative game. That's why he pulled the deal, that's why he lost so much money, that's what almost destroyed him personally.'

'But if it was solely Saul's doing, why did the relationship between you and your father break down?'

Cate shook her head in frustration. 'Because Dad thought we were in on it too. And nothing we said would make him change his mind. Can you even begin to understand how that feels? That your own father could believe you capable of such a thing?'

Fran looked at Adam. It was more or less what Saul had told her, only the other way around.

'Listen, I haven't got time to talk about this now,' urged Cate. 'Please, you have to believe me. I'll tell you everything on the way, I promise, but please, we have to go.'

But Adam stood his ground. 'How do we know you're telling the truth?' he asked. 'Everyone's seemed intent on telling us a pack of lies so far. Why should you be any different?'

'I just untied you, didn't I? I could have left you here for the police to find, or worse, for Olivia to come back for you herself.'

It was a good point and Fran knew it. She could also see from Adam's stance that he was beginning to accept it too.

'Come on,' Cate urged again. 'We need to get back to Justice House before the police arrive and catch us here. You might want to hang around and be accused of a crime you didn't commit, but I don't.'

Another good point.

Cate took a couple of steps backwards, her eyes never leaving theirs for a second. 'That's exactly what Olivia has planned, don't you see? She's trying to pin this whole thing on me – Dad's death, and now Marcus's. She's got it all worked out.'

Fran put out her hand. 'Wait,' she said. She needed time to think. 'Supposing you're right, and Olivia *is* trying to frame you, that would suggest she's the guilty party. But why on earth would she have wanted to kill Clarence?'

Cate rolled her eyes. 'The same reason as I apparently did. For the *money*... Listen, I'm sorry, I know you're old school friends or something, but she's been lying to you too, Fran. Getting you involved in this, knowing you'd help her out in her hour of need. You just need to ask yourself how well you really know her.'

Fran was having a hard time admitting she'd already been

asking herself that question. She didn't need someone else pointing it out. Particularly if that someone was Cate.

'Okay, so we haven't seen each other for years. But she and I were best friends, and I can't believe that in the intervening years she's turned into some kind of crazed serial killer. Besides, what you describe sounds planned, as if she'd worked all this out beforehand. But how could she? Until I turned up on the doorstep of Justice House she never even knew that the caterer she'd hired, a woman by the name of Francesca Eve, was actually the same Francesca Williams she knew way back when.'

A flash of understanding passed over Cate's face. 'No... no, that's not the way it happened. She *did* know who you were. Look...' She lifted the hem of her coat and began to fish around in the pocket of her jeans.

She pulled out a newspaper article, one which Fran didn't need to look at too closely to know what it said; the words had almost burned themselves into her brain by now. The article, from their local evening paper, had set her and Adam up as some kind of famous crime-fighting duo, and relied heavily on sensationalism rather than the truth. It also made reference to the fact that in both the instances of murder they had solved, the police had been singularly unsuccessful in their investigations. She hadn't ever had a conversation with Nell about it, she'd been too embarrassed to pick up the phone, but she could well imagine how that had gone down.

'You could have found this yourself,' Fran retorted. 'You could have got it from anywhere.' But even as she said it, Fran knew what it was evidence of. She just didn't want to believe it.

Cate held her look. 'I could have but, no offence, Fran, why would I want to? I don't know you, and had no reason to seek you out for the simple fact that I never had anything to do with the organising of the funeral. That was all down to Olivia, and that Margaret woman. Plus, what you're forgetting is that I live in Kent. That article is from months ago, and I haven't set foot in Justice House for nearly six years. How could I have got hold of it?'

But Adam wasn't letting her off that easily. He cleared his throat. 'So you just came across it at some point over the last day or so? What even made you pick it up?'

'Jesus…' Cate sighed with frustration. 'I found it among some of Dad's things in his room. And when I realised what Olivia was up to, and that she obviously hadn't been honest with you, I was worried.' A resolute look hardened her face. 'I still am.'

Fran shoved her thoughts about Olivia to the back of her head. Time was ticking on. 'Okay,' she said. 'Putting that aside for a minute, you said we needed to go back to Justice House. Why there? Have you worked out the relevance of the memorial?'

Cate shook her head. 'Not exactly. Just a feeling more than anything. But there's something I want to check.'

'Saul said you'd figured it out, that you'd already left.'

'Yeah, well, as I've just explained, Saul's said and done a lot of things. I wanted him to think I knew what the next clue was, just as I was trying to give him the slip. Hopefully, I've managed to do both those things.'

Fran wasn't sure whether or not she should repeat Saul's last words to them, but a part of her wanted to see what kind of reaction it would provoke.

'Saul told us that the clue *was* the clue.'

Cate looked puzzled for a moment. 'See?' she said. 'That's exactly what I mean. I remember this memorial… monument, whatever it is. I know it has some kind of significance, but I can't think what. We used to play here as children.'

'You did what?' asked Fran. 'You know this place?'

'Yes, we used to come here all the time. It wasn't like it is now, you could come and go… well, we could anyway.'

Fran shook her head. This was becoming more complicated

by the minute, when it should really be much clearer. She just couldn't put her finger on the missing piece of information, the one which would allow everything else to fall into place.

'You've obviously searched the memorial?' said Adam.

Cate nodded. 'Yes, although I was sure everyone else would have got here first. We worked out that the photo from the bothy clue was the family crest, but Marcus was sure there was one over the gate into the courtyard behind the mansion. We went there first and it cost us so much time. We hadn't long got here when Marcus heard something and went off to investigate, but he...' Cate visibly swallowed. 'He didn't come back. When I went to try and find him, and saw Olivia, I—'

'When was this?' asked Adam. 'How long ago?'

'I don't know,' said Cate, becoming more agitated again. 'Twenty minutes or so, maybe longer. And we're running out of time. Please, we have to go, you have to help me.'

With one last long look at Adam, Fran nodded, praying she was doing the right thing. 'Okay, come on.'

19

It was evident from the confident way Cate walked that she knew exactly where she was going, especially when she turned in the opposite direction from the one Fran would have taken.

'The public don't have access to this part of the parkland,' Cate explained as they headed towards what could only be another building, judging by the lights which shone from it. 'There are several cottages on the estate, all of which are tenanted. And this one in particular...' – she paused to point straight ahead – 'used to be the home of a woman called Annie Robertson. Annie virtually brought us up after our mum died. She also used to be housekeeper to the estate.'

'But I still don't understand,' said Fran.

'It's easy, once you get your bearings, and realise that the woodland behind Justice House butts up to the rear garden of Annie's cottage. We used to come here all the time.'

And suddenly Fran understood how Cate and her siblings could have roamed far and wide as the children of a man who was often away, or often preoccupied by his one all-consuming passion: his work. No doubt Annie took pity on them, the poor motherless children...

They fell silent as they passed the cottage, walking in single file as Cate led them along a path which bordered its garden. Beyond was the rear of Justice House. All Fran could think about was how much trouble they were in. Any moment now, if they weren't there already, the police would be arriving at Attingham. And, as their investigations got underway, one of the things they were sure to do was interview the people who lived at the lodge house, to ask them if they had seen anything suspicious. It was the point at which they would notice two seemingly abandoned cars that worried her the most. Because a simple check of the registration numbers would tell the police who owned them, and once Nell had that information, Fran could only imagine what the detective would be thinking.

She was also incredibly aware how vulnerable they were, essentially subject to Cate's every whim. She could be leading them on a wild goose chase for all Fran knew, but for now it was a risk they had to take. Too much about this whole situation didn't stack up and she had no idea who was really telling the truth.

Fran had only met Cate once before the family dinner, and although her first impression hadn't been favourable, it was also true that, whatever their relationship, Cate's father had just died and it was an extremely stressful situation. But beyond that first impression, everything Fran had been told about Cate, and Marcus too, had come from Olivia. Was that part of her plan all along? Had she simply manipulated them into thinking a certain way so they would jump at the opportunity to help her? Fran would have no reason to distrust her – after all, they'd been the best of friends.

Justice House lay in darkness, so if anyone was there then they weren't broadcasting the fact. If Cate was worried that someone might be lying in wait for them, however, she gave no sign of it, walking straight up through the gardens to the back door.

Letting herself in, she held the door wide. 'Here we are again,' she said. 'The very appropriately named Justice House.'

It sent a chill down Fran's spine.

Once inside, Cate flicked on the light, moving quickly into the hallway, where she turned on another to illuminate the central dining hall. Fran and Adam looked at each other, puzzled.

'I'm fed up with all this skulking around,' said Cate, reappearing momentarily with a crystal decanter which normally sat on the dining table. 'If someone wants to come and have a chat, then bring it on. Plus, I'd really rather not have Olivia sneak up on me.' She gave Fran a tight smile. 'I hope you agree it's all better out in the open.' She took a glass from the cupboard and poured herself a generous measure of brandy before throwing it back in one go.

Fran didn't know what to think, but relief was flooding through her. Never mind the brandy, just to be somewhere warm and light with food and drink was enough for now. It was nearly midnight and she was bone-tired.

Cate was watching her. 'I know how you feel,' she said. 'So first things first. Let's get cleaned up a bit, and then we can have something warm to drink. I'm bloody starving too.'

'I'll put the kettle on, shall I?' said Fran, wondering how much brandy Cate was planning on drinking.

Cate nodded and crossed to the sink, where she stripped off her coat and dumped it on the side. She rolled up her sleeves and began to wash her hands, wincing as the water flowed over them. 'My hands are cut to pieces from the brambles,' she said. 'And you've got a gash down your cheek, Fran.'

Fran touched a tentative finger to it. It was beginning to sting now they were in the warm. She pulled off her gloves, inspecting her hands. 'I fell,' she said. 'Tripped on a root. That's when we found...' She grimaced. 'Sorry.'

Cate dried her hands on a tea towel. 'They will find him,

won't they?' she asked, tears suddenly swimming at the corners of her eyes. 'I can't bear the thought of him being out there, all alone.'

'I'm sure they will. Saul said he told the police where Marcus was.'

Cate sniffed, looking around the kitchen, blinking furiously as she tried to get her emotions under control. 'I'll have a look at your cut, if you like,' she said. 'Clean it up at least. There's a first aid box in the cupboard behind you.'

Fran took it down, turning to Adam. 'Are *you* okay?' she asked.

He nodded, although he was still shivering. 'I could murder a piece of cake.'

Fran smiled at him, knowing that she looked equally tired, dirty and frightened. 'I'll find you something, don't worry.'

'We should get a move on though,' said Cate. 'Sorry, only I'm not sure how much time...' She didn't want to finish the rest.

'I know, and I can sort myself out, don't worry,' said Fran. 'Why don't you two make a start trying to figure out the significance of the memorial and I'll make some drinks and see what there is to eat.'

'Good idea,' said Adam.

Fran knew he would feel better when he was doing something.

Ten minutes later, she joined them in Clarence's Inventing Room. Someone had lit the fire and the heat was delicious. She had begun to feel as if she would never be warm again. Cate was poring over some books on one of the many sets of shelves, while Adam was looking at a display of models in a glass cabinet. She set down the tray she was carrying and crossed over to him.

'What are those?' she asked.

'Some of the characters from Dungeons of Doom,' he replied. He pointed at one which was much taller than the others, dressed in flowing green robes. 'This is Almeric,' he said. 'The mage from Aquila. And you couldn't buy him for love nor money at one stage. Every birthday, every Christmas I asked, but I never got him.'

'We need to find any references to the memorial,' said Cate. 'I'm sure I've seen something similar but I can't think where.'

Fran crossed to the bookcase closest to her. 'There are some local history books here. Some of them might have information about Attingham.'

'Good idea. I think Dad used them for research. He changed the place names, of course, but he always said the geography around here was perfect for his stories.'

Adam whirled around. 'You mean, the settings he used are real?'

Cate nodded at his astonishment. 'Didn't you know? He made some of them up, some of the earlier ones I think, but after that he started using actual locations. He said he liked to walk around the settings in his mind as he wrote and obviously that was far easier if he knew the place. That was his genius, though, that he could make them sound so otherworldly.'

'I never knew...' Adam looked at Fran, grief written across his face.

'You can still visit,' she said. 'Now you know they're real places, you can go any time. Just as long as we work out which book was set where.'

Adam crossed to her side, fired up with excitement. He had a mission now. He took down an armful of books and carried them to a chair beside the fire, all thoughts of cake forgotten.

Fran did likewise, taking her set to the desk where she imagined Clarence had once sat. First things first, however. She carried a mug and a generous slice of cake to the small table beside Adam. Putting them down with a smile, she touched a hand to his shoulder.

'Eat,' she said.

He nodded, but Adam's eye had already been caught by something in the depths of the book he was reading.

Returning to her own pile, she sat for a moment warming her hands around her mug. She still couldn't get the vague feeling out of her head that she'd seen something familiar at Attingham but, whatever it was, it was proving rather elusive. Perhaps something in one of the books would spring the trap door in her memory.

The first couple she looked at hardly gave Attingham a mention at all, but the third, produced by the National Trust itself, looked far more promising. Its focus was the history of the gardens, and in particular the walled garden which had been subject to recent renovation. When it was first created, in the 1780s, it provided fresh produce for the whole house but, after a variety of uses, became neglected and fell into disrepair. It was interesting, but not what Fran was looking for, and after flipping through the pages she moved on.

They worked steadily for some time, the room falling silent as they lost themselves in the hunt for information. At one point, Fran left the room, returning with a pile of sandwiches and the remains of the trifle, which she had to practically force everyone to eat, even Adam. The urge to continue was just too great – one more page, one more book, an almost feverish excitement growing the longer the search went on. Fran felt it as well, but it was now gone two in the morning and tiredness and hunger would help no one: they needed a break.

Partially fortified, they carried on, the hands on the clock driving them forward.

'There's just too much to look through,' remarked Cate from the other side of the room. 'I never paid enough attention to the titles of his books when I was a child. I wish I had now. But the stories he wrote down were just some of those he told us and in my head they all became jumbled. I can't remember which ones went in which books.' She sighed. 'And in many ways it was his drawings I loved the most. All those maps of imaginary worlds, full of exotic-sounding places, and funny little villages.'

She brought the book she was holding across so that they could see it, laying it on the desk. It was one of the fully illustrated versions, the colours still bright after all this time. 'I think maybe I loved the maps because once the world had been created, I recognised that any number of stories could exist within it, not just the one that Dad chose to tell. I used to make up my own when I was little.' She smiled wistfully.

Adam returned it. 'It must have been incredible watching them come to life on paper,' he said, getting up to have a better look.

Cate nodded. 'He always had a huge sketchpad on the desk here. And sometimes he said the stories came first and he drew the world around them, but sometimes he'd start drawing first, filling the page with detail and, as he did so, his mind would wander through those landscapes and stories simply rose up out of them.'

'It must have been an amazing childhood,' Fran remarked, eyes following a detail on the map.

'It was,' replied Cate, turning back to the bookcase. 'Most of the time.'

Fran shot Adam a look from under her lashes. She knew exactly what he was thinking, and how much he would have given to have a father like Clarence, someone who would have fostered his insatiable curiosity and thirst for knowledge.

She smiled, absentmindedly admiring the scent of lilies which had wafted across from a table in the corner of the room. But then she frowned, something had jogged her memory.

'Cate, can I have a look at that map again for a moment?'

'Yeah, sure.'

Fran could feel Adam watching her as she put out both hands to receive it. There was something... She turned to the page that Cate had just shown them, peering closer at one of the details. It reminded her of something. And with a click of her tongue it came to her.

Pulling her phone from her pocket, she navigated to the internet browser, still showing the map of Attingham's grounds. There was something very familiar about it, and as she compared the two images, she realised what it was.

'What?' asked Adam. 'What have you seen?'

Fran slowly rotated the book. 'I don't know yet, but it just struck me how similar these maps are. The style of them. The way the clumps of trees are drawn, the shading on the grass...' She looked up at Adam's eager face. 'When we were there, by the memorial, I said I had a feeling, didn't I? Something like déjà vu, only not... It was because I was looking at the map as a whole, showing the grounds of the park laid out in exactly the same way as Clarence used to draw his maps. That's what it reminded me of, his maps...' She carried on rotating the book, laying her phone on the desk so that she could compare the images side by side. But no matter which way she spun it, the two images were obviously different. She wrinkled her nose at Adam. 'Never mind, it was just a thought.'

'No, wait...' said Adam. 'It's a good thought. Cate, you said that Clarence often drew on real-life locations to provide the settings for his stories. So what if one of those was Attingham? We have all his other books here – all we need to do is find the one where the maps match. It won't be exactly the same, Clarence probably changed some of the details, but if it was the memorial which jogged that photographic memory of yours, Fran, in all likelihood, we're looking for a book with a similar feature.'

Excitement rippled through Fran as Adam shook his head in disbelief.

'I can't believe I missed that.' He looked quite disgusted with himself.

'It's context, that's all,' said Fran.

Cate was already at the bookcase, pulling volumes from it and stacking them on the floor. 'It could be any of these,' she said. 'Quickly, help me look.'

Fran and Adam joined her, kneeling on the floor with Fran's phone between them so they could compare images. Heart beating fast, Fran picked up the first book from the stack and began to check through it. At last they seemed to be getting somewhere.

Except that, as the pile of discarded books grew bigger, and those left to sort through smaller, she could feel her excitement slowing ebbing away. She'd been so certain they would find it immediately and yet... Fran watched carefully as Cate picked up the final book.

Elation turned to disappointment as she put it down.

'That's it,' Cate said. 'Did we miss it?'

'Maybe if we go through them again,' said Fran. 'And don't forget to turn the images in Clarence's books, the orientation may not be the same as in the map of Attingham.'

They went more slowly this time. Turning each page one by one, determined that they shouldn't miss a single detail in case it was the one they needed. But once again, it seemed they were out of luck. Cate threw down the last book in her pile in disgust, making Adam wince. He picked it up and smoothed down the dust jacket, looking at the spine. 'Maybe there are more of his books somewhere else. Are we sure we've got them all?'

'There were over thirty of them,' said Cate, beginning to count. 'I think so.'

Fran got to her feet. 'I'll start looking somewhere else.'

She crossed over to the shelves on the other wall, lifting the games and magazines she found there in case a book was nestling beneath. But there was nothing. She turned, scanning the room, her eyes narrowing as they lit on the desk. A sudden thought occurred to her. If Clarence had used one of his books as inspiration for the final treasure-hunt clue, then perhaps it was still close at hand.

She began to pull open drawers, to move papers and lift notebooks, pushing aside pens and balls of string, pots of paper-clips and old letters. She peered at one of the envelopes; fan mail most likely. And lastly, lifting a sheaf of blank paper, she found it, a copy of *The Castle of Secrets*.

'Here,' she said, plonking it on the desk. Her fingers were trembling as she opened it.

'I remember this story,' said Adam. 'They're searching for the lost Diadems of Isabeau and Nicholas finds one, set into the belt on a statue of... someone or other, I can't remember, but it's not important. It's the diadems which are, because...' His brow furrowed as he searched his memory. 'The brothers have to take them somewhere.' He took the book from Fran, flipping through the pages. 'But I can't remember where.' He looked at her for help.

She screwed up her face. 'I vaguely remember it, but not the detail, sorry.'

Adam's finger stopped on one of the pages. 'Yes! That's it. The lost Diadems of Isabeau. The village in the story was cursed when the diadems were removed from their resting place and the brothers had to return them to a hill which overlooked the village. There was a statue there.' He stared at Fran, suddenly looking bereft. 'But I have no idea what any of that means,' he said. 'What's the answer to the clue? The village? The hill above the village?'

'It has to be,' said Cate. 'But where's the village?' She stared at them in horror. 'It could be anywhere.'

'No, we need to keep looking,' said Adam. 'There'll be another map, one that shows the next part of the story, the journey the brothers have to make.' He turned the pages, eyes scanning the text, studying each illustration for clues, and he was almost at the end before he looked up again, eyes wide. 'This is it,' he said. 'Look... that's where we have to go.'

And there it was. Another map showing the location of the village with the contours of the mountain beyond, surrounded by a patchwork of fields, hedges and ditches, with groups of houses dotted here and there.

Fran looked to where Adam's finger was pointing. At the craggy rocks on top of the mountain where, carved into the rock, a statue had stood for countless years keeping watch over the village below. That is, until someone saw fit to remove the precious gems which gave the statue its eyes, and in doing so brought down a curse upon the village.

'But where is *there*?' she asked. 'In real life, I mean.'

Adam groaned. 'We're so close,' he said. 'Yet every time I think we get there, there's another step to take.'

'This is it,' said Cate. 'I know it. It all fits, don't you see? The lost diadems... and now we're on a treasure hunt too. That we should be going to their final resting place makes perfect sense.' She turned around, grimacing. 'The solution has to be here somewhere.'

'Then we search it all,' said Adam. 'Every book, every game, every magazine, until we find something.'

Fran glanced again at the books which were still on the desk but as she looked up, something else caught her eye. The desk drawer was still open and sticking out from under the sheaf of paper was something silver, something metallic. She lifted it out.

'Adam... here a sec?' She ran her fingers over the shiny surface, thinking.

'What've you got?' he asked, as Cate began frantically searching the bookshelves again. 'A laptop, obviously, I can see that, but...'

'Hmm,' said Fran, shooting Cate a glance. 'Only not

Clarence's, I would have thought. He wrote everything by hand, didn't he? So if not Clarence's, then Olivia's perhaps?'

'I'll get you in,' he said, nodding as he gave Cate a surreptitious look. 'Then you have a look, okay?'

He knelt beside the desk, opening the laptop and switching it on. With any luck it would still have some charge. She watched while the home screen loaded, knowing that the moment it did, Adam's fingers would fly into action. She didn't understand half of what he did with computers, and seeing as some of it verged on being illegal, it was probably just as well.

A couple of minutes later, Adam gave a triumphant smile and swung the laptop round to her. 'See what you can find,' he murmured. 'I'll carry on looking with Cate.'

Fran nodded, pausing slightly as she realised what she was about to do. She whispered an apology to Olivia under her breath and clicked to open her emails.

She wasn't entirely sure what she'd been expecting to find but, at the very least, exchanges with Margaret regarding the funeral arrangements. Perhaps even the email she sent to Fran enquiring about her services. Anything which gave Fran definitive proof that what Cate had said about Olivia couldn't possibly be true. But there was nothing like that at all, just what looked like a load of spammy messages from various companies. And there were no emails at all in the 'sent' folder.

Fran pursed her lips. Was that suspicious or not? She couldn't decide. But, then again, who had their default email account set to one they didn't actually seem to use? Narrowing her eyes, she opened up Olivia's internet browser, hoping she might still have some tabs open for the recent sites she'd visited. Failing that, a little check on her browser history might tell Fran something. But, as the program opened, Fran knew she wasn't about to have much luck. A single tab appeared; the home page of the browser. It was as anonymous as they come. There was no history either.

Fran thought for a moment. Okay, that didn't necessarily mean anything. She had an iPad and a laptop, both of which she used for her work, but she rarely surfed the net on either. Her phone was much handier, and generally quicker. Maybe Olivia simply did the same. But there was one last place she could check for information. And that was *very* interesting.

All the sites which Olivia had bookmarked were very curious. Very curious indeed. Fran clicked through to one or two of the pages, reading briefly before selecting another. Something was suddenly becoming much clearer.

Leaving the internet tabs open, Fran navigated to the documents folder and double-clicked. An array of subfolders opened in front of her. Each was given a simple number to identify it: one, two, three, four and so on. She clicked to open the first.

Inside was a series of documents, the kind of things that a historian might collect before starting to write: photographs, scanned articles, some handwritten notes saved as PDFs. All of which related to Clarence. Subsequent folders revealed more of the same, each pertaining to a different period of Clarence's life. From childhood, to when he began writing, got married, had children, won awards, launched games...

Olivia had been writing Clarence's biography.

Except that hadn't been all she was doing. Because another set of folders, equally vague in their file-naming conventions, revealed further documents of a far more specific nature.

Fran read on, her mouth growing drier with every document she opened. Olivia hadn't just been working on a biography of Clarence, she had also been working on a companion volume. One which introduced readers to the landscapes created by Ebenezer Doolittle. His wonderful illustrations, all gathered together in one volume, alongside explanations of why he had chosen those settings, what they meant to him, and where, if any, were their real-life counterparts. And alongside each of the explanations were a series of photos, taken recently, and by Olivia.

She had lied. Olivia had said she'd never been to Attingham Park, just like she had said she didn't know any of the other locations they'd been to, but she'd not only been to them, she'd written copious pages about them and taken photographs too.

Fran swallowed, fear stirring the hairs on the back of her neck.

'Adam,' she whispered, 'you need to see this.'

20

'I'm just going to get another drink, Cate,' she announced. 'Would you like anything?'

An airy arm waved a reply. 'No, ta, I'm fine.' She scarcely even looked up, still frantically searching through the local history books.

Motioning for Adam to follow her, Fran left the room, the laptop tucked nonchalantly under her arm. The moment they were alone in the kitchen, however, she opened it back up to show Adam what she had discovered.

Adam read silently, his mouth moving slightly as he did so.

'Well, at least we know the location of the final clue,' he said, but his eyes were sad as he looked up at her. 'I'm so sorry, Fran.'

'I thought I was a better judge of character than that,' she said. 'But seemingly not.' She silently closed the laptop lid and laid it on the work surface.

The first aid box was still where she had left it and she automatically tidied it away, not trusting herself to say anything. She was perilously close to tears. She wiped the work surfaces too, pausing when she got to the fridge. There was still a large quantity of trifle in there and right now she could lay waste to it in one fell swoop. How could she have been so blind? So stupid?

'I believed every single thing Olivia told me,' she said. 'Swallowed her story whole. What an idiot.'

Adam looked uncomfortable. 'But, Fran, why wouldn't you believe her? You had no reason not to.' He gave her a pointed look. 'So don't you dare start blaming yourself for any of this. It's one of the things I've always admired about you, you know.'

She looked askance. 'What is?'

'The fact that your first instinct is always to believe the best in people, always to help. I grew up thinking people were best avoided, and definitely not to be trusted.'

'Adam, our backgrounds are very different, that's all. You were let down by people you thought you *could* trust, whom you should have been able to trust. That's all this is.'

But Adam shook his head. 'I get that. And it is what it is. I can't change my history any more than you can, but the present, that is something we can change. I'm learning that things don't have to be the way I think they'll be, because you've shown me another side to people, another side to situations. You understand folk in a way I could never hope to. Mostly, I just think they're mad as a box of frogs.'

Fran darted a look out towards the hallway. 'In this case I think you might be right. So all that time when we were trying to figure out the first clue, when you were sneaking about at night trying to find the fountain, the what3words location, Olivia must have known exactly where we were heading. She knew how Clarence's mind worked. If he transposed real-life locations for those in his books then it was a pretty safe bet that when it came to hiding his treasure-hunt clues, he would turn to exactly those same places. Places which Olivia had an intimate knowledge of. It won't have taken much for her to work out the clues and—'

She stopped dead, eyes wide as she stared at Adam.

'Dear God... How far does this go? Did she just manipulate the old man into setting up a treasure hunt? Or did she actually go so far as to set up the *whole* thing, devising all the puzzles, laying out all the clues? We even considered the possibility that Clarence had help, too right he did.'

Adam looked puzzled. Which in Fran's experience wasn't always a good thing. He gave her a cautious look.

'That could be right...' he said. 'Which is bad enough. Except... For Olivia to do that she must have had Clarence's blessing. He had to know about it. So if the whole thing was rigged so she would be the winner, why bother with the charade at all? Why not simply make Olivia the sole beneficiary of his will in the first place? There's something about all this that doesn't stack up.'

'Yes, but if you go back to where this all started, to Clarence's will, his reasons for setting the treasure hunt were very specific. Even if he wanted Olivia to win, he still wanted the others to play, he was very determined to give them one last chance to reconcile. That doesn't change, even if Olivia had a hand in setting the hunt. And I don't believe there was anything untoward about the will, because Margaret met with Clarence on several occasions to discuss its details. It was her responsibility to ensure that everything he wanted was watertight from a legal point of view.' She frowned. 'You're not suggesting that Margaret had anything to do with this, are you?'

Adam shook his head. 'No, I just think we have to go back even further than the will, to Clarence's death itself.'

'I know... And I can't get over the fact that it might have been deliberate. But it was Margaret who was told to suspect foul play if he had a heart attack. It wasn't Olivia—' She broke off. 'Ah... there I go again, repeating what Olivia told me. This *is* where it all starts, isn't it? With Clarence's death.'

Adam's expression was grim. 'I think the question we have to ask ourselves is whether we believe that the doubts Clarence expressed were original thoughts... Or whether they'd been put there by someone else.'

'By Olivia?' Fran hung her head. 'But why would she do that if she was planning to kill him and walk off with his inheritance?'

'Because if she wasn't careful she was going to look like the prime suspect, so she needed a way to make herself look innocent. It would have been easy for Olivia to plant the suggestion in Clarence's head that his children might be capable of doing him harm. His relationship with them had broken down while his relationship with Olivia was quite the reverse, and he trusted her, implicitly. A chance remark from Olivia, therefore, however flippant it may have seemed, would have found its mark and, with some careful manipulation, the seed she planted could have flourished. But knowing how much he still wanted to be reconciled with his family, she could have then gone on to suggest a birthday party and a treasure hunt, one last chance for them all to be reunited. Clarence would have jumped at the opportunity.'

Fran was still puzzled. 'But I still don't get how that makes her guilty of Clarence's death. Why would she kill him when there was absolutely no guarantee she would win the treasure hunt?'

'No absolute guarantee, no, but a pretty good chance nonetheless, especially if you could also take out some of the other players...' Adam ran a hand over his face. 'Olivia had to be clever. She had to make Clarence's death look as plausible as possible. After all, what use is an inheritance if you're in prison convicted of murder? Best-case scenario, it had to appear as if he died from natural causes, but if there was any suspicion at all that someone else was responsible, she needed a fall-back plan. And for that she needed an audience, which is where you come in.'

Adam's eyes narrowed as he paused a moment, thinking.

'So... she's done as much as she can to remove herself from the circumstances of Clarence's death. She's made sure she isn't the outright beneficiary of his will, which would make her the prime suspect if his death was ruled as suspicious. She's planted a suggestion in Clarence's head that one of his family was responsible, a suggestion which found its way to Margaret, and then she gets you on side, agreeing that any suggestion of murder is a crazy idea, but if it isn't, that one of his children was responsible. Then, she starts playing the treasure hunt just the same as everyone else. Except that she isn't the same, because she's stacked the odds in her favour. She not only knows the probable locations, but she's also drafted in two friends, one of whom would vouch for her every action, while the other has an aptitude for solving puzzles.'

Fran held his look for a moment, but there was very little she could say. Adam's deductions made perfect sense, but she could see how reluctant he'd been to reach them. It took her a moment to find her voice.

'She even told me herself, when we were talking about the hunt, that she was no good at brain-teasers and had more of a tactical mind. That's it, isn't it? She's been playing the long game, just like in the games of chess she played with Clarence.' She paused a moment, feeling her heart sink even further. 'I just can't get my head around why Olivia would even do all of this. Is it just the money?'

'Unfortunately, that's all it takes sometimes, as well we know. I guess for some people enough is never enough. We were involved in a case only a few months ago which proved that theory conclusively.'

Fran sighed. 'And there was me feeling bad for her because she's just lost her job and her home. Except that she hasn't even lost her job, has she? She's a writer, and she's clearly been putting her skills to good use. Judging by the amount of research she's done and the notes she's written, she's been working on

Clarence's biography for quite some time. That has to have been with his blessing. The companion book too. Adam, you of all people know how popular he was, and still is. Olivia could have a bestseller on her hands, particularly now that he's dead.' She shook her head in disgust. 'Clarence has handed her future to her on a plate, in more ways than one.'

Adam nodded. 'I think you're probably right.'

'But she seemed so upset over Clarence's death, so genuinely fond of him. That's what I don't understand.'

'Some people are incredibly good actors.'

Fran looked at him, realising the truth in his words. 'Or they live a lie so long it becomes the only truth they know.' She inhaled a deep breath. 'So what do we do now?'

'There's only one thing we can do, and that's see this thing to its conclusion. You might not want to bring Olivia to justice, Fran, but you will, because it's the right thing to do.'

'Justice House...' she said. 'How bloody ironic is that.'

Adam's brow furrowed. 'Yes, isn't it?'

'Okay,' said Fran. 'So we go and tell Cate that we know the location of the last clue, and then what? Because something else has just occurred to me: Where are Saul and Olivia?'

'Probably standing on top of Caer Caradoc as we speak,' replied Adam. 'Saul obviously worked out the meaning of the memorial clue while he was at Attingham. That's what he meant when he said the clue is the clue. And if he remembered the story of the lost diadem, then all he had to do is come up with a location. He grew up around here, Fran, he has just as good a knowledge of the local area as we do.'

Fran paled. 'Then he's walking into a whole heap of trouble,' she said. 'Because Saul doesn't suspect Olivia, does he? He thinks Cate killed Marcus. He thinks she's the one he needs to stop. And he's going to think that all the way to the top of that hill, because he thinks that's where Cate's already gone. He doesn't realise that in all likelihood Olivia will already be there.

And I don't want to think about what she might do when she realises that Saul might be about to claim the prize.'

Adam nodded, swallowing.

She held his look for a moment and then nodded towards the door. 'Right, come on then. Let's go do this.'

She'd taken two steps when Adam touched her arm.

'Fran... let's not tell Cate what we've seen on Olivia's laptop.'

Her brow furrowed. 'Why not?'

'I don't know... humour me. I simply want to keep what information we have to ourselves, for the time being at least. Cate knows we suspect Olivia, so essentially nothing has changed. I don't think we need to tell her, that's all.'

Fran's eyes narrowed. 'What are you up to?'

'Nothing,' said Adam blithely. 'Honestly, I'm not. Put it down to my natural cynicism, if you like. I feel happier when the balance of knowledge is tipped in our favour, that's all.'

Fran stared at him, pursing her lips. The seconds ticked by. 'Okay,' she said. 'Let's go.'

It took no time at all to convince Cate that Adam had simply had a eureka moment while in the kitchen with Fran.

'I don't know why I didn't think about it straight away,' he said. 'Caer Caradoc is one of the most famous landmarks around here. It has to be that. And the setting all fits – the layout of it, the location of the village in relation to the hill, the fact that it has an iron-age hill fort on the top. Substitute that with a statue which has diadems for eyes and you're right there.'

Cate nodded. 'Of course... I went up there countless times as a child.'

Fran was already searching through the local history books for proof, and it was easy to find. 'Look,' she said, holding open a double-page spread for them to see. 'There are countless aerial photos taken of the summit, in almost every book, and the similarities to Clarence's map are obvious to see. Clarence has even used the lines of the old fortifications.'

Cate's eyes lit up, every trace of her tiredness gone. 'We need to get a move on. Quickly, grab what we need.'

Fran cast about her, picking up her phone. Her gloves and coat were still in the kitchen where she'd left them and... She suddenly realised that Adam hadn't moved.

'What?' she asked, eyebrows raised.

'There's just one problem,' he said, turning to stare pointedly out the window. At the still-black night outside.

Fran could cry. All of this and now they were scuppered at the final moment.

Cate checked her watch. 'It will be light in just over an hour. We have to go. We can't risk wasting any more time.' Her voice had taken on a pleading tone as she looked first at Adam and then at Fran.

'I don't know,' said Adam. 'Going up there in the dark is asking for trouble. It's too dangerous.'

Fran pulled a face. 'Adam's right,' she added. 'Even in the daylight, it's a hard enough climb. There are paths... but not nice, neat gravelled things which are easy to follow, we're talking trails, and rough ones at that. It will be almost impossible to see where we're going. I don't think even Olivia would have been daft enough to go up by herself.'

Cate looked as if she were about to cry. 'Please,' she begged. 'We can't let Olivia get away with what she's done. I don't even care about the money any more, but Marcus and Dad—' She broke off, sudden tears spilling down her face. 'Oh God... Where's Saul?'

'We don't know,' said Adam. 'But we think he might be on his way up there too.'

'Then we have to find her!'

Fran gave Adam an uneasy look. 'Listen, Cate, the truth is

that Olivia is probably way ahead of us,' she said gently. 'She could be long gone by now.'

'Yes, but we don't know that. It might have taken her just as long to work out the final location. We have to try. It's the only place we know for certain she might be. She's tricked everyone. She's going to claim the inheritance for herself and pin Marcus's murder on me, I know it.'

Fran dropped her head.

'I'm right, aren't I?' demanded Cate. 'That's what she told you, isn't it? Yeah, I bet she did,' she added, her lips a thin hard line. She took several steps forward. 'Please, can we go now?'

Fran nodded, stealing a look at Adam. There was no possible reply other than to agree. And time was running out.

'Yes,' she said. 'Come on.'

Caer Caradoc was only twenty minutes away by car, but that was by far the easiest part. Because the site of the old hill fort was, not surprisingly, on the summit, and the only way to get there was on foot. Uphill. All the way.

Fran had only done it once, when Martha had been much younger and she had stupidly volunteered to accompany her on a primary-school trip. Her impression then had been that everyone else seemed to be far fitter than she was, or perhaps they were just better at hiding it. Fran was cursed with a complexion that turned bright red the moment she did any exercise. Today, however, what she looked like would be the least of her worries.

Cate was the first from the car, climbing out before Adam had even switched off the ignition. She would have left them standing if Fran hadn't stopped her.

'We go together,' she said, her hand on Cate's arm. 'It's safer that way.' It wasn't just the terrain that was worrying her.

The cloudy sky of the earlier part of the night had given

way to an inky blackness, studded with stars. Dawn was still over half an hour away by the time they arrived. Once their eyes were accustomed to the gloom, however, it was much easier to see than Fran had feared. The trail was well signposted and moments later they set off without a word. As expected, Cate took the lead, setting a cracking pace which threatened to leave both Fran and Adam behind. Fran understood the need to get to the summit as quickly as possible, but they had no idea what they were walking into. If Olivia was already there, then finding the final clue would be the last thing on their minds.

Half an hour later, the three of them had strung out into a line, with Fran bringing up the rear. To her left, lights glittered from the town below – houses filled with ordinary people, safe and secure in their ordinary lives, comfortable in warm beds, snuggled against partners or dogs or cats. She had sometimes wished for a life less ordinary but, right now, she'd trade places with them in a heartbeat.

Up ahead, Adam had slowed to a stop and she renewed her efforts.

'Adam, my legs are virtually half the length of yours,' she complained as she reached him, puffing visibly in the cold morning air. She motioned ahead. 'You go on, and I'll just follow as best I can.'

'How much further is it?'

'Just keep going,' she replied, trying to draw breath.

The summit was blind. That was the worst thing about it. They were following a ridge on a seemingly never-ending upward trajectory, and ahead lay only sky. They would have to almost reach the top before a final crest revealed a sudden expanse of land which fell away on all sides. She remembered how it had taken her by surprise before. With any luck it would be the only thing which would.

Her eyes followed a car on the road below, its headlights tracing a path through the dark. A second later it was lit by a blue flashing light and she shivered. Someone else was in trouble too. She gritted her teeth and pushed her thigh muscles onwards. She would get there, she had to.

It took another fifteen minutes or so before she finally stumbled over the last ridge, chest heaving and exhausted. Blinking, she took in the thin molten line of the dawn, a bright band of orange just grazing the horizon. Above it a strip of milky pearlescence faded back to the dark purple haze of the night.

In front of her Cate had also drawn to a halt. 'Is this it?' she asked, gazing around her. 'Are we even at the top?'

The annoyance in her voice was plain and Fran had a feeling that the wild and windswept hills were not Cate's natural habitat either. In fact... Fran frowned. Now that she thought about it, it did seem a very odd choice for the final clue. On the one hand, it made perfect sense, given that its location mirrored the one in Clarence's book, but clearly Clarence wouldn't have been able to put the clue up here by himself, so who had? Which brought her back to Olivia, who they had already decided hadn't actually engineered the hunt at all... None of it made sense. She was about to ask Adam the question when he spoke.

'It's over there,' he said, pointing to a pile of stones atop another rocky outcrop. 'There's no trig point, but that's always been regarded as the summit.' His heavy breaths appeared as puffs of white in the dim light. He was standing a little way from her, or rather bent over, hands on his knees. Despite his age, the early-morning hill climb had obviously taken its toll on him too.

Cate wasted no time. 'Quickly, help me look. What are we even looking for? Another film canister or...? I don't even know if this is the right place. Perhaps we should be searching in the remains of the fort, wouldn't that be more akin to the location Dad used in his book?' She stared as neither one of them moved. 'What? Come on, we're wasting time.'

Fran stepped forward. 'Cate... there's no one here.'

'Yes, *and*? I'm not going to worry about something I don't have to.'

'But we were so convinced that Olivia would be up here, possibly Saul too.' Fran turned in a circle. 'So where are they?'

'I don't bloody care,' replied Cate. 'I need this last clue, I can deal with Olivia later. Or the police can. If she's not here then it's a bonus as far as I'm concerned.'

Fran looked anxiously at Adam before giving Cate a soft smile. 'Do you not think we might be wasting our time? There was no sign of them on the way up, and there's obviously no one here now. Olivia was way ahead of us, Cate. I'm sorry, but I think she's beaten you to it.'

Cate's face was grim. 'She may have, but she's a lying, cheating... She's a murderer, for God's sake, and she's not getting her hands on my money... I mean, it's family money, it's...' She trailed off, hands on her hips. 'Well, I'm going to look even if you aren't. I reckon it must be hidden in the remains of the fort.' She ran over to the jumble of rocks and began to climb them, stumbling as her feet slipped on the uneven surface.

Fran and Adam joined her, there wasn't much else they could do and there *was* a chance that Olivia hadn't got here yet. Anything could have happened. She could have run into Saul and he could have worked out what happened, maybe tried to apprehend her... It didn't bear thinking about.

'I'm pretty certain we'll be looking for another canister,' said Adam, eyes on the ground. 'Something that would withstand the elements up here at least. Look for something it could be secured to as well, or hidden under, it wouldn't be out in the open where anyone could have picked it up.'

From behind them a throat cleared.

'Hi,' said Olivia. 'Are you looking for this?'

21

Fran stared at the figure in front of her, wondering how Olivia had managed to appear without anyone noticing her; so silently, and with a degree of stealth which made Fran very uneasy. There'd been no one in sight and yet...

The truth of it was that the area was filled with grassy knolls and it was conceivable that Olivia could have hidden behind any one of them, unseen, as she lay in wait... Fran shivered.

With the brightening dawn behind her, streaks of orange radiating out from behind her head, Olivia's face was in shadow. Fran couldn't see her expression, but then she didn't need to, the sky and Olivia's stance were working well enough together to fuel Fran's imagination. Avenging angel – the description popped into her head before she could stop it. But what was Olivia here to avenge? Fran shook her head. It was quite possible she was delirious. Or had been reading too many of Clarence's books.

Olivia was still holding something aloft, and, as the light caught one side of it, Fran could see it was a cylindrical container, long and thin, one end tapered to a point.

'Sorry, Cate,' Olivia said. 'You're too late. I win.'

'No, you haven't, you'll never win,' snarled Cate. 'Who cares if you got here first? When I tell everyone what you've done, there's no way you'll inherit.'

Olivia gave a tight smile. 'Maybe I won't, but then this was never about the money for me. For you on the other hand... Isn't that right, Cate? And the lengths you've gone to ensure all that lovely money ends up in your bank account. There's quite a list: lying, cheating, bashing people over the head, tying them up... oh and murder, best not forget that one.'

Cate took a step forward. 'Give me that!' she hissed. 'That clue is mine. I'm Clarence's daughter. You're nothing. Hired help, that's all. Do you really think it's fair that you should inherit right under our noses?'

'Stop trying to change the subject. You're not getting the clue, Cate, and that's all there is to it. So could we just get back to the subject of murder for a minute, I—'

Cate's face twisted with hatred. 'You're accusing *me*?' she said. 'What about you? It's the oldest ploy there is, Olivia. Middle-aged woman befriends vulnerable old man, whispers lies in his ear, insinuates her way into his life, bumps him off and then robs his family of his fortune. I'd say the lengths you've gone to are pretty extraordinary, but then—'

'I wasn't actually talking about Clarence,' said Olivia smoothly. 'I was talking about Marcus. But that's very interesting, that you think Clarence's death wasn't natural. Thanks for bringing that up. Maybe we should have a chat about it.' Her eyes were locked on Cate's.

Fran's head had been whipping back and forth between the two of them as if she were watching a tennis match. 'Just shut up!' she yelled. 'Both of you.' She took a deep breath. 'Will someone please tell me what on earth is going on here?'

Olivia's face lit with a soft smile. 'Hi, Fran,' she said. 'And Adam... I'm so sorry I had to drag you into all of this, but things will become clear, I promise. Please, just bear with me.'

Fran shot a glance at Adam but his face was unreadable. She had no idea what he was thinking. 'Why should I believe anything you say?' she replied. 'When it looks as if you've killed two people.'

Olivia's face grew sombre. 'I know that's what it looks like, but I promise you that isn't the truth, Fran. It's just the version of it that Cate wants you to believe.'

Fran was indignant. 'Well, I've been taken in by one of you. And I used to think I was a pretty good judge of character.'

'But you are, Fran, you really are,' said Olivia. 'You just need to trust your instincts. As a child you always had everyone sussed – the good guys and the bad guys – but, more importantly, the bad guys who were trying to look like good guys. We were the best of friends and, right now, I know I'm asking the impossible, but you have to trust me. You always did do the right thing, whatever the cost.'

Fran swallowed. How could she possibly know what was right? Of course Olivia would play on their friendship, using it to sway her judgement. And if Olivia was guilty of what they thought, then why should she care about betraying their friendship? It was just another in the long line of crimes which Olivia had committed. And yet... She *did* want to trust Olivia. Underneath it all, she knew she did. But who did she listen to? Olivia or Cate? She needed to think clearly. To calmly and rationally run through everything that had happened, because the clues were there, they always were.

'Don't believe a word she says, Fran,' said Cate. 'She's trying to trick you, just like she has all along.' Cate's retaliation was fierce. 'You know what happened back in the woods. You'd still be there if it wasn't for me. She'd have left you, tied up, for God knows how long. You're lucky you're still alive.'

Fran frowned. 'Actually, Cate, it was Saul who tied us up.'

She turned to look at Adam, who hadn't moved a muscle. His gaze was fixed on Olivia, deep in thought.

'Saul?' Cate faltered.

'Yes, your brother,' said Olivia. 'You know, the other one who was in the running for the inheritance, aside from Marcus, that is. I wonder where he is...?'

Fran looked around her. It was a very good question and a flicker of fear curled around her neck. Was he dead too? Had Olivia done what Fran feared she had?

'It's okay, Saul, you can come out now.' Olivia's raised voice carried clearly across the open space.

She was bluffing, she had to be, but, as Fran watched, peering past Olivia, another figure emerged a little distance away, straightening up from where he'd been hiding. Fran hadn't a clue what was going on.

'You might as well give it up, Cate,' said Saul, coming closer. 'Olivia's right, you're never going to win, so now it's more about what you stand to lose.'

Cate's face was full of confusion. And, for the first time, looking a little less confident. 'What?'

'Olivia has explained everything to me,' he replied.

'And you believe her? Jesus, you always were stupid.' Cate shook her head in disgust. 'There'd have been more money in the pot too, if you hadn't been so greedy all those years ago. Betraying Dad like that. Betraying Marcus and me as well.'

Fran blinked. They were talking about murder and Cate was still harping on about the money. Yet for Fran it hardly seemed as if that mattered any more.

'Not as stupid as you think, actually,' said Saul. 'Or as desperate. And I've already told Fran and Olivia what happened. What you and Marcus did to Dad.'

'What *you* did, you mean. We helped Dad build up his company and then you destroyed it in one fell swoop. Dad only had a fortune in the first place because we helped him build it, yet he cut us off from it without a second thought.'

'That's what this is all about, isn't it?' said Saul. 'It's always been about the money. Money you think you deserve. Money you think you should have now.'

'Dad was in his eighties, for God's sake. He'd had a life, and he was one of those people who was going to go on and on and on... Why shouldn't I have what was coming to me? You certainly didn't deserve it. Not after what you did. I told you what happened, didn't I, Fran?' Cate's head turned from one to the other.

'Your memory of things certainly seems a little different from Saul's,' Fran replied. 'He told me that you and Marcus betrayed your father, leaving him with the prospect of either losing the intellectual rights to one of his bestselling lines or footing an enormous legal bill to break the contract. No choice at all really.' She tipped her head on one side. 'It's funny though, because now we have two people who say your version of events is wrong, Cate.'

'I'm being set up,' she screamed. 'For God's sake, can you not see what's going on? They're in it together. It's obvious.'

'Is it?' said Olivia. She paused. 'Actually, you could well be right. It *is* obvious what's going on. What do you think, Fran?'

Fran searched Olivia's face, wanting so hard to believe she was telling the truth. She didn't know what to say, and before she could open her mouth, Olivia cut back in.

'Well, this is lovely,' she said. 'Talking about the good old days and what awful children you all were, but can we get back to the subject of your dad's death, Cate, seeing as how you very kindly brought it up in the first place.'

'*Again?* When are you going to stop being so utterly ridiculous? How on earth could I have killed him when I haven't been anywhere near the house in years? I live in Kent, for goodness' sake.'

Fran stared at Cate, a scene from the wee small hours of the morning suddenly coming back to her with utter clarity. 'But that's not true, is it?' she said. 'You *have* been to the house. In fact, you know it very well.'

Cate shook her head angrily. 'This is crazy, I don't have to listen to this.'

'Where are you going to go?' asked Olivia, widening her arms to take in the expanse of hillside. 'Go on, Fran.'

Fran marshalled her thoughts. 'You said you hadn't been to the house in years, so the first occasion would have been for your dad's funeral. You paid one very brief visit on the morning I first met with Olivia, and then you didn't return until the day of the funeral itself, on Friday, the same as I did. You were shown to your rooms, went to the funeral and then came back to the house for the dinner. By seven that night, the will had been read and you'd been told about the terms of the inheritance. All three of you later went to the pub.'

'What's that got to do with anything?' demanded Cate.

'Because I was in the kitchen virtually that whole day. And I don't recall seeing you in there except when you were passing through.'

'And?'

'So how did you know where the first aid kit was kept?'

Adam turned to stare at her.

'When we got back from Attingham with you, Cate – cut, bruised, cold and wet – you told me where the first aid kit was. *In the cupboard behind you, Fran,* you said, cool as a cucumber. Didn't even stop to wonder if there was such a thing, or where it might be kept. No, you knew exactly where it was. And the only way you could have known that is if you'd used it before. Recently.'

And suddenly it was as if all the tumblers in a lock fell into place, unlocking the memories in Fran's mind.

'And there was the perfume too. I didn't notice it when we were at the house last night, because there was a vase of lilies in Clarence's room. Their scent was so powerful it masked yours.

But I did smell it, when you came over to the desk. And Saul did too. Remember when you bashed him over the head? He said he thought he'd smelled something sweet. Olivia had a scent bottle in her handbag and I thought that meant it was her.'

'This is all absolute rubbish,' said Cate. 'None of it means anything. Yes, I may well have cut my finger on something, I don't remember. My mind was on other things. Like the fact that my dad had just *died*.' Her face was twisted into a vicious sneer.

'Except it isn't rubbish, is it, Cate?' said Saul, stepping forward. 'I said you were desperate, and I was right. You *did* kill Dad.'

She shrugged. 'Well, one of us had to. You didn't have the guts and Marcus was too clumsy, he didn't have nearly enough imagination.'

'No, and you were different, weren't you?'

'Too right I was. And I learned my lessons at the knee of the best teacher there was – Dad himself. *You want things in this life, Cate*, he said, *you have to go out there and make them happen*. So that's exactly what I did.'

Fran stared at Cate, a wave of revulsion rising up inside her. From the corner of her eye she saw Olivia raise a hand, holding it to her face as if in shock. But there was something about the movement, as if she'd been trying to attract Fran's attention, but surreptitiously... And then Fran saw her eyebrows raise, just for a second, as if to say *look at me*, and there in Olivia's eyes, Fran saw the message she'd been trying to give her. And she knew exactly what she had to do.

'That's how you did it,' she said, turning directly to Cate, eyes wide. 'You're a pharmacist.'

'Mmm, with an almost encyclopaedic knowledge of drugs and their uses. Drugs I can get my hands on quite easily, I might add. Well done, Fran. You'll never work out how it was done though, that's the absolute gem in all of this.'

Fran stared at her. Cate was discussing the killing of her father as if it was all a game. She swallowed, flicking a glance at Adam. 'I can think of one or two things,' she said, praying that Adam might realise what she was trying to do. They had caught a murderer in the past by taping the confession on a phone. She hoped with all her might that he had set his to record. 'Insulin for one. Isn't that a murderer's weapon of choice?'

'Not bad. But it only really works if the victim is diabetic. Too many questions asked otherwise. No, there's something far more useful. Something which can't even be traced post-mortem, and do you know why? Because it's the very same chemical that's pumped into the body by muscles when they're damaged. And the heart is just one big muscle essentially...'

'So, a heart attack—'

'Exactly. A dying heart pumps the body full of potassium chloride, the very thing which has been given to cause the heart attack in the first place. It's very clever, don't you think? Dad would have loved that. It's ironic, 'cause he'd probably be proud of me... one last mystery for you all to solve.'

'So what did you do?' bated Fran. 'Slip it in his cocoa?'

'No, that was just the sleeping draft, in the glass of water he always kept by his bed. I needed to make sure he slept right through the injection. That's the only thing about potassium chloride, you see, you can't give large doses of it orally, our stomachs have a kind of failsafe to prevent us from overdosing.'

'Is that why you needed the first aid kit? Pricked your finger, did you?'

Cate just smiled. 'I forgot the antiseptic wipe,' she said. 'I used a little anaesthetic cream to make doubly sure Dad didn't feel the needle prick, but I needed something to clean it off afterwards. Just in case. You won't find it though, I hid the site very well.'

'Then we'll just have to hope you also forgot to wipe off your fingerprints from the first aid box, won't we?'

'You really think I'm that stupid,' replied Cate, although Fran was pleased to see her pale a little.

'It doesn't matter anyway,' said Olivia. 'Because I kept the glass.'

'What glass?' Cate's head swung in her direction.

'The glass Clarence had by the side of his bed. I don't know why I did, really, I guess something must have made me suspicious.'

'Oh, for goodness' sake,' spat Cate. 'What do you think you're going to find?'

Olivia smiled. 'Well now... if you were really stupid, your fingerprints will be on it. There might even be a face of the sleeping powder. And if you weren't stupid... then the glass would be wiped clean. Except that it shouldn't be clean of fingerprints, should it? Clarence's should be on it at the very least.'

Cate looked from one to the other and then a slow smile made its way up her face. 'It doesn't matter what you say because who's going to believe you? All you have is circumstantial evidence and that's not enough. Nothing about any of that leads to me.'

'Actually,' said Adam, 'that's not quite right.'

It was the first time he'd spoken and all four heads turned in his direction.

'See, the thing is...' He fished in his pocket and pulled out a smallish object. Fran had to squint to see what it was. 'Marcus was on to you, Cate, and that's why you killed him. He worked out what was going on, so when you'd bashed him over the head you smashed up his phone too.' He held up the object in his hand. 'And that's because there's something incriminating on it. Did he message you, Cate, asking you why you'd done it?' He paused to let his words sink in. 'That was a big mistake, leaving his phone back there in the woods. Fran and I found it, close to his body. You thought we'd all assume the phone had become damaged when Marcus was attacked, when he fought for his life. I think you also thought that whatever's on here would be destroyed along with the phone. A reasonable assumption. Trouble is, whatever's on here is still on here, very much so. In fact, it won't take long to find it at all.'

'Give me that!'

Cate shot forward, lunging at Adam, but not before Saul caught her arms, holding her firm.

'Oh no, you don't,' he said.

'I should never have gone back for you,' Cate added. 'I should have left you tied up.'

'You made another mistake there, didn't you, sis? Bumping off Marcus so early. You had to go back for Adam and Fran because you realised you could never work out the clues by yourself.'

'So bloody what? There's nothing on that phone at all, you're just making it up to try and spook me. You still won't be able to prove anything. And we're standing on the top of a hill, Saul, in case you hadn't noticed. Who are you going to tell?'

'Er, how about the police?'

'And say what? Call them. Call the police. They'll never prove anything and all I have to do is say I'm innocent. Say that I was scared of what you were going to do to me. I had to confess, it was the only way I thought I'd get away with my life. You have no evidence and you'll never find any.'

'On the contrary, I think we'll find plenty.'

It was a new voice, coming from behind Fran.

'You see, we can get fingerprints from wood too, did you know that, Cate? And I don't suppose your hands were all that clean when you murdered Marcus. Mud, sweat, dampness from the wood itself, any of these things could have conspired against you, leaving a lovely set of prints on whatever you hit him over the head with. It might take some time, but we'll find the murder weapon, and when we do, we'll find the prints. Besides which, you might also be interested to learn that the police have been here the whole time. There's a cave up here as well, did you know? Quite nice, actually, a bit damp and chilly this time of the morning, obviously, but comfortable enough. My detective constable and I have been listening to your entire conversation and your taped confession is probably all we'll need.'

The woman coming forward paused, her colleague beside her. 'We haven't met before, Cate, but my name's Nell Bradley, Detective Chief Inspector Nell Bradley.'

22

Fran wasn't sure who looked the more surprised, Cate, Adam or herself. Only Olivia and Saul looked unperturbed by the latest set of events. But Cate's surprise didn't last long. It soon turned to abject misery and her whole body sagged.

'DC Holmes, perhaps you'd be so kind as to read Ms Lightman her rights,' said Nell. 'Then take her away, I'd quite like her out of my sight. Saul will accompany you to the foot of the hill.'

The voice of the DC droned in Fran's ear as she stared at Nell. 'Cate Lightman, I'm arresting you on suspicion of the murders of Clarence and Marcus Lightman. You do not have to...'

Nell took a step forward. 'Fran, Adam... it's good to see you,' she said, a bright smile on her face. As usual, Nell scarcely had a hair out of place. Even her walking boots looked polished to within an inch of their lives. 'Sorry about this, it's all a bit... complicated. But I will explain fully in due course. Just as soon as we get off this bloody hill.' She turned to Olivia. 'How are you holding up, Livvy?'

To Fran's even greater surprise, the two women hugged.

Fran's mouth hung open. 'But how do you...?'

Olivia smiled. 'I mentioned when we first met that I'd been married but it hadn't worked out. And I'd also been very careful to keep my married name from you in case you made the connection, but Nell here is the only thing good that came of it. My husband was exactly what I said he was, a ne'er-do-well, and a lying, cheating one at that. And it's odd because his family are the nicest people you could ever wish to meet... especially, his sister. A bit scary at times, but when you're in a spot of bother, absolutely the best person to have on your side.'

Nell grinned. 'Too bloody right I am. This is my day off, I'll have you know. First proper weekend I've had in ages. And what am I doing? Hiking up a hill and hiding in a damp smelly cave in the wee small hours of the morning.' Her voice was light-hearted though, despite her grumble, and Fran could see the compassion and warmth in the detective's eyes as she smiled at her sister-in-law.

Most of the time, Nell kept her soft spot very well hidden, but Fran had seen it on a few occasions now, and she heartily agreed with Olivia. You wouldn't want to get on the wrong side of Nell, but if she had your back, you were very lucky indeed.

Fran pursed her lips, looking up at Olivia. An awkward silence began to grow, but then Olivia flung her arms around Fran and squeezed her so hard, she thought she might have to check her ribs for damage. It felt good though, given everything that had happened.

'I'm so sorry, Fran,' she said. 'But I couldn't tell either of you what was going on.'

'Why are you sorry?' asked Fran. 'I'm the one who—' She stopped then swallowed. 'I'm the one who got duped into thinking you were a murderer. I mean, I didn't really think that, obviously, but I...' She paused. 'No, that's not right, I *did* think you'd murdered Clarence, and Marcus, and I'm so sorry I didn't trust you, didn't—'

But Olivia held up a hand.

'Then our plan worked beautifully,' she replied. 'And you really don't have to apologise. There was no reason for you to trust me, not really. Yes, we were the best of friends, but that was a lifetime ago, why should that make a difference now?'

'Even so, I should have given you more benefit of the doubt,' replied Fran, frowning, determined not to let herself off the hook quite so easily.

Olivia shook her head. 'I always knew that when it came to it, you would do what was right, even if you thought that meant bringing a friend to justice. And you came through, Fran, just like I knew you would. The minute you worked out what was really going on, you stepped right up.'

'Plus, I've used you and Adam quite shamelessly,' added Nell. 'But I hope when we explain it all, you'll realise why I had to.'

'I think I already know that,' replied Fran. 'But I would like to know exactly what's been going on. My head is scrambled.'

Beside her, Adam was quiet. He was always wary around Nell. It wasn't that Nell didn't like him, far from it, but, not surprisingly, Nell had taken a dim view in the past of some of his 'antics', as she called them; the ones which weren't exactly legal. But now Nell's smile turned on him, full beam.

'When did you first twig?' she asked.

Adam pulled a face. 'Not nearly soon enough,' he replied. 'But it was when we got back to the house and Cate made the comment about the name of it being ironic. It suddenly occurred to me that Clarence and Olivia may well have said those same words once upon a time. Perhaps when they were talking about justice, or just deserts, for a family who had seemingly grown up without a shred of decency about them.' He smiled. 'Nope, Fran definitely beat me to it on this one.'

'I did not,' retorted Fran. 'What was it you said when we decided to keep our discovery about Olivia's work from Cate?

That you liked to keep the balance of knowledge in our favour. You knew then, didn't you?'

'I began to suspect there might have been more to this whole situation than we were being led to believe, yes. Particularly when we already knew that Olivia was aware of our background as far as solving murders was concerned. It made me wonder why she would knowingly invite us in if she had committed murder herself. It seemed far more obvious that there was another reason.'

'See...' said Fran. 'When I found that out, it just convinced me of Olivia's supposed guilt all the more.'

Nell smiled. 'Fran may have been the one who garnered Cate's confession, and that was very smart detective work, Fran, but don't underestimate your role in all of this, Adam. I needed you to work out all Clarence's lovely clues and bring everyone here. Which you did, admirably.' She stared ahead of her, at the three figures already descending the slope of the hill. 'Come on, it's bloody freezing up here. Shall we walk and talk?'

'So when did all this start?' asked Fran, as they began to pick their way down the ridge line.

'It *was* a chance remark made by Clarence which sparked it,' said Olivia. 'That much is true.' She smiled. 'Anyway, that comment was made months ago, and I had no reason to think about it afterwards until the day when Clarence actually *did* die from a heart attack. Then it became a sentence I couldn't get out of my head. What if something I'd dismissed as a throwaway comment was true? It wasn't until the day of the funeral itself, however, when my imagination really went into overdrive...'

'So you never knew about the contents of Clarence's will?' asked Adam.

Olivia shook her head. 'No. I knew about the party and the planned treasure hunt. I shared that with you on the day we met, Fran, if you remember, but I didn't know what Clarence had planned until the will was read. As soon as I heard it, however, I realised that Clarence was setting into motion a plan of his own. He was a wily bird. And don't forget, he lived and breathed puzzles and games, so it was obvious that he had some sort of ulterior motive for doing what he did. I had no idea what any of the clues were, or where they were hidden, but Clarence knew that the locations at least might be familiar to me...' She smiled fondly. 'But that aside, there was no guarantee I would win. I had to try though, because the more I thought about it the more it seemed as if that's what Clarence wanted me to do – to use the treasure hunt, when the family would all be together, to somehow flush out Clarence's killer. Which is obviously where Nell came in.'

Nell nodded as she picked up the story. 'Olivia rang me at some ridiculous hour, jabbering like a crazy idiot, but once I'd got her to calm down, it didn't take much for her to convince me her concerns were genuine. Livvy isn't one for being overly dramatic and I could see that she really believed there was something untoward about Clarence's death. But she also knew that the circumstances of his death and the subsequent pronouncement of the cause of his death gave absolutely no reason for concern. So she came to me. I nearly fell over when she told me who had catered for Clarence's funeral, and that Fran had a friend who had come to help because he was good at puzzles.' She gave a wry smile. 'No need to tell me who *that* was. And that's when I realised the perfect solution was staring me in the face.'

'Does this mean we're officially consultants?' asked Adam.

'No, it does not,' said Nell. 'The police don't work with consultants.' But her subsequent smirk made Adam grin even more. 'I had to work fast, however. Once the treasure hunt started there was no way of knowing how soon everyone would work out the clues. Olivia obviously had to win, and I had to take care of what I could behind the scenes. Trouble was, as well you know, Fran, I couldn't commit any officers or time to investigate something my superiors would view as the whim of an employee addled by grief. So up until this point everything I've done has been off my own back. Olivia had already planted the suggestion that Clarence's death wasn't natural, so I just had to hope that your brilliant deductive powers would begin to work, solving both the clues and the murder. Which of course they did.'

'But wouldn't it have been a lot simpler to have told us what was happening in the first place?' asked Fran.

'There just hasn't been time,' Nell replied. 'Olivia called me in the wee small hours of Saturday morning. It's only Sunday now.'

Fran stared at her. She was right, of course, but somehow it seemed as if a week at least had gone by.

'I had to let the game play out, while at the same time do what I could behind the scenes. Not that there's been much, but I have made arrangements for Clarence's body to be exhumed. He chose to be buried, thankfully, and if there's any evidence of foul play still on his body, we'll find it.'

'You have the glass as well,' added Fran. 'The one from Clarence's bedside table.'

Olivia coughed. 'Er... that might have been a lie,' she said. 'Did the trick though, didn't it? Put the wind up Cate, that's for sure.'

'Marcus's phone then?' said Fran, rolling her eyes. 'Or did you make that up too, Adam?'

'I'm making no promises, but I'll do what I can. There'll be phone records too, won't there?'

Nell nodded. 'Absolutely. Calls and texts made. Murderers always slip up. Always. I should have foreseen Marcus's death though, the poor man. That lack of foresight is something I'm going to have to live with, but it all happened so fast and up until that point none of us really knew quite how desperate Cate was, or how ruthless.'

'I saw Cate running away,' said Olivia. 'And when I stumbled over Marcus and realised what had happened, I went after her. That's when I left you two behind. I was convinced she had already worked out the next clue and I knew I couldn't let her get ahead of me. But I didn't realise until afterwards that Saul had doubled back and tied you up until he caught up with me a little while later at the house. He'd seen Cate with Marcus too and had pretty much worked out what had been happening. He genuinely thought he was helping by keeping you out of harm's way while he went after Cate himself. I had expected to find Cate when I got to Justice House, but obviously by then she was back in the woods convincing the pair of you that I was the murderer. She needed you, you see, because she had no idea what the memorial clue meant. She needed you to work out the location of the final clue. Once Saul and I met up, however, and I realised he knew Cate had murdered Marcus, I had to come clean about what had been going on. We spoke to Nell and together we hatched the final part of the plan.'

'Which was to sit up half the night in a dirty, cold and smelly cave waiting for you guys,' put in Nell. 'And here we all are.' She sniffed. 'God, I could murder a bacon sandwich.'

Two hours later they were all back at Justice House, where they were met by Margaret and Saul's wife, Jo, a petite brunette, who didn't know whether to look upset, horrified or pleasantly pleased by the outcome. It was much how Fran was feeling herself.

From the moment they got to the bottom of Caer Caradoc, Nell had switched into detective-inspector mode and started firing instructions to her team, which was, after all, what she was very good at. Cate had been taken away and, although they would all need to be questioned and give statements, they had at least been allowed to return to Justice House. It didn't take long at all for the kettle to be pressed into service.

For a while no one said very much. Having congregated in the kitchen, they were all too busy thawing out, cleaning up, drinking tea like it was going out of fashion and stuffing their faces. That, and trying to make sense of the last couple of days. Eventually, Olivia got to her feet and, crossing to her coat which was still dumped where she'd left it, she withdrew something from a pocket.

'I think perhaps it's time I gave you this,' she said, handing Margaret the slim cylindrical object she had found at the top of the hill.

'The final clue,' said Margaret, smiling softly. 'Which must mean you're the winner, my dear. And the inheritor of Clarence's estate.'

'Perhaps,' said Olivia. 'Although Saul and I have already decided we're going to split it between us.'

'Rather, she told me that's what she was going to do,' said Saul, squeezing his wife's hand. They'd been glued to each other since he arrived. 'And, after a bit of persuasion, obviously I agreed.' He gave a sheepish shrug. 'Olivia's keeping this place,' he added. 'Jo hates it, so...'

'And the rest will go to Saul,' said Olivia.

Margaret nodded. 'Clarence always knew you would do what's right,' she said. 'I think he'd be very pleased by your decision. And you'd certainly have his blessing.' She gave Olivia a swift glance before looking back at Saul, her expression warm. 'Incidentally, did you read your father's letter to you? I think now might be a good time if you haven't.'

Saul looked confused for a moment before letting go of Jo's hand and fishing in his jeans' pocket. 'I didn't, I... I couldn't face it at the time. Shoved it in my jeans and forgot all about it.' He pulled out a crumpled envelope and ran his hands over it, straightening out the creases at length before finally turning it over. He gave a wry smile. 'Crazy, isn't it, given what's happened and the fact that I'm a grown man, I'm still scared of hearing what Dad might say.'

'Maybe you don't need to be,' said Olivia, smiling at Margaret, who nodded.

With a swift movement, Saul undid the seal and pulled out a sheet of paper. He lay it flat on the table and began to read.

Fran watched as he did so, noticing the slight shake of his shoulders as he reached a particular point. When he'd read to the end, he sat for a moment, head still bowed, struggling with his emotions. Wordlessly, he slid the letter along the table to sit in front of Jo. She pulled it closer, her lips moving slightly as she too began to read Clarence's last words to his son. Her hand reached out, her fingers lacing with Saul's.

When she'd finished, she looked up, her eyes shiny-bright with tears. 'Did you know that's what he'd written?' she asked Margaret.

The solicitor shook her head. 'The context, not the words,' she replied. 'But I suspected it was a letter which Saul would want to read, and that perhaps now might be the perfect moment to do so.'

Saul cleared his throat, and drew in a deep breath, which he then blew out slowly. He straightened and reached out with his free hand to reclaim the letter. 'Perhaps you'd like to read it, Margaret? Aloud, if you wish.'

Margaret hesitated a moment, but then she dipped her head in acknowledgement.

Dear Saul,

Death is a funny thing. It happens to us all, and yet, even though we know this to be a fact of our lives, we give it so little thought. If we did, perhaps our lives would be better. Perhaps we would live always striving to make the best of every moment, knowing that it could be our last. Perhaps we would make the most of every relationship we have, knowing that, if we are lucky, those people might accompany us on our journey to its end. Perhaps...

Yet, life is rarely like that. Life comes with hurt and sorrow, in equal measure with joy and happiness, and, truly, you never know what each day might bring. The trouble is that we humans know so much, while also knowing so little and we allow the scales of our lives to become unbalanced, to only see the hurt and sorrow, forgetting everything that is good on the other side. And so it is with you, my son. I've spent far too many years being concerned only with the wrongs which lay between us, failing to see all the times where you strove to redress the balance and bring our relationship back into all that was right and good. And for that I am truly sorry.

Of course, the greatest irony is that in saying these things to you now means I am no longer around to enjoy what I know could have come to pass. It's been a good life though, none-theless, and in many ways I've been truly blessed. But, Saul, you still have your life, so use it wisely. I've known for a long time that you are the one who knows how to do this best of all and it's that knowledge which will sustain me on my journey to the next place. I'm leaving you a gift, Saul, a gift of opportu-nity, and I know that you will grasp it to you and never let it go. I hope it brings you everything you ever desired. It's all I ever wanted for you, after all.

Margaret laid the letter gently down on the table, her face openly showing the emotion she was feeling, the emotion they were all feeling. Fran wasn't the only one dabbing her eyes.

For a moment, no one spoke, but then Saul's face creased into a wide smile and he chuckled. 'Dad always did have a way with words.'

'Hear, hear,' said Olivia firmly, and with that the poignant bubble of tension broke.

'One thing I still don't understand about all this though,' said Fran, catching the look in Olivia's eyes, 'is who planted all the clues. There's no way Clarence could have walked to the top of Caer Caradoc.'

'You're perfectly correct,' said Margaret. 'And this is where Clarence called upon the services of his dearest friends, all of whom shared dinner with you on Friday night. Some of them had simply agreed to be at the end of the phone numbers you rang to obtain the next in the sequence of clues, but others around the table provided assistance of a different kind. Paul Iveson might be in his seventies, but he's been a keen rambler for years. He knows the hills around here like the back of his hand, and it was a simple afternoon stroll for him to place the final clue on top of Caer Caradoc. Francine Collins, similarly, may be retired, but she still volunteers at Attingham Park gardens, where she worked for so many years. It was where Clarence met her, actually, and when the bothy was renovated recently and the brickwork repointed, she who placed the USB stick where it was so cleverly hidden.'

'And you knew all of these locations, of course,' added Fran, looking at Olivia.

'I did. My research for the book I was writing with Clarence took me to all the places he used as inspiration for the settings in his books. But Attingham was a particular favourite. I guess that's why he used it for the treasure hunt the way he did and, as you all worked out, it was also the location he used for the setting of his favourite book, *The Castle of Secrets*.'

'It was also a place we knew well as kids,' added Saul. 'We spent hours there, roaming around. It was very different back then, and we pretty much had free rein.'

Fran nodded. 'Cate told us about Annie. She was the house-keeper there, I gather.'

'She was. We were in and out of her cottage too. It was like a second home for us.' Saul stared at the table a moment, toying with a half-eaten biscuit in front of him. 'Which is something else I have to own up about,' he added.

Fran frowned and looked at Adam.

He shook his head. 'Nope, I'm not sure what he's talking about either.'

'It's how I got the key,' explained Saul. 'The key to the shed where I left you, Fran. I'm sorry about that, by the way.'

She dipped her head. 'I forgive you, although I'm not sure what would have happened if Adam and I hadn't got out. You didn't know he was in there though, did you?'

'No, and that *was* Cate's doing, I'm afraid. But as to where we both got the keys from... When we were kids we used to help Annie sometimes. As the housekeeper she had keys to the place and, although it was open to the public, it wasn't at all like it is now, there were far fewer facilities for visitors. But one thing they did have was a hut which sold ice creams in the summer. They still do in fact. Annie used to take stock over to the hut from the main house, and we'd help her carry it sometimes. Boxes of the stuff. I think it was all too much for three kids who liked ice creams. We pinched her spare keys, and when no one was around, used to sneak back in and help ourselves to ice lollies. We hid the keys under a loose floorboard in the hall cupboard and they were still there. I took one when I came back to the house to try to solve the clue hidden in *The Shadow of the Wind*. Cate must have too, right after she bashed me over the head. I had a feeling we might end up at Attingham somewhere along the line.'

'The final mystery solved,' mused Fran.

'Not quite,' replied Adam with a grin at Olivia. 'There's still one thing we don't know.' He leaned forward and tapped the canister that still lay on the table. 'Come on then, put us out of our misery. What's the answer to the final clue?'

Margaret unscrewed the cap and carefully drew out the slip of paper which lay rolled inside. She smoothed it out, smiling as she placed it on the centre of the table so that everyone could see it. 'There was only one thing it could be really. Although, of course, when Clarence revealed it to me, I had no idea just how much significance it would have.'

Fran stared at the paper, at the single word written there in black ink. 'Of course,' she murmured. 'What else could it be?'

'Justice,' read Adam. He looked up and caught Fran's eye. 'I'd say that's the perfect end, wouldn't you?'

A LETTER FROM EMMA

Hello, and thank you so much for choosing to read *Death on the Menu*. I hope you've enjoyed reading it as much as I've enjoyed writing it. If you'd like to stay updated on what's coming next, please do sign up to my newsletter here and you'll be the first to know!

www.bookouture.com/emma-davies

There is no getting around the fact that writing a book involves a huge amount of sitting in a chair, either typing, or writing longhand. It's also true that, while I would never want to do anything else, the mechanics of writing are not good for the mechanics of the body. Quite some years ago, therefore, I realised that walking was the perfect solution for not only ironing out the kinks in my back and neck, but those in my plots as well. And I'm incredibly lucky that one of the places I'm able to walk most often is in the grounds of Attingham Park itself. Now owned by the National Trust, its beautiful surroundings extend through a deer park, areas of woodland and also cross a winding river, twice. It's here that I notch up roughly fifteen miles in a good week, walking through every season, which means there's always something new to see. Even a change in the time of day, or the angle of the sun, is enough to bring about a brand-new perspective.

So, when I was thinking about the numerous settings I

would need for *Death on the Menu*, Attingham Park provided obvious inspiration. I think it's fair to say that, over the years, I have walked every path, in all directions, and so while my characters were busy creeping through the grounds as they searched for the location of their next clue, I was very much with them, literally walking those same paths in my mind. It was huge fun to be able to direct them here and there, although, if you're lucky enough to have visited Attingham Park, you might spot the odd occasion when I had to bend reality a little to fit the requirements of my story. Any 'mistakes' therefore are deliberate and mine alone. I might also add that in the course of my research, I have never broken in at night – I leave that mischief to Adam, who is able to do these things in the name of fiction!

In the writing of my books I'm also incredibly grateful to my wonderful publishers, Bookouture, for enabling me to bring you these stories and for their unfailing support. Thanks also to my wonderful team of editors and, in particular, Susannah Hamilton for her sage advice.

And, finally, to you, lovely readers, the biggest thanks of them all for continuing to read my books, and without whom none of this would be possible. You really do make everything worthwhile.

Having folks take the time to get in touch really does make my day, and if you'd like to contact me then I'd love to hear from you. The easiest way to do this is by finding me on Twitter and Facebook, or you could also pop by my website, where you can read about my love of Pringles among other things.

I hope to see you again very soon and, in the meantime, if you've enjoyed reading *Death on the Menu*, I would really appreciate a few minutes of your time to leave a review or post on social media. Every single review makes a massive difference and is very much appreciated!

Until next time,

Love, Emma

www.emmadaviesauthor.com

 facebook.com/emmadaviesauthor
twitter.com/EmDaviesAuthor

Made in the USA
Las Vegas, NV
15 January 2023

65683243R00166